The Feather and the Lamp

An Imperceptibility Happenstance Adventure

By L.N. Hunter

Three Ravens Publishing
Chickamauga, GA USA

To Ann and Kathryn,
for making life an adventure.

Credits:

The Feather and the Lamp was written by: L.N. Hunter

Cover art and graphics by: Mike Armstrong

THE FEATHER AND THE LAMP by: L.N. Hunter /Three Ravens Publishing – 1st edition, 2022

Trade Paperback ISBN: 978-1-951768-55-3

Hardback ISBN: 978-1-951768-60-7

Table of Contents

Author's note ix

Chapter 1: Prelude—The Adventurers' Guild 1

Chapter 2: The Djinn Appears 25

Chapter 3: Take Care What You Wish For 43

Chapter 4: A Sailor's Life for Me 64

Chapter 5: Interlude—The Adventurers' Guild 86

Chapter 6: That Sinking Feeling 92

Chapter 7: Down Under 112

Chapter 8: Deeper Underground 134

Chapter 9: Village Life 158

Chapter 10: Dragon 182

Chapter 11: Flight 202

Chapter 12: Yossburg 218

Chapter 13: Rille 236

Chapter 14: Dark 252

Chapter 15: Dam! 270

Chapter 16: Fuel 292

Chapter 17: Nice Doggy 314

Chapter 18: An Old Friend 332

Chapter 19: Escape 350

Chapter 20: Second Chance 372

Chapter 21: Interlude—The Adventurers' Guild..... 388

Chapter 22: Schankenkrausloftenisburg 394

Chapter 23: The Three Villages.....................408

Chapter 24: Sir Oscar de Montford...........................426

Chapter 25: The Deal..440

Chapter 26: The End, Almost..................................454

Chapter 27: Back at The Adventurers' Guild 472

Author Bio 491

Author's note

This novel began life as a short story in 2017, and it's thanks to feedback from members of the OUSA Write Club that I knuckled down to expanding Imperceptibility's adventures. The first novel-length draft appeared in 2020, and those same OUSA folk helped me bash it into shape over the next couple of years, as did many talented writers on the critique site Scribophile. Thank you, everyone who commented on the story; it wouldn't be here without you.

Thanks, are also due to Mike Armstrong for his amazing cover art—you can find more of his work at https://mike-armstrong.com

Lastly, thank you to the team at Three Ravens for helping to bring this novel to life.

Chapter 1: Prelude—The Adventurers' Guild

Who Will Become This Year's New Adventurers?

On the eve of The Adventurers' Guild's annual rare objects contest, your intrepid reporter had the opportunity to sit down with Sir Stanley Livingbore, senior assembly member of the Guild. The world-famous explorer explained that, although there are other methods of entry, 'Having one's offering displayed within the Museum of Rare and Unique Objects is the most prestigious way to join the Guild. The contest brings back fond memories of locating the source of the river Daloon and becoming an Adventurer thanks to the map I presented to the Guild.' As readers may be aware, Sir Stanley's new book, *How I Lost My Tune and Found Daloon*, is available in all good literary bureaux now. Quote voucher code KHTIM16 for a 10% discount on the hardback deluxe version.

'If an offering is insufficient to grant admission, the candidate will not be permitted to reapply and may be executed as a deterrent to the rash and foolish,' he warned, reminding us how seriously the Guild treats the competition.

We at *The Khaleshkan Times* offer best wishes to all contestants and urge our readers to pick up tomorrow's edition for full coverage of the results.

Page 7, *The Khaleshkan Times*, 16th day of Nontemps, 39th year of the 8th Emperor.

'Next!'

The strident voice echoed across the hall, instantly hushing the audience. It was the sort of voice that would emanate from a face endowed with horn-rimmed glasses, a long sharp nose and thin, humourless lips. The kind of impatient and quick-tempered voice that might cause adults to cry or babies to fill their nappies, and sometimes vice versa. A voice, indeed, which could etch worry wrinkles in the marble busts of senators and statues of heroes within the alcoves dotting the high walls. Even the sentries at the entrance stilled themselves to avoid drawing the attention of its owner should their swords or armour clank.

The voice belonged to the gatekeeper of The Adventurers' Guild, a severe woman tasked with ensuring that only the best, the most worthy, the very *crème de la crème* would be permitted to join the esteemed society. She glared with disdain over her tall, narrow desk at the group of petitioners near the entrance.

Even before her exclamation had finished resonating across the stone chamber, another sound could be heard.

Pok. Pok. Pok.

The echoing footsteps crossed the marble floor towards the circle of light around the gatekeeper's imposing desk. The footsteps slowed, faltering under the disapproval radiating through the glasses, and stopped with a final, nervous shuffle.

'Name?' the gatekeeper barked.

'Heron–' the wispy-bearded owner of the footsteps attempted, his voice dissolving into a croak. After a clearing of the throat, he tried again, in a more controlled, but still flustered, voice: 'Heronicus Fizzlewick, Your Maj– er, Your High– er, ma'am.'

The gatekeeper stared at Heronicus as if mentally dissecting the young man organ by organ to decide whether he genuinely needed them all. After a painfully long moment, her gaze swivelled away, down to the large book on her desk. As he dared to breathe again, her quill could be heard making a precise tick mark on the page. The gatekeeper's eyes flicked up to resume their inspection of the perspiring petitioner, who was perhaps regretting heavy brocade as his choice of clothing today.

'What treasure have you brought us today, Master Fizzlewick?' The curve of the bright red lips on her alabaster face was more threatening grimace than inviting smile.

Heronicus Fizzlewick swallowed, then gingerly opened a small, polished wooden box. He held it aloft in hands that were almost hidden within the wide lacy cuffs of his best shirt, taking care not to let the contents touch his bare flesh. 'The p-poisonous tongue of the lesser-spotted Obstruvian c-calciferous newt,' he squeaked.

The gatekeeper riffled through her book, then slid her finger down to the relevant line and tapped on it.

Tap. 'The Guild's museum already has one.'

Heronicus' face dropped.

Tap. 'You are dismissed, Master Fizzlewick.'

His shoulders slumped.

Tap. 'And, Master Fizzlewick, be glad you walk away with your life.'

Heronicus Fizzlewick gulped and bowed to the gatekeeper. Closing the box with a barely audible click, he took two trembling steps back before bowing again. Under the silent gaze of the audience in the hall, he turned and started his crestfallen walk out of The

Adventurers' Guild, undoubtedly wondering what he was going to do with a poisonous newt's tongue now. He flinched as the scratch of the gatekeeper's quill crossing out a line in the book of names cut through the sound of his shuffling footsteps.

'Next!'

It was a grey day of intermittent drizzling, typical of autumn weather this far north. A sharp wind made the flags atop the gate to The Adventurers' Guild—or to give it its full title, The Imperial Guild of Adventurers, Explorers, Inventors, Scientists, and Sundry Seekers of Knowledge—crack and snap. Lower down, the wind heartlessly whistled through the clothes of the hopefuls awaiting an audience, as if urging those individuals to abandon all hope and leave.

Applicants for the Guild's annual contest had been waiting in the damp chill since before dawn, clustered in front of the imposing bronze gates. Some huddled in solitary clouds of apprehension, staring blankly at the ground. Offerings that had looked so grand to their owners when setting out now seemed unworthy and inadequate in comparison with everyone else's. Several candidates' places in the queue were maintained by their serfs, while they relaxed in tents, tended by a further entourage of servants. All of this added to the misery of those unshielded from the dreary weather and the scrutiny of curious onlookers.

Dozens of inhabitants of Khaleshka, along with a good many visiting tourists, had assembled to spectate. Gawping at potential Adventurers of the Future, they gossiped in anticipation of stories of success or otherwise. Tales of failures, especially those resulting in executions, always elicited more generous offers of drink in the taverns. Bookies—

speculative entrepreneurs, as they preferred to be called—took wagers on which of the waiting applicants would be accepted and who would be sentenced to death. While senior journalists from *The Khaleshkan Times* were comfortable inside the Guild's chamber, junior members of the press shivered in the cold outside the gates, relegated to snatching interviews with applicants on their way in and out.

Among the spectators, several young ladies—and a few doe-eyed young lords— were neglecting their schooling for the promise of a glimpse of the handsome Prince Ollipher. The prince's sumptuous gazebo shielded him from the hoi-polloi, while he calmly drank dainty cups of sweetened ginseng tea. His audience sighed in unison behind delicate folding fans when the wind fluttered the tent fabric, offering them a fleeting view of their heartthrob's chiselled jaw and long-lashed, ice-blue eyes.

There was no ginseng tea for those waiting outside. They had to make do with the suspicious-looking brownish-grey beverages and equally questionable edibles available from street vendors. Such purveyors of debatable sustenance popped up anywhere people congregated, but the Guild's annual Rare and Unique Objects contest was the pinnacle of their year.

Coincidentally, the city's rodent population was at its lowest point annually in the days surrounding the contest.

Unlike most of the other contestants, Ollipher, son of Queen Agronetta of neighbouring Plenipont, hadn't actually traversed the world to seek his entrance gift to The Adventurers' Guild. He—to be more precise, his mother—had sent teams of explorers in all directions to gather the most unusual items they could find. Often returning disease-ridden or with fewer limbs than when they'd set out (more limbs in one case, though he had made a satisfactory recovery and was carving a name for himself as a one-man orchestra), the dutiful searchers brought back rare gems, bizarre creatures, exquisite perfumes, intricately woven textiles, and ornate jewellery. One came back carrying a sugary substance called chok-lit by the locals of the region in which it was found. Prince Ollipher liked this peculiar brown, waxy confection so much he'd consumed all of it while waiting in his tent.

'Olly, you *do* want to be an Adventurer, don't you?' the queen hissed, wary of being overheard by those outside the tent. 'Did you really have to eat it all?'

'But, Mother…' the prince drawled. 'It was soooo delish.'

She sighed. 'Sometimes I just want to smack you. It being, as you put it, *soooo delish* is precisely why it would have been certain to get you in. Thanks to your mediocre self-control, now we have to choose among these.' The queen gestured towards the table. 'What do you think of the dew-worm?' She held up a small glass specimen jar, peering at the rainbow-striped worm it contained.

'It's not very exciting. It doesn't do very much; just wriggles, and every now and then, burps clouds of coloured dust.' Ollipher tapped the jar with an elegantly manicured fingernail. 'At least, I think that's the head end.'

'It doesn't have to be exciting, you dullard; it only has to be *unique*. There are no more than five of these in the whole world.'

'I like the Amulet of Wallaberne, Mother. So many weapons hidden in a brooch—three blades, five spikes, and a poison capsule.' The prince picked up the somewhat plain-looking piece of jewellery and held it up to the light. 'Soooo elegant and soooo deadly.'

'Yes, dear, but can we be certain the Guild's museum hasn't got one already? I'm sure I heard rumours of something very similar at last year's event: four blades, poison, and a device that explodes. No, no, we have to rely on our wits for this one.' She paused to wipe a spot of chok-lit from her son's chin. 'My wits,' she corrected herself. 'We'd be doomed if we were relying on yours.'

The queen took the amulet from the prince's hand and placed it back on the table. She stared at the meagre collection, tapping her finger against her lips. After a few moments, she said. 'I think you should go with the shroud.'

Ollipher reached for the fragment of the death shroud of Amoncolata, last of the ancient Parathian God-kings. The queen and prince would have preferred a piece of the mummy itself, but loyal McKenzie had been lucky to return with his life, only just managing to snag the shroud and tear off a handkerchief-sized patch of cloth as he fled from temple guardians. The prince examined it sceptically. 'I suppose…'

'We can hope that McKenzie's difficulties in retrieving it are a sign that no one else has been able to find Amoncolata.'

Prince Ollipher turned the piece of grey fabric over and sniffed at it. He grunted, dropped it on the table, and slouched back in his chair, sipping tea and dozing until it was his turn.

The prince was called mid-afternoon, by which time the rain had stopped and the sky had brightened all the way to a middling grey. After a final look in the mirror to check that his cravat was symmetric and his waistcoat smooth, he picked up the frayed rag that had once covered a dead god and left the tent. Waving to his admirers, he entered the Guild building and strode confidently towards the gatekeeper. He stopped in front of her desk with a smart click of his heels.

'Madam, Charming Lady, Prince Ollipher of Pleniport at your service,' he oozed as he bowed low.

'Hmph. What have you brought, *Master* Ollipher?' Within The Adventurers' Guild, all were equal, regardless of rank or title in the world beyond its walls. At least, all who were male, since adventurers were always men.

Ollipher flourished his ragged square of cloth. 'A precious fragment of Amoncolata's death shroud, thought lost seven centuries ago, and reputed to have powers of–'

'Yes, yes, we know what it is,' the gatekeeper snapped. 'And I don't have to look at the book to know that this is something not yet in our museum. Well done in "locating" it.' The gatekeeper was clenching her jaw as she spoke—the prince's questionable tactics were well known. She paused, then slyly asked, 'Can I ask how you acquired this particular item?'

Ollipher swallowed and began to relay McKenzie's story *exactly* as he'd rehearsed it with the queen. He described how he risked his life visiting well-protected, hidden libraries in far-flung ancient cities to uncover rare books and scrolls containing any reference to Amoncolata's final resting place, no matter how tenuous. He explained how, after decoding maps and cryptic clues, he followed tortuous trails through burning deserts and ice-bound mountains.

The prince strode back and forth across the floor like an actor on a stage, gesticulating widely to demonstrate the complexity of negotiations with countless dangerous and dubious characters. Finally, he reached the prize in a temple deep in the sweltering rainforest of Queliqueliaq, only to be discovered by Amoncolata's guardians. As the audience in the chamber gasped, the prince completed his story with a breathless description of a daring race through stone passages and escape under a hail of poisoned arrows.

'All for this.' He held his treasure aloft, and applause burst from the audience.

The only teeny-tiny difference between McKenzie's story and this yarn was Ollipher's portrayal of himself as the hero.

The gatekeeper narrowed her eyes and inspected Ollipher for a few moments. After writing something in her book, she looked back to the prince, smiled coldly and uttered a grudging, 'Welcome, Master Ollipher, to The Adventurers' Guild.'

Late in the evening, as the sun—not that anyone had seen much of it that day—began to set, the queue was finally gone, and all but a few spectators had dispersed to the warmth of homes or taverns. The Guild had accepted three new adventurers during the course of the day, and rejected forty-seven. This year, only one applicant had fled, pale-faced, from the hall the moment he laid eyes on the gatekeeper. These were better numbers than the speculative entrepreneurs predicted, so there was coin-jingling happiness within the pockets of a few lucky spectators and a measure of disconsolate scraping at the bottom of the bookies' emptying purses. The junior *Times* journalists were pleased with the stories they'd be writing for the first print run the following day: two of the rejected had been locked up to await their executions for blatant foolishness and time-wasting.

One of those destined for capital punishment, a tall youth with gangling limbs and a wispy pencil moustache that looked like it really wanted to be an eyebrow, had brought a life-sized origami chariot model in which the horse's head nodded and legs moved when the wheels were turned. Unfortunately, horse and chariot had disintegrated in the day's rain and wind. The young man similarly wilted under the gatekeeper's glare as he'd tried to describe the former magnificence of his model while holding up a sodden mass of papier-mâché. The other, a sleek-haired man who titled himself a micro-biologist, whatever one of those might be, presented a glass of water containing what he called back-teeriums. Some sort of invisible disease-makers, he'd claimed. More like *non-existent* disease-makers, everyone agreed, laughing at the very idea.

The journalists in the chamber packed away their notebooks and prepared to leave as the gatekeeper made her ceremonial last calls, the traditional signal to indicate the contest's end.

'For the penultimate time. Next!'

Silence.

'For the final time. Next!' the gatekeeper bellowed louder than before.

More silence.

She harrumphed and looked around. 'Well, that seems to be that.' She leaned back on her stool, looking forward to relaxing at the end of a long day. 'Guards, close the gate.'

'Wait! Wait, please!'

The tik-tik-tik-tik of eager footsteps on the stone floor followed the breathless shout.

With a sigh, the gatekeeper sat up straight again and called, 'Na–'

'Imperceptibility Happenstance, Your Gatekeeperiness. Itty Happenstance,' a panting but cheerful voice cried out. 'I hope I'm not too late.'

The gatekeeper harrumphed again and peered over the edge of her desk. A brief frown of confusion appeared above her glasses, while the lips below pursed. She leaned across the desk and adjusted her gaze further downwards, to settle on a rather short young woman in her late teens, with a round, chubby-cheeked face split by a wide, confident grin.

The woman's upper half was clothed in an eye-watering scarlet and gold striped waistcoat. Below, bright lemon pantaloons with turquoise polka dots assaulted the gatekeeper's eyes. These two items of garish clothing met at a lime green sash where her waist would have been, had she tapered in the middle. As if to make certain she offended the entirety of the visual spectrum, a blue and orange checked handkerchief protruded from her breast pocket.

The gatekeeper sniffed. 'You want to be an adventurer? But you appear to be *female*. Are you sure you're not here for another position? Kitchen staff, or administration, or…'

'Yes, Madame Gatekeeper, I do indeed. Yes, I am a female. And yes, I'm sure; an adventurer is what I want to be. Is that a problem?'

There was a pause as the gatekeeper consulted another book on her desk, muttering to herself, 'I suppose not. There's nothing in the rules. But we've never… There are women working here, naturally, but there's never been a female *adventurer*…'

While she waited for the gatekeeper to address her, Itty looked around the hall, eyes wide as she took in the numerous busts and portraits of adventurers she'd only seen in books back home. She was so absorbed by the images of the famous faces that she didn't notice the chamber was designed to be intimidating—harsh stone walls, tall columns with crows nesting on top, and gloomy lighting.

The gatekeeper cleared her throat. 'Never mind. Tradition exists to be challenged. What have you brought, young lady?'

Itty jumped as if she'd forgotten what she was doing here. She patted the pockets of her pantaloons before finding and extricating her treasure from inside her waistcoat. Smiling, she carefully smoothed and flourished what looked to all like a feather. Surely, the audience was thinking, it must be a very special feather, a uniquely remarkable piece of plumage…

'I have brought a feather from the underside of a Common Arcanian goose.'

As one, the remaining spectators in the hall gasped. Prince Ollipher, standing with the other two new adventurers, sniggered. One of the journalists withdrew her notebook from her satchel; this was going to be worth writing down.

The gatekeeper stared at the young woman in front of her. 'A feather? From a common goose? You are aware that the penalty for time-wasting is execution?'

Itty gulped, and several expressions crossed her face as if she was trying then discarding appropriate responses. In the end, she simply nodded.

The gatekeeper riffled the pages of her ledger, then riffled some more. She sniffed, harrumphed, looked at her feather quill in its holder, and sniffed again. Finally, she removed her glasses and peered down the slope of her narrow nose at the nervously smiling, round face. 'We don't have one of those listed in our catalogue, that is true. However, the question is, Mast– er, Mistress Happenstance, why on Earth did you bring one to the Museum of Rare and Unique Objects?'

'Well, Honourable Gatekeeper, that's an interesting story. It all started on my way to the library one morning...'

Chapter 2: The Djinn Appears

Such that a binding contract with a djinn (hereinafter referred to as the First) requires that the receptacle wherein the First resides (hereinafter referred to as the Lamp) should be passed, either freely given or for a nominal sum, to its new owner (hereinafter, the Second), the agreement between both Parties shall not materially commence until the making of the first wish; this measure is intended to protect the Second, giving the Second a period sufficient to become acquainted with the nature of the First, since it is highly likely that the First will attempt to place the Second at a disadvantage.

While not mandatory, it is recommended that the Second read 'Tricks of the Djinn' and 'Wishes: Phrasing, Fulfilment and Failures' before attempting a wish.

Once the First has granted the final wish, the First shall return to the Lamp, to be transferred forthwith to the next owner, who will then become the Second.

> Wherein three shall be the maximum number of wishes granted, the Second should be aware that the death of the Second before the third wish will null any prior commitment to the Second and, furthermore, permit the First to break entirely free from djinnic service to the Second.
>
> *Standard Djinn Contract*, found among the writings of the lawyer-philosopher, Avelgard the Mighty, believed to be the first person to capture a djinn.

On one thoroughly normal morning in the Estalian capital of Hyrhia, Imperceptibility Happenstance was ambling across the market square for her daily visit to the city's central library, wearing her customary bright clothing.

Having spent her childhood in the Convent of the Ethynites' orphanage on the outskirts, where clothing was chosen based on functionality and availability, she had developed no fashion sense. Nor had she any desire to spend time coordinating her wardrobe if she could be reading instead. When shopping by herself, her gaze automatically settled on the garments with the most vivid colours, so that's what she tended to buy. This also made for speedier shopping than trying to choose among all the drab greys and browns and greens—she wasn't very good at making decisions at the best of times, so shortcuts like heading towards the brightest colours saved a lot of time. The most important attribute of suitable clothing, she thought, was that it came with ample pockets—book-sized pockets, ideally. That the colours clashed with each other and hurt onlookers' eyes mattered not a whit.

The market in the desert city of Hyrhia might have been crowded and bustling, or it might have been empty in the oppressive heat of the morning. Or was the day merely pleasantly warm; perhaps it was unseasonably chilly. Were the tall palm trees that surrounded the square swaying in a gentle breeze? Itty didn't notice. As usual, she was busy daydreaming, valiantly defending her city from attack by fierce pirates while still fiercer dragons filled the sky. Absent-mindedly, she alternately munched an apricot croissant purchased from *Pierre's Patisserie* and brandished it as a sword, silently mouthing, 'Begone foul fiends, this city is under my protection.'

Those occupants of the city streets who existed outside her imagination were well-used to the oblivious wanderings of the oddly-dressed dreamer. Without conscious thought, they moved aside to avoid being bumped into or sprinkled with crumbs from baked goods used as weaponry against non-existent foes.

At the age of almost seventeen and living by herself now, Itty Happenstance believed she knew a great deal about the world.

This wasn't entirely accurate.

Although it was true, she knew a lot about the worlds of the many stories that she'd been devouring since she first picked up a book, those worlds were somewhat different from reality. This didn't matter in any appreciable fashion to the young woman, as she tended to pay little attention to what was going on around her much of the time. This isn't to say that she couldn't tell fact from fiction; she knew what was real—well, she had a fairly good idea, anyway. It's just that the realms of her imagination were much more exciting.

Many of her favourite stories involved the great explorer Sir Stanley Livingbore, who discovered too many jewel-encrusted artefacts to mention and claimed to have visited the moon. Although unconvinced about that last part, she was certain that Livingbore was real; the library contained several biographies of the man (biography section: upper floor, third room, north wall shelves—most definitely non-fiction) and they all agreed upon the main facts. He had travelled the world, finding hidden monuments, sources of many rivers, countries even, and had braved horrors beyond count. And he was a member of The

Adventurers' Guild, an organization comprising the most talented and famous explorers in the world, as well as accomplished scientists, inventors, archaeologists, and—of course—adventurers. Itty's dream of dreams was to join the distant Guild, though she knew that it never would, or could, happen except within her imagination.

Her imagination was in fine fettle on this pleasant morning.

Itty glanced up at the top of the clock tower on the corner of Pinculas Avenue and Westfaring Way, imagining that the clouds and occasional dirigible dotting the azure sky beyond it were hordes of storm dragons preparing to rain fire on the city. Across the market square stood the marble-columned Municipal Bank, where the bronze-armoured guards at either side of the door had been transformed into a pair of bloodthirsty pirates, sporting eye patches, wooden legs, and hooks for hands.

'You'll never get my treasure,' she mouthed.

They waved their viciously sharp cutlasses and well-oiled flintlock pistols in her direction, though her imagination glossed over the question of how they could brandish such weapons with only hooks at the ends of their wrists. The calls of street hawkers and stall owners were the defiant cries of the brave rag-tag army she'd mustered as the city's last line of defence.

A loud 'Psssst!' cut through her personal soundscape of bloodthirsty shouts and fire-filled roars. The interruption almost made her drop her breakfast pastry, which was no longer a sword, having become the precious treasure the pirates and dragons lusted after.

She turned to see a tall, tanned figure beckoning her. He wore loose linen trousers and a matching waistcoat, unbuttoned to reveal a broad, hairy chest. On his head sat a white turban with a sparkling emerald set in the front, its colour exactly matching the man's piercing green eyes. His clothes and skin were lightly speckled with the dust of the marketplace. He sported a long, drooping white moustache above a wide smile packed with such dazzling teeth they seemed to have a glow of their own.

The moustachioed giant bowed deeply towards her and wrung his hands in a curiously liquid manner. 'Young mistress, if it pleases you, come closer, come closer.' He gestured towards a small drab tent, just visible behind his bulk. His voice was as oily as his hand movements. 'Please, this way.'

Itty wasn't sure if she'd seen the tent before that day, but had to admit to herself that she seldom noticed what was in the market most days. She looked around, but only a cud-chewing camel on the far side of the square was paying any attention to what was happening here. Shoving the last of the croissant into her mouth and dusting the crumbs off her hands, she pointed to herself and raised her eyebrows at him.

'Yes, yes, young mistress.' He nodded. 'Come, come. I can tell by your demeanour and distinctive attire that you possess an appreciation for the unusual and unique. And, on this most auspicious of days, I happen to have such a thing that will most certainly pique your interest and enrich your enthusiasms. Come, please, this way.'

She approached the obsequious giant, who bowed again and moved aside to reveal a small polished wooden table just inside the tent's opening. Whether by accident or design, a beam of light coming through the roof of the tent precisely illuminated the lone object on the table. Itty's gaze followed the light and landed on a grubby old-fashioned oil lamp. Dust motes hovered around it, shimmering in the sunbeam, tickling and teasing at the edges of her vision.

'Ah, what a perceptive young woman you are—I see you have already spotted my treasure. It is one of the last remaining djinn lamps in the vastness of Estalia, young mistress, if not the entire world. It is a most beauteous object. I can tell by your eyes that you are interested, yes? It can be yours for a mere trifle, a handful of coins.' Clasping his hands together below his chin, he leaned forward. 'It is truly a treasure and would be a bargain at ten times the price, yet all I ask is a paltry five dinari. Surely, I do not see you hesitate, esteemed mistress.' Barely pausing, and certainly not giving Itty a chance to say anything, he gasped and spread his hands. 'No, you are right, young mistress. I should not ask five, but *two* dinari, for you seem to be such a worthy noblewoman. Do not look surprised! I can tell that you are noble to have such discriminating sensibilities.'

The man's voice blurred and faded as the small lamp engulfed Itty's senses. Her field of view contracted to exclude everything else, and her hands stretched towards the lamp of their own volition as if they were so eager to touch it that they couldn't wait for her floundering brain to command them.

Nothing else existed beyond the lamp.

Its surface felt perfect, a tingling combination of smooth and rough patches—strange though not unpleasant, and exactly the right size to fit her hand. The lamp looked perfect as well, with eye-capturing, swirling patterns detectable beneath a layer of grime. It even smelled perfect, a subtle aroma of spices: vanilla and cardamom, with a hint of cinnamon.

'Lamp. Want. I. I. Lamp…' she mumbled, all conscious thought banished from her head. Her own voice seemed to come from a long way off and was somehow beyond her control. 'I'll take it!'

She didn't remember handing over any money, but she must have, because when she turned away, the lamp was in her possession.

Walking away from the tent, attention locked on her acquisition, Itty failed to detect the grin easing its way across the shopkeeper's face.

A few moments later, still dazed, she glanced back and saw… nothing unusual. She felt there was a gap, a space where a tent might have been. There had been a… something—white, smiling, sunlight, cinnamon—hadn't there? But now it was gone. She couldn't put her finger on what it might have been. She looked back at the lamp, and all other thoughts faded away again.

Her feet took her home, the daily library visit forgotten for the first time in her life. Even her imaginary pirates and dragons failed to provide companionship on the short journey.

Itty's cramped room contained only a small bed, her untidy clothes drawer, an overflowing sink and several bulging bookshelves. A framed sketch of her adoptive parents, Magnar and Dolcia Happenstance, hung on the wall by the door, so that she could smile a goodbye to them each time she left and greet them on her return.

This time, though, she ignored the sketch and books, choosing instead to sit on the edge of the bed and attempt to clean the lamp. Her vigorous rubbing caused a fragrance of spices to infuse the air, tickling her nose and making her eyes water.

A flash of light snapped her out of her trance-like state. She fell off the bed, landing on the floor with a thud. A billow of smoke emanated from the lamp, and Itty sneezed as the intensity of the cardamom and vanilla scent overpowered her nostrils.

From within the haze, a voice boomed, 'What is your desire, O mistress?'

The smoke cleared, revealing a tall figure who looked exactly like the shopkeeper from the market, right down to the drooping moustache and the glowing white teeth. He peered around the room, squinting in confusion, before he eventually spotted Itty lying beside the bed.

The figure closed his glowing emerald-green eyes and sighed. 'Your desire, what is it?'

Itty's mouth flapped open and shut, but no sound came out.

'Nothing…? Weren't you paying attention back in the market? This is a djinn lamp, yes?' he said, tapping the lamp with one long fingernail. He spread his arms wide. 'And I'm a djinn. You know how this all works, right? *Everybody* knows how this works. I'm here to grant you three wishes.'

She gawped at him from the floor, struggling to disengage her attention from the lamp and focus on this stranger in her room.

'Well, mistress? What do you want? Chop-chop. Riches? A palace? Anything at all.' The djinn stared at her for a moment, then shrugged and wiggled his eyebrows. 'Maybe a love interest?' After a glance around the room, he muttered, 'Though, first, you ought to wish for larger accommodations. I don't know how you can live in this hovel.' He gingerly lifted a wrinkled woollen stocking from the end of the bed, sniffed it, and recoiled. He flicked it into the corner of the room before wiping his fingers on his waistcoat and tentatively sitting on the bed. 'You're quite short, aren't you? You could wish to be taller. I can do that, you know.'

She pushed herself off the floor and stood with her hands on her hips. 'How did you get in here?' Her voice rose in volume as she summoned her courage. 'Get out, before I scream!'

The djinn's face dropped. 'But, mistress, I'm your djinn now. I'm at your service.' He was almost pleading.

Her eyes widened. 'Do you really expect me to believe that?'

The djinn scowled at her and puffed out his chest. 'Haven't you been listening to anything I've said, girl? I mean you no harm—quite the contrary, in fact.' He pointed to himself. 'Me, djinn. Me grant wish.' Then he pointed to Itty. 'You, djinn mistress. You make wish. Is there something you want, O mistress, or shall I come back later?' Under his breath, he added,

'When your brain's working again, assuming it does work.'

'I'm dreaming, aren't I?'

'Nope.' He reached out as if to pinch her, but she jerked back.

'I'm here, and I'm waiting.' He spoke more sharply this time, then tilted his head back as if addressing the heavens, and muttered, 'I was bound to get a stupid one eventually.'

Itty didn't register the insult; she was too busy struggling to fit the idea of a djinn into the real world—surely, they belonged only in stories. She remembered one about a princess with a magic carpet and a djinn; and there was the one with the thief, the sesame seeds, and the djinn. The books containing these stories were all in the south wing of the library, the fiction section, weren't they, shelved between demons and duck-billed platypuses? She'd have noticed if they'd been misfiled. Right?

'This has to be a trick. You're not real. I mean, you *are* real—that's obvious—but you're not a djinn. You're the man from the market.' A huge smile spread across her face. 'You raced ahead of me and managed to hide behind the bed before I came in, didn't you? You're trying to trick me.'

'Aargh!' The djinn ground his teeth together and pulled on the ends of his moustache. 'Look, watch this.' He twirled his arms above his head and produced a cabbage in each hand.

'A trick. Quite an easy one at that. You had them hidden up your sleeves.' Itty scowled at him, more confident now. She'd seen street magicians before.

With a flick of his wrists, he shook the cabbages. They vanished, to be replaced by a pair of startled capuchin monkeys. The monkeys chirped angrily at Itty and the djinn before knocking over a pile of dirty crockery and departing through the window.

'Mere trickery.'

The djinn took a deep breath and blew out a plume of smoke, which formed itself into a human-like shape on the other side of the room. As Itty's jaw dropped, the smoke solidified into an exact copy of the djinn, while the original faded away.

'Well?' the second—and now only—djinn said and crossed his arms.

'Wow,' Itty whispered.

Chapter 3: Take Care What You Wish For

The powers of the First are not infinite nor are they unchanging. If the Lamp should be passed on prior to the realization of three wishes, the strength of the First's djinnic powers will increase, and the First may eventually be able to take actions beyond the confines of the Lamp in advance of the act of summoning by the Second. The actions may be both physical, such as but not limited to endangering the life of the Second, and mental, such as but not limited to, removing any memories the Second may have about the actuality of the First and his Lamp.

Addendum to the Standard Djinn Contract, found among the later writings of the lawyer-philosopher, Avelgard the Mighty.

In words any normal human being can understand: once you've made your first wish, you're committed. The djinn will try to kill you until you make your next two wishes and pass the accursed lamp to someone else. It is important to take action quickly, since a powerful djinn can make you forget he exists!

Note scratched in the margin of the Djinn contract and attributed to Avelgard's assistant, believed to be the second person to capture a djinn, shortly after Avelgard the Mighty's untimely and unexpected death.

Itty stared at the djinn, and after several seconds, remembered to breathe again. A number of incisive responses cascaded through her brain, but got lost in a tangle of thoughts before reaching her tongue.

'You're real. Actually, really, real,' she uttered, eyes wide.

'About time! Sheesh. Give the girl a bisc— What do you eat in these parts, anyway? Do you have biscuits here? Cookies? Topeki cake? Chocolate? You don't look like a stranger to a sugary treat.' The djinn clapped his hands. 'Never mind. Let's get on with the show.'

'What's chocolate?'

'A sweet food made from roasted cocoa pods and sug– That doesn't matter.'

'You really came out of the lamp? That tiny lamp?'

'Yes, yes, now you're getting it,' The djinn nodded eagerly, causing the ends of his moustache to dance up and down. 'Well, missy, what do you want? I haven't got all day, you know. The clock's ticking.'

'How'd you get in there? Did a magician imprison you?'

'Magician, yes. Spells and magic, that sort of stuff. Long time ago, doesn't matter anymore. Come on, make a wish.' The djinn made hurry-up gestures. 'Please.'

'Who was he?' If djinn were real, she wanted to find out as much as she could about them.

The djinn stopped waving his arms, and his brow wrinkled in apparent confusion. 'Who was who?'

'The magician who imprisoned you.'

'Never mind; he's long dead,' the djinn spluttered. 'Even his ghost is dead. Stop wasting time. What do you want most in the whole world?'

'What were you before?'

'Before what?'

'Before the magician trapped you.'

The djinn froze briefly, then murmured, 'I was… I can't remember. Warmth, bliss, I think. Belonging.' He blinked, then said more loudly, 'It doesn't matter now. What *does* matter is your wish.'

'Did it hurt?' The thought crossed her mind that she could write a book about real djinn. An actual book—or at least, a pamphlet! How exciting would that be, having her own writing on a library shelf?

'What?'

Itty pointed at the lamp. 'Did it hurt when you were put in there?'

The djinn stared at her for several seconds with his mouth open, then blinked once and said, 'Yes, a bit…' He winced. 'A lot.' He smiled and clapped his hands again. 'But that doesn't matter right at this moment.'

'What's your name?'

'What? Why?'

'I've got to call you something…'

The djinn heaved his shoulders. '*Djinn* will do. Just. Make. A. Wish! Anything, anything at all.'

'Anything?'

He pressed a hand on his forehead. 'YES!'

She frowned. 'Are you really so powerful that you can do *anything*?'

The djinn scowled at her. 'Well, yes, OK, I'm not a god. But then gods don't offer you wishes. Believe me, O mistress, my powers extend well beyond the bounds of your imagination.'

'Hmph.' She squinted at him. 'Is there some sort of trick here?'

'What is it with you and tricks? Young people are so distrusting these days.'

He produced a long parchment from behind his body and waved it at her too quickly to read. He shuffled the scroll through his hands until he reached the part he wanted. Then, still holding it just out of her reach, he said, 'Look, standard djinn contract. See. Blah, blah, three wishes, blah, blah, boilerplate, the agreement between the djinn—that's me—and the owner—oh, how I hate that term; by the way, that's you—*begins upon the granting of the first wish* and yada, yada, within the spatial and temporal limits of his power, blah, blah, once the djinn has granted the final wish, he will return to the lamp, to be passed on to the next owner. And-then-there's-some-small-print which we can ignore.'

He'd not taken a breath while the words poured out and inhaled deeply before smiling and leaning towards Itty. 'So, let's get on with it. What's your first wi–?'

She snatched the contract from him and skimmed it. 'Wait! What's this bit about *removing memories?* And here, it says something about *endangering the owner's life?*'

He grabbed the parchment back and ground out through clenched teeth, 'Nothing. To. Worry. About.' A shudder passed through his body, then he took a deep breath and smiled sweetly at her.

'It just means you might forget about me, that's all, but don't worry. Everything will come back when you touch the lamp again, and the lamp'll turn up when it's needed. As for that death thing, put it out of your mind. It's never happened with me, cross my heart, but you know lawyers and magicians… They always make things sound complicated and alarming so that they can charge premium rates for their services. Besides, if it had happened—death, I mean—would I be here at all, having been released from my tortured life of servitude? Those trifling details are totally unimportant, nothing to fret about. All you should be thinking about is what you want to wish for.'

I'm not stupid. I know I probably can't trust him. In the stories Itty had read, fictional djinn always interpreted wishes in ways that didn't quite meet their owners' expectations. *Real djinn might be different*, she said to herself, *but I'll just take my time and be careful not to say the first thing that comes into my mind.*

'Well, I've always wanted to be an adventurer and travel the world. That'd be nice,' she mused.

What was it she'd been thinking about earlier…? Pirates. But real pirates would be a bit scary. I've never been on a ship—that's it! An exciting journey to somewhere exotic, a treasure island like in pirate stories. But absolutely no pirates.

'I want to go on a sea voyage.' *A nice safe voyage—with treasure, maybe, but no pirates. Right, now to ask for this carefully. All I want is calm, relaxing travelling, and perhaps visiting places where pirates have been. And finding treasure. That would be nice. Oh, this'll be so much fun!*

Caught up in her building excitement and forgetting her own sage advice, she blurted, 'My wish is to travel the seas.'

'As you wish, O mistress,' the djinn said in a deeper than normal voice and clapped his hands once more, making a boom much louder than should have been able to fit inside

Itty's small room. There was another flash, and smoke poured from the lamp, smelling of vanilla and cardamom.

By the time the flash faded, the djinn had disappeared, and the echo of his clap transformed into a hammering on the door.

Itty flapped her hands to disperse the smoke as she hurried to see who was knocking. Before she reached the door, it burst wide open, almost smacking her in the face. Two huge men tried to enter at once, getting stuck in the doorway. After some futile struggling, the larger of the two pushed the other back and squeezed himself in.

Unable to work out what she should do now, she could only watch as, with his heavy-browed head grazing the ceiling, he lifted a piece of paper close to his eyes. His lips moved as he squinted his eyes at it. He grunted, 'Are you Impelcep– Impersens– Your name Happenstance?'

The second man had entered the apartment by now and clamped a sweaty, ham-sized hand around her arm before she could reply. 'You're coming with us,' he growled.

The first man grabbed Itty's other arm, and the pair easily lifted her off the ground. They got stuck in the doorway again while trying to exit, then turned sideways and eased out.

'What's going on? Who are you? Put me down!' Itty's feet dangled a good distance from the ground as she struggled between the men.

'The prisoner will be quiet!' the larger man bellowed.

'The who– What?' she squeaked, head snapping around to face him.

'QUIET!'

Droplets of spittle hit Itty's face. She attempted to remove them by rubbing her cheek against her shoulder. It might be better to say no more, she decided, until she worked out what was happening.

Outside, a pair of bored-looking horses stood harnessed to a shabby canvas-covered wagon. One dull-eyed animal cast an indifferent glance at Itty as the men fastened shackles around her wrists and ankles. They hauled her to the rear of the wagon, where they threw her into a cage already full of chained men and women sitting on wooden benches.

Her fellow prisoners sat hunched over, heads bowed. A few flicked their gaze towards her while the remainder continued to stare at, or perhaps through, the bottom of the cage. Without looking up, two women shifted to make room for her to squeeze between them on the hard bench. Feeling sick, she took her seat.

What am I doing here? What do I do now? Who are these people? She wanted to call out to the men, to explain that they'd got the wrong person, but the reaction just now suggested that would not be a good idea. She gulped down air, trying to calm her nausea. *They've got to stop sometime—I can speak with whoever's there when we get out. They're bound to be reasonable.*

The wagon creaked and bounced as her captors climbed up on front. With a snap of the reins and a 'Hya!' the wagon set off, rocking from side to side in time with the slow, even clopping of the horses' hooves.

With clammy hands, she rubbed her arms where the men had gripped her and studied her companions in the dimness of the wagon. They all appeared worn down and resigned to their fate, dressed in grimy rags, some sporting bruises and cuts. None looked particularly friendly.

When the churning in her stomach had settled down a bit, she asked in a trembling voice, 'Where are we going? Who are those men?'

One woman glanced at her before turning her gaze back down to her manacled hands in her lap without answering. No one else reacted at all.

If she strained, Itty could hear parts of the conversation between her captors sitting up front.

'Tell me why we… that last one. She's tiny… never make a sailor.'

'This.' Coins jingled. 'A tall… white moustache… turban gave me this 'ere bag o' gold to kidnap 'er… dump 'er with the… Didn't ask why, don't right care. Means nothing to me if she's thrown to the fishes… a day out to sea.'

Moustache and turban? That sounded familiar, but she couldn't conjure up memories of where or who it might have been. *Sea?* Panic sent her thoughts spiralling. *I can't go to sea—I should be… What time is it? Oh, no. I'm late!*

'Excuse me, sirs,' she called. 'There's been a mistake. I'm supposed to be in the library. They're expecting me, and–'

The two men laughed and a few of her fellow prisoners rolled their eyes at her, but the slow, plodding journey continued. The gentle rolling of the wagon did little to settle the queasiness in Itty's stomach. She concentrated on the floor of the wagon, trying hard not to throw up. *I just have to wait until we stop. There'll be someone to explain things to, and that'll go better if I don't smell of vomit.*

When the wagon stopped some interminable time later, she jerked up to the smell of fish and the sound of people shouting. The calls of gulls added to the cacophony.

The downcast prisoners were ushered out of the wagon and lined up on the docks, an area of the city Itty had never visited before. She squinted in the bright sunlight and found herself facing one of the largest ships in the harbour. 'Invigilator' was painted on the side. Its varnished wooden hull reflected the morning's light, and its brass railings gleamed. Twenty cannon ports along the vessel's side announced that this was a ship not to be ignored. The Estalian flag, a blue seven-pointed star on a yellow background, snapped proudly at the top of the tallest of its three masts.

A sour-faced man in a port official's uniform of blue frock coat and breeches eyed them up and down and muttered, 'I suppose they'll do.' He handed a bag of money to Itty's two captors.

'A pleasure doin' business with you, guv'nor,' the larger man said, tapping his fingers to his forehead in salute. 'Another dozen next week?'

The official nodded, almost dislodging his powdered wig, and turning to the prisoners, pointed to the *Invigilator*'s gangplank. 'You lot, get up there,' he yelled. 'Move it!'

Itty made to call out, but the official had turned away, and the burly men corralling the prisoners didn't look like the sort of people who'd pay attention to her.

The ship buzzed with activity; sailors rushed from station to station, winding winches and scrambling up and down ropes to tie and untie things Itty couldn't identify. This chaos was nothing like the quiet, tidy ports and ships in the elegant pictures hanging in Hyrhia's library. Trolley wheels and capstans squeaked, feet stomped, sails flapped, and everyone was shouting.

The captives were taken below deck, into a muggy dimness filled with even more noise. She had little time to think as sailors removed their shackles, handed each prisoner a uniform of pale green blouse and slacks with a lime green belt, and ordered them to clean themselves and change into their new clothing. The bathing water was cold and salty, having only just been hauled in buckets directly from the sea by the first of the prisoners.

Itty tried several times to ask what was going on. 'Excuse me–' was met with a shove to keep up with the prisoner in front of her. 'I shouldn't be–' garnered a blank look. 'There's been some sort of mista–' resulted in a clip around the ear and a 'Get in there for delousing with the rest of these fine ladies and gentlemen or you'll get more than that.'

None of the other prisoners said anything.

After they'd changed into their green naval uniforms, the prisoners' old clothes and belongings were collected in small bags which they were told would be returned when their sentence was up, if they were lucky.

Soon after, hair still dripping, they all stood in a line on the deck, looking like a row of peapods in their green naval uniforms. Ships were elegant and filled with excitement in the books she read, not like this rough and terrifying place. Itty's legs shook from more than just the cold.

The ship had set sail already, and the earlier furious activity had slowed down. Itty gazed at the Port of Hyrhia, her home for the past sixteen-and-a-bit years, as it receded into the distance. She felt empty. *It's too late to escape now. I'm stuck here.*

A shout wrenched her out of her reverie. 'Prisoners, attention! Captain on deck!'

With his hands clasped behind his back, a thin, aristocratic man with grey hair tied in a loose ponytail strode along the line of prisoners, scrutinizing each of them, before stepping back to inspect the whole group. He was wearing white breeches, shirt and waistcoat, with an ornately embroidered green frock coat sporting gold epaulettes.

'I am Captain Smart. I bid you fine people welcome aboard the *Invigilator*.' He curled his lips in an approximation of a smile. He pointed at the sailor who had shouted earlier. 'This is my first mate, Mister Ansif. You will do everything he says. You will act on his orders without question, and you will do it instantly. Am I clear?'

He glared at the prisoners.

'The Estalian navy needs people like you—men and women who aren't afraid of a scuffle. The fact that you've been sent to me indicates that you're the most despicable and violent prisoners in the country. You have thereby amply demonstrated your ability and willingness to fight, albeit for purely selfish reasons. Nevertheless, giving you the chance to start a new life on the sea is preferable to letting you rot in our jails.'

He paced up and down the line, staring off into the distance. 'I'm a fair man and I run a fair ship. I expect you to earn your freedom by working hard and obeying orders. If you choose not to, you may attempt to swim to shore, voluntarily or otherwise. No one will stop you. The closest land is'—he glanced back towards where Hyrhia was barely visible—'currently seven leagues distant and increasing.'

'C-captain? Sir?' Itty raised a trembling hand.

'Silence, vermin! Speak only when you're spoken to,' the first mate roared directly into her ear.

She jumped—she hadn't noticed him move from behind the captain. Once again, she felt the unpleasant sensation of spittle hitting her face, and gagged at the mate's horrendous breath.

As Mr Ansif stepped back, Captain Smart strode up to Itty and stared down at her for a few seconds. He rubbed his chin and mused, 'You're very small for a murderer. You must be more bloodthirsty than you look.'

'But, Captain, I shouldn't be here—I was kidnapped. I'm innocent,' she said meekly, trying—and failing—not to whine.

Everyone laughed, including the other prisoners.

The captain's eyes widened. 'Innocent, you say? Oh dear, I'm so sorry. Mister Ansif, please be so kind as to prepare a first-class cabin for this young woman.'

When the first mate saluted and said, 'Aye-aye, Cap'n,' Itty sighed in relief.

'Oh, wait.' The captain smiled, but his eyes remained dark as he leaned in close to her. 'We don't have any first-class cabins on this vessel. A navy ship has no room for comfort, and my crew has no time for luxury. And *you*—she shrank back under his glare—'are part of my crew.' He stood up straight and scowled at all the prisoners. 'You all are, and do not forget it. Take them away, Mister Ansif.'

Chapter 4: A Sailor's Life for Me

There's many a sailor who's robbed and fought,
Serving the navy 'cos they've been caught.

Scrub the decks, ye scurvy knaves.
Hoist the sails, ye scurvy knaves.
Sing for me, ye scurvy knaves,
Or ye'll be drowned beneath the waves.

Time on the sea will make ye a good 'un,
Wasting in prison most certainly wouldn't.

Scrub the decks…

The captain is king; ye does as he says.
He judges ye fair; no crime ever pays.

Scrub the decks…

Estalian Imperial Navy sea shanty (Trad.)

Before her first hour aboard the *Invigilator* was up, it was evident to everyone that Imperceptibility wasn't strong enough to be effective at anything

involving heavy lifting—or moderate lifting—
when she had to be rescued from underneath
the coils of an empty cargo net. Not very long
after that hour, they also discovered that even
light lifting was beyond her, so the first mate
put her to work on the rigging instead.

Within a quarter of an hour, however, they
also discovered that she was petrified of
heights. When she had climbed as high as the
main mast's first cross-spar, an odd waft of
vanilla and cardamom tickled her nose. At the
same time, she heard a faint, 'Look down.'

She wasn't sure if she imagined the words
on the breeze, but she made the mistake of
glancing downwards. Her vision blanked, and
her hands slipped. She screamed as she tipped
over. Only her legs, caught in the netting,
prevented her from ending up a smear on the
deck. Three sailors had to untangle her and
carry her frozen-rigid body back down.

Mr Ansif opened his mouth to shout at her,
but closed it again, before stalking off, shaking

his head and mumbling something about useless landlubber wastes of sea air.

Once she'd recovered, a less traumatic third introduction to a sea-faring life was devised, consisting of scrubbing decks, polishing brass, scrubbing decks, being shouted at, and scrubbing decks. Although a little careless about cleaning right into the corners and utterly incapable of remembering which side was port and which starboard, she was deemed sufficiently competent in carrying out her duties as a swabby that she wasn't tossed overboard. And she was never asked to climb the ropes again.

She cried herself to sleep the first and second nights, missing a city that probably hadn't taken much note of her disappearance. At most, someone in the library would be mildly annoyed when her current loans weren't returned in time, earning her a black mark in the ledger. Or perhaps her landlord would notice her departure when he came to collect the rent; maybe the library would get its books back when he eventually cleared out her room to make way for a new tenant. She hoped she hadn't left the water running or any candles burning. Or lamps… *Lamps?* Why did lamps pop into her mind? She had only candles, not lamps. Still, something about a lamp tickled the back of her mind, but she couldn't work out what it meant.

After those first days, she was so exhausted when her work shift was over that she fell asleep almost instantly, despite the loud singing of sea shanties up on deck and hissed conversations below. The conversations would stop when she came down through the hatch, and restart when she climbed into her bunk at the opposite end of the sleeping quarters. She was too tired to wonder what they were about.

Shipboard life was nothing like any of the stories she'd read. They never mentioned scrubbing decks for a start. Apart from that, she did have to admit it was similar to growing up in the Ethynites' orphanage: there was a constant buzz of sound; she worked all the time; meals were uninspiring but filling; most people didn't say much and kept to themselves. Like the Ethynite nuns, the senior sailors weren't cruel, but they also didn't go out of their way to be friendly.

As she got used to performing her daily duties, Itty was able to let her imagination roam, though she took care not to wave her mop around too violently when attacking imaginary crack-ins, small but vicious cephalopods who would climb into ships via cracks in the woodwork. If they weren't dealt with quickly, the myths said, so many would sneak aboard that a ship would capsize under the extra weight. She also tried not to flick her cloth too wildly when eradicating all traces of the aftermath of bloody battles with Short Jack Sliver or Cutthroat Rainbow Beard from the brass work. Still, all things considered, she thought she would prefer *not* to encounter these sea monsters and pirates she recalled from her books now that she was at sea herself. Perhaps she wasn't cut out to be an adventurer after all.

Her other daydreams were about what she really wanted: to be back home, in a city surrounded on three sides by sand, and where she would do her best to ignore the docks on the fourth side. She'd even settle for any city, as long as it had a library and plenty of bookshops. And delicious breakfast pastries; saliva filled her mouth at the thought of *Pierre's Patisserie*.

Of course, where there were pastries, there should also be a wide market space or a few longish roads to amble along while munching them. Not only was the *Invigilator* lacking in baked goods, the distance from bow to stern wasn't long enough to properly enjoy even an imaginary apricot croissant.

But there was little prospect of dry land and long walks, let alone Pierre's pastries, in her future.

Itty often saw Captain Smart on the wheel deck, looking through a spyglass and pointing a direction to the steersman or passing orders to Mr Ansif. The first mate then relayed those instructions to the common sailors, typically at the top of his lungs—though sometimes he seemed to have a whispered huddle with a select few of the sailors when the captain wasn't on deck. Most of those orders related to the maintenance of the ship, since there was little other work for the sailors on the quiet seas. The captain also patrolled his ship, ensuring he was familiar with the state of his vessel and crew, having a word with each sailor whose path he happened to cross.

The first few times he met any of the new sailors, he made a point of saying that it didn't matter what their crimes were; being on the *Invigilator* was a chance to forget that past life and become a new person. The captain himself seemed to have forgotten his outburst the day Itty came aboard, and when he bumped into her now, he would tell her that she reminded him of his granddaughter who was of a similar age. Not that his granddaughter was a hardened criminal, of course, he would laugh, nor had she ever set foot on a ship crewed by criminals.

Itty smiled and mumbled thanks at him, though she was never sure what she was thanking him for. Not being thrown overboard, perhaps. Each time the captain left, she mentally kicked herself and wished she'd been brave enough to repeat her claims of innocence. Actually, she admitted to herself, it was the ever-present Mr Ansif she was frightened of; if the captain had been unaccompanied, she would have spoken up. She'd got as far as opening her mouth once, but a growl from the first mate made her clamp it shut.

Early on the fifteenth morning—or was it the sixteenth, maybe the seventeenth, she'd completely lost track—she was busy outside the ship's sickbay, putting a shine on the brass railing, when the door at the end of the passageway burst open.

A sailor was half-carrying, half-dragging a screaming young man with a leg injury. Red-raw flesh peeked through torn trousers. 'Galleyman's burned hisself. Poured boiling fat all down 'is leg, he has,' he called as they pushed past Itty.

'Let me help,' she said, grabbing one of the stricken man's arms and supporting him into the sickbay.

A few minutes later, the ship's surgeon tied off the last of the galleyman's bandages. As Itty was cleaning up the mess of soiled dressings and globs of salve, Captain Smart and Mr Ansif arrived.

'How is Jackson?' the captain asked.

The doctor replied, 'He'll live, sir, but he won't be working for a few weeks.'

Mr Ansif gave Jackson a friendly punch on the shoulder and said, 'Jackson here's a sturdy lad. He'll be up and about by daybreak, mark my words.'

Jackson groaned, then threw up into the bucket Itty managed to get in position just in time.

'We'll need a replacement galleyman,' said Captain Smart.

'I can do it,' Itty chimed, hoping that working in the galley would mean less deck scrubbing. She also mentally crossed her fingers that the captain would look on her more favourably, too, and consider reducing her sentence in the Prisoners' Navy.

Jackson attempted to sit up, sweat breaking out on his forehead. 'No, sir, I can work. I know where everything is.'

'Nonsense, you need to rest,' said the captain, before turning to Itty. 'This girl will do. Happenstance, isn't it? Can you cook?'

'A little.'

'Can you wash up?'

Itty thought about her messy accommodation back in Hyrhia. 'A little,' she mumbled.

Mr Ansif said, 'Sir, she's obviously unqualified. She'll be useless. Jackson's your man.'

Captain Smart turned his gaze on the first mate and, through gritted teeth, said, 'Do not contradict me, sirrah. Jackson's staying here, and this girl won't be missed on deck. And, Mister Ansif, you will do well to remember who is in command of this ship. I have stated that Happenstance will be the new galleyman, and that's the end of the matter.' He glanced at Itty, who stared back with wide eyes. 'You'll do, won't you, my girl? Breakfast's in an hour, so get yourself down to the galley right away. Go.'

Mr Ansif scowled at Itty.

Jackson moaned and fell back onto his pillow.

Itty gulped and ran.

She knocked on the galley door less than a minute later. The ship's cook was an enormously fat, red-faced woman, barely fitting into the narrow galley. She grunted at her new assistant and nodded towards the mop and the splashes of oil on the walls and floor.

Itty's shoulders drooped. So much for an escape from deck scrubbing.

It was fortunate that the oily mess was on this side of the cook, because there was no way she could have squeezed past in the tiny ship's kitchen.

She offered a tentative smile. 'I'm Imperceptibility, Itty to my friends. What should I call you?'

'Cook.'

'Oh. Keeping an entire ship's crew of sailors fed must be a very important job.'

Cook stared at her through narrowed eyes, her lips forming a tight line. 'Harrumph.'

Itty blushed and turned back to the mop.

After cleaning up the spilled oil, Itty was put to washing and drying dishes. So far, working the galley wasn't very different from working on deck, except there was less shouting.

Cook said barely a word as she reconstituted dehydrated eggs and boiled porridge, basic fare for a hundred and twenty men and women, but warm and filling.

Itty and Cook doled out globs of both to the sailors streaming past the galley hatch. None of the sailors seemed to object to dollops of porridge and eggs on the same plate, but Itty thought she would prefer to keep hers separate. After the crew had been fed, she resumed cleaning while Cook prepared the captain's breakfast.

The captain didn't get porridge and reconstituted eggs. Instead, taking considerably more care than she had over the crew's breakfast, Cook hummed to herself as she boiled two *fresh* eggs, fried five rashers of crispy bacon, lightly buttered two slices of toast, and squeezed a glass of fresh orange juice.

Itty asked, 'Where did the eggs come from?'

'Duck.'

Instinctively pulling her head down, Itty wondered what new hazard could be found in the galley. She looked up to see Cook rolling her eyes.

Cook opened a cupboard in the far corner of the small ship's kitchen, and a duck's head popped out.

Itty blushed again.

Cook fed the duck a morsel of bacon fat and scratched its head affectionately before closing the cupboard again. After a brief period of banging other doors open and shut, muttering, 'Where'd that idiot boy put it?' she found the coffee jar and brewed a pot, strong and hot. She almost smiled as she laid the plates and coffee on a tray. After covering the food with a cloth, she set a small vase on the tray. Retrieving a single daffodil from an icebox at the back of the galley, she held it carefully, pinkie finger raised, and gently placed it in the vase.

'Girl, take this to the captain. Quickly now, before it gets cold.'

Itty balanced the heavy tray on one hand, holding on to the railing with the other as she navigated the narrow passages and ladders from the galley to the captain's cabin. Although she'd developed her sea legs by now, she didn't want to risk spilling anything. She wanted to make a good impression on the captain, hoping to have a chance to explain how she was innocent and needed to return home.

As she knocked on the door, she heard a faint giggle and a vaguely familiar aroma of vanilla and cardamom wafted from nearby.

'Enter,' the captain called.

Itty eased the door open and stepped in. A faint snigger came from behind as her feet tangled together and something pushed her forward. She yelped and fell, launching the entire tray towards the captain.

Eggs, toast, and bacon landed on the finely woven red and blue Souf carpet, mingling with the seaweed pattern like some bizarre breakfast fish. Coffee spilled on the varnished mahogany floor beyond the carpet, while the orange juice ended up on the captain's trouser leg, dripping onto his shiny black boots. She found herself staring at the vase Cook had so delicately placed on the tray; it had managed to land, upright, directly in front of her, mocking her with its cheery daffodil.

Captain Smart's initial expression of surprise turned to dismay as he surveyed the mess. He bellowed, 'You imbecile, you clumsy, good-for-nothing cretin! I'll have you clapped in irons. I'll have you keel-hauled!'

'Oh no, please, sir. Sorry, sir,' Itty pleaded. She caught sight of something bubbling on the floorboards. 'Captain! Captain, look!'

'I'll have you fl– What?'

She pointed at a blistered, hissing patch of varnish where the coffee had spilled. 'Look at the floor, there.'

The captain paused, then carefully picked up the almost empty coffee pot. He sniffed at it and jerked his head back. 'Where did this coffee come from? What did you put in it?'

Itty replied, 'N-nothing, Captain, sir. Cook gave it to me just now.'

Then the captain shouted through the open door, 'Mister Ansif! Find Cook and bring her here.'

A few minutes later, the first mate entered along with a pale and limping Jackson. Both pointed pistols at the captain.

The captain regarded them calmly. 'Mister Ansif, Mister Jackson,' he said quietly, 'what's the meaning of this? Where's Cook?'

'Captain, I'm sorry to do this to you. It would've gone easier if you'd just drunk the poison,' the first mate said as he waved his gun in Itty's direction. 'But it seems this useless shred of an idiot wasn't capable of carrying out her one simple task.'

The captain's gaze snapped to Itty. 'You're part of this, too?'

Getting up from the floor, she frantically shook her head, then stopped with the sudden realization that she might be better off siding with the majority. Nonetheless, she couldn't bring herself to lie to the captain, not even by nodding.

He turned his eyes back to the first mate and calmly asked, 'What's this all about? You've been my first mate for—what?—ten years now, and you've been loyal all that time. It's been a good life on the sea, hasn't it?'

Mr Ansif grunted. 'Maybe for you, Captain, but we're still prisoners here. No shore leave for us. No freedom!'

'But this is better than wasting away in a jail cell, surely, and you'll be a free man once your sentence is served.'

The first mate growled, 'That's not good enough. We're going to have our freedom now.'

I've got to do something, Itty thought. She tentatively raised a hand, then cleared her throat to attract everyone's attention. Her mouth went suddenly dry when all eyes focussed on her. She ran her tongue across her lips and spoke quickly, before she could change her mind. 'I wonder if you've ever read Warren Piece's *The Economic Value of Discord and Cooperation*. It's a magnificent book and talks about how short-term opportunistic gains can lead to long-term losses. I say we should give Piece a chance and come to some amicable arrangement which would involve killing no one and perhaps a reduction in sentences.'

She smiled weakly as she looked across at the hostile faces staring back.

After a moment, Mr Ansif smiled.

Then he laughed, Jackson joining in.

'Little girl,' he said, 'if we could read, we wouldn't be here in the first place. Even though you're not much use on the ship and couldn't even do something as simple as delivering a poisoned coffee pot, we were going to keep you on, as a mascot, like. But if you're going to keep spouting nonsense like that, we're better off without you. You can join the captain. Get over there.'

He waved his gun at her. 'I don't want to have to shoot either of you. It'll make a mess of this fine carpet.' He scowled at the captain's breakfast on the floor. 'More of a mess.'

Itty squeaked, unable to persuade her mouth to form words.

Captain Smart stood up straight. 'Mister Ansif, hand over your weapon. You are relieved of duty.'

Jackson and Mr Ansif glanced at each other, then the first mate said, 'No, sir. You are. All things considered, I think I will keep my weapon.'

'Why now, Mister Ansif?'

Mr Ansif shrugged, 'Didn't get the poison until Sally Oakes brought it with her in the last prisoner intake. You remember her? Widow Oakes—poisoned five husbands before she was caught. Too good an opportunity to pass up, though it didn't work out as planned, thanks to this girl.'

Mr Ansif and Jackson took the captain and Itty at gunpoint out to the deck, where they were surrounded by the scowling faces of the rest of the crew.

The captain paled. 'All of you?' he choked. 'No…'

Mr Ansif called out to the sailors, 'Shall we kill the captain?'

The surgeon stepped forward. 'Mister Ansif, we have the ship now, but I, for one, would prefer not to see the captain dead. He's done a lot for us and has not been cruel.'

A few of the crew shouted, 'Throw him overboard,' and 'String him up,' but most murmured that they'd had enough of killing.

'Very well,' Mr Ansif said. 'We'll cast him and the girl adrift, with enough fresh water for a few days. We'll let the tides decide if they should live or die.'

Three of the sailors manhandled Captain Smart and Itty into one of the ship's dinghies and lowered the boat off the side as the others cheered.

The captain barked, 'This is mutiny, damn your souls. I'll have the lot of you hanged!'

The crew responded with laughter and jeers.

'So long, captain,' called Mr Ansif—now Captain Ansif—as he tossed the Estalian Navy flag down to fall on top of the captain. 'May your voyage be brief, and see you in the afterlife.'

As the ship disappeared into the distance with a skull and crossbones flag atop its central mast, Itty was sure that she heard chuckling over the splashing of the sea. Hints of vanilla and cardamom mingled in the salty sea air, and the waves seemed to whisper, 'I'll be free soon.'

Chapter 5: Interlude—The Adventurers' Guild

The most exciting place in the world for any aspiring explorer has got to be *The Adventurers' Guild*. Where else can you expect to find the most astonishing discoveries in the world, or meet the bravest explorers and most brilliant scientists who ever existed?

There's never a moment's boredom in The Adventurers' Guild.

> *The Little Explorer, Activities to Entertain Budding Adventurers*, Dame Octavia Bluminsheim, Gatekeeper to The Adventurers' Guild.

The gatekeeper interrupted with a polite, 'Excuse me, Mistress Happenstance.'

'Yes, Madame Gatekeeper?'

'I confess I am slightly confused about some aspects of your story. Let me see if I've understood what you've told us so far…' The gatekeeper coughed gently. 'You were going about your normal business one morning, enjoying your breakfast on the way to, of all places, a library. And during this perfectly normal journey that you made every day, somehow—you can't remember precisely how—ended up press-ganged into the Estalian navy.'

Itty nodded.

The gatekeeper leaned forward and narrowed her eyes at the young woman.

'Are you certain you hadn't been—how shall I put this?—engaging in criminal activities in Hyrhia, and that's why you ended up in the *Prisoners'* Navy? I must warn you against trying my patience.'

Someone in the audience shouted, 'She looks like a right bad 'un, she does.'

'Aye, I wouldnae trust her,' another voice added.

'Frankly, this is ridiculous, Madame Gatekeeper,' Prince Ollipher called out as he stood up from his seat with the other successful candidates. 'The girl's obviously lying or delusional. She doesn't look like she could possibly survive life on a ship, let alone in a mere dinghy. I doubt if she's been to sea at all, or even knows where Hyrhia is.'

Before Imperceptibility could respond to this, the gatekeeper bellowed, 'Master Ollipher, please keep your opinion to yourself.' She glared at him, then let her eyes scan the chamber. 'And that goes for the rest of you, too. The Guild is a dignified institution, and we owe it to each candidate to treat them with a modicum of respect until such time as *I* can make a decision about their suitability. Is that understood?'

There was a subdued murmuring among the audience, and the prince's cheeks reddened.

'But, madam,' he blustered, 'it's getting late.' He gestured at the darkened windows. 'The contest should have ended ages ago, but instead, we're listening to this nonsensical wittering. The good people here should be released to their evening activities.'

'Master Ollipher, I am in charge of the contest, and it is over when I say it is. Anyone in the audience is at liberty to leave whenever they want.' The gatekeeper's eyes swept the hall. No one made any moves to depart, though it was unclear how much of this was fear of the gatekeeper and how much was interest in Imperceptibility's story.

She returned her gaze to Ollipher and smiled sweetly. 'I can also change my mind about who is and is not accepted into the Guild. Is that clear?'

Ollipher swallowed, and his face paled. He nodded meekly and sat down.

The gatekeeper called to someone standing at the edge of the chamber, 'Steward, would you be so kind as to request the presence of the lamplighters, so that we might have some more illumination? I suspect we could be here for quite some time more.'

The steward saluted and scurried away.

'Now, Mistress Happenstance, for the moment, let us put to one side your life in Estalia, for we are far from there. Rest assured that if we find it necessary to do so, we will dispatch a dirigible to your home city to make enquiries about your background, but pray continue with your intriguing story.' The gatekeeper's voice became sterner. 'And please ensure that your words are truthful.'

Someone in the audience snorted derisively. Itty suspected it might have been Prince Ollipher, but when she glanced across at him, he was doing his best to look innocent.

At this point, the steward returned with two somewhat soot-smeared youths in tow. The pair set about lighting lanterns on pillars throughout the chamber as well as replacing the torches on the walls.

Itty licked her lips. 'Thank you, Madame Gatekeeper. Well, we had been cast adrift…'

Chapter 6: That Sinking Feeling

There are many theories about the underworld, but one thing they all agree on is the existence of the River Sticks. This river, the boundary between the upper world and the lower, takes its name from the complex and ever-changing maze of razor-sharp plants growing just below the surface. These unyielding wooden spikes would shred the hull of any boat and thus prevent anyone from crossing the river. Anyone, that is, apart from the lone ferry pilot, the dark and terrifying Kharon, whose knowledge of the maze patterns permits safe passage of souls across the Sticks to their final resting place.

It is unclear what the form of this resting place might be. Depending on the theory one chooses to study, it is deemed to be either some form of eternal paradise, or conversely, excruciating and everlasting punishment. However, the premise of reincarnation notwithstanding, the lack of concrete evidence of anyone's return from this place does suggest that it is, indeed, ultimately final.

Myths of the Underworld, Professor Marian
Gesenhalter, DTheol.

'Damn and blast them!' Captain Smart was still fuming as daylight faded and stars began to dot the sky.

When heroes were cast adrift in the books Imperceptibility read, it always occurred within easy reach of a convenient island, but there were no islands here. Of course, sometimes the heroes then had to contend with cannibals and other dangers, such as in Deffo's story *The Robbing Son of Crewso*. Still, land would have been preferable to the empty sea stretching as far as the horizon in all directions.

'What do we do now, Captain?' she asked quietly.

His brow unfurrowed and his anger morphed into a grim smile. 'We're in a bit of a pickle, Happenstance, my girl. There's no doubt about that. You must have committed a serious crime to end up on my ship, and I'll warrant you wish you'd held your tongue instead of intervening on my behalf.'

She was about to protest when he held up his hands.

'But none of that matters now. Your past is none of my business, and there's no point in us being uncivil to each other while we're stuck here in this rather small boat.'

He glanced at the sky, then rummaged in his pockets, producing a compact sextant and a compass. 'Perhaps, my girl, we can occupy ourselves with a navigation lesson… You know your stars, don't you?'

Itty recognized some of the constellations: the Great Triangle of the Hippopotamus, the Faded Blossom of the Rhododendron, and just peeking over the horizon, the Face of the Sludge Farrier. She already knew that if you drew a straight line from the top of the Rhododendron through the left eye of the Sludge Farrier, and extended it as far as the

Hippopotamus, you'd reach the North West Star, the one fixed point in the sky.

Captain Smart pointed out the Flenser, the Effulgent Dragonfly, the Querulous Bodkin, and so many others that Itty suspected he was making some of them up.

She had the impression that the captain was talking to keep her mind—and probably his, too—diverted from their current circumstance. It seemed to be working. She found herself forgetting about their predicament as she listened to his soothing voice.

'Happenstance, the night sky is a rich tapestry of myth and story, but the truth is, all you need is the North West Star as long as you have a sextant.'

After telling her this bit was the index lever, which moved the corresponding index mirror, and this the micrometre drum, and several other parts which she promptly forgot, he lifted the sextant to his eye and aimed at the horizon. 'Thanks to our compass, we know where north is, and sighting the sextant to the North West Star, we can get an angle that will tell us exactly where we are with a bit of arithmetic, which is a bit simpler in a small boat like this one since we are pretty much at sea level and don't have to take deck elevation into account.' He lowered the instrument and deflated. 'Unfortunately, even if we know where we are, without my charts, I can't tell which bearing we should take.'

The captain went on to explain that he was familiar with the locations of the major continental ports, but the nearest of those was surely too distant to reach in a dinghy. He knew there were several clusters of small islands much closer, but not precisely where they were.

None of that mattered anyway, since they had no means of propulsion. All they could do was drift wherever the currents happened to take them.

'Now, we've got enough water for several days, but no food,' Captain Smart said as he fiddled with the buttons on his jacket. 'The Navy likes jackets with shiny brass buttons, but do you know what that means, young Happenstance?'

She looked at him blankly.

'Hooks!' He held up a curved piece of metal, the wire from the edging of one of his buttons. 'Now, if we tie these to our bootlaces and dangle them off the side of the boat, with any luck we'll catch a fish or two.'

He also used a hook to unpick some of the threads in his jacket and then ripped it in half. Handing her one of the pieces, he said, 'Soak this in the sea and use it to cover your head during the daytime. The sun can be quite vicious.'

Three days and three nights passed. They used the flag from the ship as additional protection from the sun during the day and from the chill during the night.

They caught two fish during that time, much to Itty's surprise. The captain sliced each one open using a piece of metal he'd twisted off his sextant. They didn't eat all of the fish in one go, instead eking them out because they didn't know when the next would come along. Itty found the meagre bites less unpleasant after they had dried in the sunshine for a while, but that might have been primarily because she was so hungry.

At the beginning, the captain filled the time with stories of the sea: myths of David Johnson's Locket and the ghosts of the lost ship, the *Celestial Marie*. He included some tales of his own battles with pirates and terrifying demons. Itty reckoned that those 'demons' were probably just more pirates, though that didn't make the captain's tales any less enjoyable. In return, she told him stories from her favourite books back home, about pirates and thieves, dragons and djinn.

As time passed with little food and water and no sign of land or rescue, they both became weaker. They could summon energy for little more than blankly gazing at the blue sea and bluer sky. Itty drifted off into dreams about being back home, curled up in a snug corner of Hyrhia's library surrounded by books. She dreamed of *Pierre's Patisserie* in the marketplace, especially those sweet, sticky fruit croissants. Her cramping stomach seemed especially reproachful after those dreams.

During the chill nights, nightmares of white teeth in a laughing mouth and the smell of cardamom and vanilla pushed her dreams aside. Piercing green eyes stabbed at her, while the mouth formed words beneath a twitching moustache. She couldn't make out what the chortling demon said, but there was something about wishes and promises. When she woke to the morning sun and the slap of waves against the boat, her nightmares always evaporated before she could make any sense of them.

On the fourth day, they drank the last of the fresh water. Itty suspected it had lasted so long because the captain wasn't drinking his fair share.

'No, my girl, you finish it,' Captain Smart croaked through dried and cracking lips. 'I've had a long time on this Earth, but your entire life is ahead of you.'

Not wanting to upset him, she didn't say that in their present situation, perhaps her entire life wouldn't end up being all that long.

'Let's pass the time with another story,' the captain wheezed when they were both awake the following day. 'One about why I chose to employ prisoners on my ship.' He pushed himself upright and extracted his compass from his pocket again. 'This was handed down from my grandfather, who got it from his. And *he* was Captain Estobilius Argonistas Smarrette.'

Itty perked up. 'Wasn't he a pirate? I read about him. He terrorized ports in half the world, didn't he? He was famous for sacking the city of Durogne and stealing the world-famous Ulangian diamond, wasn't he?'

She loved the swashbuckling tales she'd read featuring the infamous pirate, with his magic compass and crew of ruthless cutthroats, or possibly intelligent monkeys and sleek mermen, depending on which book she read. Smarrette cropped up in both the fiction and non-fiction sections of Hyrhia's library, so she was never sure how much was fact.

'Oh, you've heard the story already.' The captain sagged. 'Never mind. He's the reason I'm trying to rehabilitate prisoners, attempting to do some good to make up for his deeds. Not that it seems to have worked out very well for me.' He looked out at the empty seascape. 'Or you, I'm afraid.' With a trembling arm, he reached the compass towards her. 'Here, take this, please. Recognize that good can come out of evil, and may you never again be as lost as we are now. I'm sorry you're in this mess.'

Closing his eyes and lying back in the boat, he whispered so quietly Itty could barely hear him, 'There's a legend, passed down through my family, that the compass will show you where you need to go when all else is lost. Perhaps you should try it.'

His laboured breathing became gentle snoring, which slowed and then stopped.

No, please no. Itty felt like her mind had stopped, too.

She looked at the captain for several minutes, then at the worn-shiny compass in her hand. After a few moments, she returned her stare to his body.

You can't leave me alone.

The only sound came from the waves gently slapping the side of the small boat.

She leaned across and touched his knee, then shook it gently. 'Captain?'

Nothing.

She crawled across the boat and shook his shoulder. 'Captain Smart!'

It was true she knew about death—her foster parents had died only two years before, and there were the incurably ill children in the orphanage in which she'd been raised—but she'd never actually *seen* someone die. Itty felt cold and more alone than ever before.

What do I do now?

She curled up in the other end of the dinghy from the captain. She wanted to cry, but her body was so parched that no tears would come.

How did I get here? I should be in a city surrounded by desert, not a boat surrounded by water. I wish I was back there now. I wish… I wish…

She clutched the compass tight in her hand—it reminded her of something she'd held, ages and ages ago, something shiny and mesmerizing. Something that smelled of spices when she rubbed it and made smoke and… something else. No, some*one* else…

Calling to mind the captain's final words, she wondered even if the compass did show her where to go, how would she get there? She flipped open the lid to find the needle whirling around rapidly.

The noise of the sea became louder, distracting her from her thoughts. Waves smacked harder against the boat. Suddenly alert, Itty grabbed the sides of the boat as a rushing, churning sound surrounded her. The sky became heavy with thick, dark clouds. A bolt of lightning streaked past, illuminating boiling waves as a whirlpool took shape nearby.

The vortex widened and sped up, sucking at the boat's hull and pulling clouds across the sky. Gusts of wind beat at Itty and propelled the dinghy ever faster towards the deepening hole in the sea.

She screamed—at least, she felt that she was screaming, but she heard only thrashing water and shrieking wind.

The dinghy tilted, throwing her backwards, and pointed itself directly into the whirlpool's centre. Lightning transformed the roiling sea into a blur of impenetrable dark and flashes of angry white. The world spun around as the vortex extended deeper and deeper. The sky shrank and vanished. Flickering in the lightning flashes, the seabed lay bare far below. She gripped the sides of the plummeting boat so hard her fingers were numb. The seabed disappeared, revealing a matt blackness. She closed her eyes tight.

'Ahhhhhhhhhhh!' She could hear her voice again and stopped screaming.

Silence echoed in her ears.

Itty lay on something hard and rough. Everything hurt.

She opened her eyes and pushed her aching body upright. Blinking and spitting sand, she found herself beside the dinghy on a featureless shore under a reddish sky. She checked all her limbs for injuries: no more than a few scratches and some bruising.

She blinked. *Sky? Didn't I fall through…?* Squinting upwards, she tried to detect some sort of hole above her, but there was nothing other than a uniform red glow.

The briny smell of the sea had been replaced by a sweet, minty scent. This must be a lake or a wide river. Fresh water! Hurrying to the water, she drank three sloppy handfuls then forced herself to stop—too much on an empty stomach would be unwise, she remembered reading somewhere.

Somewhat refreshed, she stood up and looked around. *Where am I, now?*

Lost! Lost and alone.

At least aboard the *Invigilator*, there were other people and the possibility of leaving the ship when it next docked.

That sky… She wasn't sure if she was still on Earth.

Mouth suddenly dry and palms sweaty, she gave an involuntary shudder. Was this the end?

'Hello,' she shouted. 'Captain, where are you? Is anybody here?'

The only sound was her own voice echoing back as if mocking her: '…lo …lo …lo …oo …oo …oo …ear …ear …ear.'

'G'day, mates!' a different voice called behind her.

Itty whirled around and tripped over her own feet. She pushed herself up to see an odd-looking flat boat on the water—narrow and raft-like, with a curved prow—piloted by a tall, slim woman with skin so dark it was like night under her hooded cloak. Captain Smart stood on the shore, looking at his surroundings and scratching his head.

She ran towards him. 'Captain, you're alive!'

Before she reached him, he shook his head sadly, and she noticed his body was translucent. Through him she could see a duplicate captain lying on the ground beyond, slowly being absorbed into the sand along with the overturned dinghy.

The woman brought her boat to the shore and wedged a staff she'd had strapped across her shoulders into the ground to anchor it. She called out, 'Nah, mate, he's kicked the bucket. You should've croaked too. Something's not right here.' She pulled an enormous ledger out from her cloak; Itty couldn't see how it could possibly have fitted in there. The woman tapped on a page. 'Captain Smart, Captain Augustus Smart, son of Vannevar and Persephone Smart, yeah?'

The captain's ghost nodded.

'You're early. I wasn't expecting you for another… Well, never mind. You're here now.' She put the large book inside her cloak again and looked at Itty. 'You, on the other hand… The living shouldn't be here, but that's your problem, girlie, not mine. At least for now—people don't tend to *stay* living for long around here, so I'll catch ya later.'

'Where are we?'

'You must have heard of the River Sticks.'

'The Sticks? That means you're Kharon?'

'Yep, that's me.' She seemed to think for a bit. 'Actually, it's Karrin, but no worries, you're close enough. Everyone gets it wrong.'

'You don't look like how I imagined.'

'Yeah, I get that a lot,' Karrin said drily.

'Do you ferry every soul across the river?'

'Well, not every single one. But most, for sure.'

'Is it tiring? That boat looks like hard work.'

Karrin scratched her head. 'Crikey, you ask a lot of questions.'

'How do I get back home?'

Karrin shrugged. 'If you were on the other side of the Sticks, there's a way out—probably—but I can't take you across. I don't deal with the living. Sorry. Maybe when you're, you know, not living anymore…' She turned to the spirit of the captain. 'Right-o, Cap'n, time to go. Got the cash for the crossing?'

Captain Smart pulled out his pockets to show they contained nothing but his sextant and a neatly folded silk handkerchief and shrugged.

'Well, Bruce, that's a bit of a no-go. This thing's not cheap to run, y'know. I can't be giving people rides for free.' Karrin pulled up the staff being employed as an anchor, replacing it over her shoulder, and let her boat drift away from the shore. 'You're up a gum tree, you two.' She jerked a thumb over her shoulder. 'There's not much to do on this side, but I guess you'll see people coming through. Maybe someone will have a spare coin to pay for you, Cap'n.'

Itty looked at the captain, then at the strange boat receding from them, then around at the lack of anything at all between her and the distant horizon. *Hold on, this isn't fair. I've got to do something.*

'Wait!' she called. 'Is there another way we can pay to get across? What if I offer my services for a month, and you take both the captain and me to the other side, and you can let me return to the surface at the end?'

Karrin stroked her chin, murmuring to herself, 'Well, there's the dog, and I really don't like cleaning and tidying.' She brought the boat back and said out loud, 'Make it two months, girlie, and it's a deal.'

Itty nodded.

'Hop on me surfboard, mates.'

Chapter 7: Down Under

In life, as in nature, all things descend, and do so absent of the influence of gods or any other imagined supernatural forces. As rain falls and stones sink in lakes, so the structures of man collapse and reach equilibrium in the form of mundane heaps of matter. Even one's very features droop as one ages. Everything that goes up must come down, probably injuring bystanders along the way.

To explain this phenomenon, I have formulated a Theory of Sagginess, articulated as three natural laws of the fundament, thusly: first, unless interfered with, an entity will sag at a constant rate due to a universal force I have termed *saggity*; second, the rate of change of sag depends inversely on the expenditure of effort in combatting it; and third, there is no equal and opposite to sag—everything does it. Whether you like it or not, you will end up underground.

Tough. Live with it.

From *Principia Naturae*, the collected
knowledge of Sir Isaac Oldson.

Karrin murmured a song to herself—
something about dancing and
boiling billy-bongs, whatever they
were—as the water behind them rose up to
propel the narrow craft forward. Just as they
were about to reach the far side of the river,
Karrin abruptly leaned low, steering her heavy
surfboard back in almost the opposite
direction.

Either because of his many years at sea or
because he was incorporeal, the captain
seemed to naturally sway as the boat turned.
Itty, however, had to cling to Karrin's cloak to
avoid being thrown into the water.

There were several further twists and turns
in the intricate route of the stick maze's safe
channel before they finally docked by a rickety
pier on the sandy riverbank. After tying up the
boat, Karrin told Itty to settle herself at a

shack standing a little way inland, while she dealt with the captain's spirit.

To distract herself from thoughts about the captain's death, Itty walked around the shack as he and Karrin wandered off into the woods beyond the small building. Its walls were made of corrugated metal and covered in paintings of stick people and intricately patterned animal outlines: turtles and lizards, fish and birds. Everything was coloured in earthy browns and reds, with contrasting bright yellow, green, and white highlights; no surface of the shack was blank. She wondered if even the roof was painted, but she couldn't stretch high enough to see.

Besides the hut, there was a fire pit, presumably for cooking, with a ring of flimsy, canvas chairs surrounding it, and a small white box, about waist-high with a door on the front. Itty was about to open the strange little cupboard when Karrin returned.

'Go ahead, help yourself to a stubby,' Karrin called out. 'And open one for me while I light the barbie. There's soda in there if you fancy that instead.'

As Itty opened the white cupboard, finding four shelves stacked with ice-cold bottles and cans, some of which must be this mysterious soda thing, Karrin struck a match and threw it into the fire pit. Once the initial whoosh of flame had died down, she placed a metal grille on the top and went around the back of the hut. She returned with a tray piled with T-bone steaks and tossed them on the makeshift grill, sprinkling some seasoning on top.

Itty sipped her pineapple soda—a bright yellow, sticky concoction so sweet and fizzy that she could feel her teeth dissolving. The smells of grilling meat, coated in garlic, mustard and coriander, teased her nose, and her stomach rumbled.

Karrin put her index and little fingers in her mouth and whistled loudly. A huge, jet-black dog, taller even than Karrin, with three identical, enormous heads bounded out from behind the hut.

Itty whimpered and dropped her half-finished can of soda.

'Oh, don't mind him; he's a big softie, all three of him.' She scratched his shoulder. 'Aren't you? Who's my cutesy-wootsy poochie-wootchie, then?' She thwacked the dog's rear end, and the three heads turned and covered her in slobbery licks.

'Let me introduce the scallywags. This is Kerr.' She patted the head on the left. 'Bey.' She patted another. 'And Russ here in the middle.' She scratched the third between the ears. 'Come and say hello to my babies.'

The dog heads barked a greeting, deep resonating raawwrfs, and looked at Itty expectantly.

She tentatively held out a hand to be sniffed and found herself being whiffled, butted and enthusiastically slobbered on. Laughing, she pushed the wet, tickly noses away. She thought the title Kerr-Bey-Russ sounded familiar, something she'd read in a book, but Karrin informed her that the names went in order from left head to right: Kerr-Russ-Bey. Krispy for short.

As Itty scratched Russ's chin, all three heads went cross-eyed, and with a grunt, the beast dropped an enormous load of unpleasantness.

'Strewth!' Karrin groaned, holding her nose. 'Bad boys! What have you been eating? Girlie—what's your name? I can't keep calling you *girlie*.'

'I'm Imperceptibility. Imperceptibility Happenstance.'

'Well, Imperceptibility—nah, that's too much of a mouthful. I'll stick with *girlie*.' Before Itty could tell her her nickname, Karrin continued, 'Might as well start your work right now and clean that up. You'll find a shovel and a wheelbarrow behind the shack. Off you go!'

Itty hurried and got the shovel, wondering how her work here might compare with being on the ship. More dog poop and less poop deck, she supposed.

By the time she'd disposed of the dog mess and scrubbed her hands, the steaks were ready, and they smelled wonderful.

Karrin threw three of them to Krispy and grabbed a slab for herself. She kicked off her boots, revealing white socks covered in little blue flowers and hearts, and pulled back her hood. She had short, tightly curled hair, large dark eyes, a slightly crooked nose, and a wide, wide grin.

'Welcome to the Down-Underworld, girlie,' she said around a mouthful of steak as she sat down on one of the canvas chairs. 'Grab something from the barbie and tuck in.'

Life in the underworld wasn't all that different to being aboard the *Invigilator*, but with less shouting and more shovelling. As with her time as a sailor—and it must be said, living in Hyrhia—she didn't have to think very hard. There were few decisions to be made, and she simply followed a daily routine.

Besides cleaning up after Krispy, Itty's duties included tidying the hut every few days. This took surprisingly long for such a small building, since Karrin was incredibly messy and never seemed to discard anything.

On the first few cleaning sessions, Itty carefully made piles of corroded coins, unusually-shaped bottles, broken crockery, wooden false legs, a 'Sooveneer Frum Uckly' snow-globe, and all the other odd things she found in the shack. They looked like junk to her, but she wasn't certain, so she asked Karrin if they should be thrown out.

'Nah, girlie, just chuck 'em all back in there somewhere. They're sentimental, they are. Presents from souls who've passed through here. I can't get rid of those.'

She got used to finding spaces for the new bric-à-brac Karrin would return with now and then. Once every windowsill and table were full of trinkets and knick-knacks, Itty fetched several flat pieces of wood and put up additional shelves—it took several attempts before the shelves were horizontal and stable. After discovering several partly filled pots of paint in Karrin's clutter, she touched up the pictures on the shack's walls. She also painted her new shelves with what were intended to be depictions of Captain Smart and Krispy, but the paintbrush seemed to have a mind of its own. The end results were more like a small, fluffy-eared bear clinging to a tree and a giant rat standing on its back legs.

Itty did most of the cooking now, and the majority of the meals featured huge amounts of grilled meat, since Karrin and Krispy really liked their barbies. These were accompanied by a beer or soda from the never-emptying white cupboard that kept the drinks cold, though sometimes Itty refilled her bottle from the river just to have something that wasn't sweet and sickly.

When she wasn't working, Itty spent time playing with, bathing, or grooming the dog;

activities which both—or all four in total, depending upon whether you counted the dog's one body or his three heads—enjoyed greatly. It could be exhausting at times, since she had to throw each stick and toss each ball three times. If her attention wasn't given equally to each head, at least one would sulk. She managed to train the dog to do tricks: roll over, play dead, beg, and balance sausages on the end of his noses. The last of those was particularly tricky because Bey was eager to grab the titbits from the other pair's noses, but Itty found that a light tap on the snout would get his attention.

There was, of course, dealing with what Krispy's other end produced. The vast quantities of food entering three mouths meant there was an awful lot making its way through the dog's alimentary canal. After the first week of shovelling, she spent some time training the dog to go off to a corner of the woods a little distance from the shack and dig his own hole. She did have to admit, however, that the smell of one of Krispy's loads wasn't much worse than what she'd encountered when cleaning the ship's head aboard the *Invigilator.*

At first, it was a quiet time for Itty. Karrin wasn't used to having anyone else around and didn't say much to her guest. She was away most of the day, ferrying souls across the Sticks or trimming the spikey thorns that gave the river its name. That job was necessary, she said, so that the plants wouldn't poke above the water; she needed to ensure that the safe route through the maze remained invisible.

Itty asked her why.

'I don't want souls crossing over willy-nilly when I'm not ready for them,' Karrin replied. 'They're hard enough for me to manage on me lonesome, and it'd be a lot worse if a bunch arrived at once and went walkabout this side of the Sticks.'

Most evenings, Karrin's work stretched long into the night, and she would sit at her desk, writing in her ledger of souls.

At dinner, Itty would talk about events in the world above. She had read Hyrhian newspapers as avidly as storybooks and did her best to bring Karrin up to date with world events, at least what had been happening up until Itty was press-ganged. Not that Karrin had asked to be informed.

Gradually, Karrin joined in, telling Itty about the souls who'd passed through each day. She seldom learned much from them, as they tended to be somewhat preoccupied by their recent deaths.

In a lull in one such conversation, Itty asked Karrin what happened to people's souls in the underworld.

'Dunno. None of my business. My job's to take them into the bush, and that's not as simple as it sounds. It's tricky to get each soul to the right place at the right moment, and I haven't time to hang around after that.' Karrin shrugged. 'When we get to the proper spot, a door appears, and they go through it. The door's in a different place each time, and each seems to open for just that one person, vanishing as soon as it closes. I tried to go through one once, but it slammed before I could. That's why me nose is like this. Stung like a bu– a lot.'

The white cupboard also intrigued Itty—she guessed this was something like the cold box in which the captain's daffodils had been kept on the *Invigilator*, only this one needed no ice. She'd asked Karrin how the cupboard worked, but Karrin shrugged. 'Just part of the Down-Underworld's nature. Drinks stay cold in the fridj, and there's a never-ending supply of steaks and charcoal out back as long as I keep leaving the coins the souls pay me. Just lie back and enjoy it as it comes.'

'But where do the steaks come from? Is there a way down from the surface?' *One I can climb up*, she added to herself, wondering how she would get out when her time was up.

Another shrug. 'Dunno, girlie. Making sure I help souls pass on is the only important thing here; nothing else is worth worrying about.

Your way out will come when it needs to—that's how this place works. Now, bring me another tinnie, will ya?'

For the next two days, Itty spent as much time as she could at the back of the shack, watching the handful of coins sitting in the space where the meat would appear, but nothing happened as long as she was observing, even when she hid herself behind the corner of the shack. However, as soon as she turned away, the money would be replaced by food and fuel. She tried staring without blinking, but eventually, her eyes would snap shut, and then the steaks were there when she opened them again.

With a sigh, she gave up; there was no route out of the underworld that way.

I guess I'm just going to have to be patient. Still, it's not too bad here. She glanced at where the meat had appeared and sighed again. *It'd be nice if books and newspapers came down this way, too, or if people gave Karrin books as gifts every now and then. But if I can't read, maybe I can write. Yeah, I could tell the* real *story of Karrin and the Down-Underworld. We've got so much wrong about her up on the surface. I wonder if she has any spare paper.*

The days blurred into each other, but one day, when Itty's two months were almost over, Karrin asked if she would help guide souls to their doors: 'Something big's going off up top; there's a lot of souls coming through at once.'

Indeed, about thirty spirits were milling about the far shore of the Sticks, requiring several surfboard trips. She recognized some of them from her time on Captain Smart's ship—Mr Ansif and Jackson, for a start, both of whom looked surprised to see her. She spotted Cook as well, cradling a bedraggled duck in her arms.

'What happened?' Itty asked, thoughts torn between justice being served and sorrow at the deaths of people she knew. She wondered what the captain might think about it all.

Mr Ansif tried to speak, but although his mouth moved, no sound came out. He picked up a pebble and started to write on the sand.

Caught on reefs trying to reach land without being seen. Capsized. Half the crew saved. Rest are here.

Itty and Karrin led the sailors through the forest and across deserts, and one by one, doors would appear, and a spirit would pass through.

When it came to Jackson's turn, he stopped and picked up a twig. He wrote, *weer sory for wot we dun. you an the captn wer good foke. heers sumthin wot I fink is yors.* He slid a small bag off his shoulder and handed it to her.

It became solid as it passed between them, crossing from one world to the other.

'Good luck, Jackson.' Itty waved as he entered his door. 'Goodbye.'

Intrigued, she opened the bag. It contained her belongings from when she'd boarded the *Invigilator.* clothes, a purse, a couple of books, pencils, and... something else... *Why did Jackson think this is mine?* Was it a grimy lamp?

She thought she heard angry muttering and smelled cardamom and vanilla, with a hint of brimstone.

Her ruminations were interrupted by Karrin saying, 'Looks like you got off that ship at the right time after all, girlie,' and the thoughts vanished.

Back at the hut, Itty examined the bag again. The lamp fell out, chiming like a shop bell when it hit the ground. Her fingers tingled as she touched it, and the memories of the djinn and her wishes came flooding back: the tent in the market, meeting the djinn, her first wish, and how she'd been press-ganged. Odd how she'd forgotten all of this since then. *Perhaps,* she wondered, *the memories fade when the lamp is out of sight. Maybe that's how djinn manage to stay so well hidden.*

Then there was a mental snap, and everything came flooding back, including the bit in the contract about forgetting. *I wonder if there's some way I can keep the lamp in view all the time.*

As she pondered and more memories returned, she absently rubbed at a mark on the side of the lamp, and smoke began to leak from the spout.

The djinn's shape formed, accompanied by a faint scent of spices. But before the semi-transparent cloud could become solid, Karrin shouted, 'Whoa, timeout! That's not allowed. No manifesting down here.'

The djinn shrugged and started to drift back into the lamp.

'Before you go, I…' Itty frowned and tried again. 'Back on the ship, did you trip me when I entered the captain's cabin?'

The djinn's lips tightened, and his gaze slid sideways as he vanished without replying.

Itty sighed and emptied the rest of the bag. She changed into her old trousers from Hyrhia but decided to keep the navy's blouse and transferred the rest of the items from the bag to her pockets.

'Time to go, eh, girlie? Hard to believe your time's up,' Karrin said a week later.

Itty's eyes welled up. 'I do want to get back to my home, but I'm really going to miss you.' She turned towards the dog. 'And you, you rascals!'

Krispy jumped up and licked her face, hiding any sign of tears behind a triple film of slobber.

'Got something for ya,' Karrin said in a slightly husky voice. She handed Itty a small whistle she'd whittled from one of the stick plants from the river. 'If you're in trouble, blow this and Krispy will come running, no matter where you are.'

'Can I come back and see you again?'

'I'm afraid the only way that can happen is…' Karrin ran a finger across her throat. 'This is the Down-Underworld, after all, and people get here by… y'know?' She half-smiled. 'You landing here, alive and all, was a chance in a million, and those don't happen every day. I'll miss you.'

'Oh.' Now Itty's tears did come, and with a wail, she embraced Karrin.

'Now, now, girlie. Let's have none of that. Look, here's your door; it turned up today, and you can't keep it waiting. It's different to the soul doors—it'll take you back to the world above.'

The door matched the others Itty had seen in the underworld: plain wood with a simple knob halfway up. Perhaps there was a difference only Karrin could see. More likely, Itty suspected, Karrin was trying to draw attention away from her own slightly reddened eyes.

'Where will I come out?'

Karrin shrugged. 'Dunno. I don't see what happens up there. I just know it'll be somewhere in one of the monasteries of the Humble Monks. They're not far from the Down-Underworld.'

'The who?'

Karrin shrugged again. 'Just people. Bit strange, but friendly. You might not meet them, anyway. Take care, girlie; be seein' ya.'

Itty opened the door and stepped into darkness. She turned around to say a final goodbye, but the door slammed just as she opened her mouth. Heart thudding, she frantically groped for the door in the sudden blackness. Her fingertips brushed the wall, but however she searched, she could find only smooth rock. She turned and pressed her back into the wall, breath coming in loud gasps that left her dizzy.

It was dark. Very dark. So dark that everything pressed down on her, heavy and dull. Even the musty air she was breathing felt thick and slow.

'Hello there!' a chipper, high-pitched voice called out.

Chapter 8: Deeper Underground

O, Great Lord—or Lady, for We Do Not Know,
We are not worthy of Thy Attention.
We are insects. No, we areth less than that.
Parasites on insects, verily,
Remaining far distant from Thy Being, or possibly Beings,
So as not to cause offence in Thy Gaze.
Not that we merit an acknowledgement within Thy Sight.
Of Thee, we beseech nothing,
For we deserveth not even of the scrapings of Thy Boots,
If, that is, Thou wearest Boots and not, say, Sandals or Flip-flops,
For we desire not to maketh assumptions on Thine Apparel.
Or anything else.

*One of the few documented prayers of the Humble
Monks.*

Itty whirled around, eyes straining to make out anything at all in the pitch blackness. 'Who…?'

'Over here!' the high-pitched voice said.

'Where…?'

'Ooo, sorry. I didn't realize you were an over-lander. Hang on a jiffy.'

Itty could hear some rustling and scratching, then the *tschh* of a match being struck. Light flared from a torch held by a skinny, tonsured man wearing a grubby brown cassock and carrying a carpetbag. The light from the bare-footed monk's torch illuminated no more than a few yards of featureless corridor: grey stone walls joining overhead in a smooth curve and a scattering of small rocks on the ground.

'I'm Brother Nobody. Brother Nobody 231, actually.' His unusually large, pale eyes blinked at her. 'And you are…?'

'Imperceptibility Happenstance, sir—er—brother. Where am I?'

'You're in the lowest part of Monastery 1,195.'

'How do we get up to the– Wait, are there really a thousand monasteries?' she asked.

'Ooo, many more than that. Tens of thousands. All over—I mean, under—the world.'

'But where are we?'

Brother Nobody said, 'Where we need to be.'

Itty's jaw tightened, but she decided to be polite. 'I mean, where in the world? Are we near any cities? What country are we in?'

The monk shrugged. 'The surface doesn't mean much to us down here. Come, let's walk. Choose a direction.'

Itty peered left and right, unable to make out any of the tunnel beyond the range of the torchlight.

'Which way takes me out quicker?'

Brother Nobody shrugged.

She tried hard to not grind her teeth. 'Which direction did you come from?'

The monk pointed left.

She asked, 'Did you come from the surface?'

A shake of the head.

'How about we go the other way, then?' she said, struggling not to scowl.

Brother Nobody nodded and set off at a leisurely pace. Despite her impatience, Itty forced herself to walk slowly to match his speed.

'Um,' Itty started. 'You don't seem very surprised that I'm here.'

'No, no, I suppose not. Things are what they are, and one should accept them for what they are. We Humble Monks don't expect much, nor do we upset ourselves by worrying about the unexpected. Lo-La looks after us in the way He or She deems necessary. Or possibly They. By the way, we monks never seek to impose, but should you feel a desire to do so, please go ahead and tell me how you got here.'

Itty quickly told him about accidentally ending up in the Down-Underworld, working for Karrin for two months, and coming through a door just now to find herself here, in the depths of the monastery.

'Ooo, you have been a busy little pilgrim, haven't you? Some of our scholars, Brother Nobody 35 and Brother Nobody 180, I think, might like to talk to you about Kharon's underworld. If we happen to bump into them, Lo-La permitting.'

'Excuse me for asking, but are you all called Brother Nobody?'

'Yes. We're not worthy of names of our own. Same goes for the monasteries; no need to name them individually.'

They'd been walking through narrow twisty passages for a while now, sometimes up, sometimes down. Mostly, any slopes in the tunnels were so gentle that Itty barely noticed them, but twice they'd climbed runs of four or five shallow steps, worn in the middle by what must have been centuries of footsteps.

The gentle *slap-slap* of their feet on the ground jostled Itty's thoughts in a hypnotic rhythm. Hyrhia and the *Invigilator* and the Down-Underworld cycled around her head in this quiet, dark space as if they were nothing more than dreams.

The tunnels were comfortably warm, and she found her head nodding forward as her breathing became more and more relaxed.

In an attempt to stave off sleep, she said, 'I hope you don't mind me asking another question.'

Brother Nobody nodded his assent.

'We're very far below ground, aren't we? How long before we reach the surface?'

'Ooo, I don't know. We walk wherever the Great Lord, or Lady for We Do Not Know— that's Lo-La for brevity, but only when speaking *about* Him or Her, or possibly Them, of course, not when speaking *to* Him or Her or Them. We walk wherever the Great Lo-La takes our feet.'

'Could we perhaps go up, or walk a little faster?' Itty couldn't contain her impatience any longer. 'I've been in the Down-

Underworld for two months and I'd like to see some stars and actual sunlight.'

Brother Nobody sucked his teeth. Coming to a standstill and setting down his bag, he raised his eyes and performed a complex spiralling gesture with his free hand.

'Forgive her, O Ineffable Lord or Lady for We Do Not Know, she understands not what she is saying,' he called upwards. To Itty, he continued more quietly, 'We mustn't rush things. Perhaps I should tell you something about the Humble Monks.'

They had stopped beside a small wooden door, which he opened to reveal a little room containing two soft armchairs and a table.

'Ooo, here's as good a place to park our posteriors as any other.'

A row of candlesticks above an unlit fireplace gave the room a cosy glow. The table was laid with two cups on saucers, a teapot kept warm underneath a knitted cosy, and an inviting plate of biscuits of various kinds. The crockery all rested on delicate lace doilies, and a napkin was folded neatly alongside each cup.

He sighed. 'If you were older, we might have found some of Brother 63's most excellent brandy behind the door. Very smooth, it is. But never mind; things are what they are. Make yourself comfortable. Tea?'

Itty was about to say she didn't think she had time for tea when she realized it had been ever so long since she'd tasted a biscuit. Or eaten at all, for that matter. She sat down and reached for the plate.

Mumbling, 'Mustn't forget,' Brother Nobody opened his carpetbag and extracted a small, neatly wrapped package. He placed it on the mantelpiece and turned to Itty. 'Just something for the next person to come here.'

'What is it?'

The monk shrugged. 'Don't know—I didn't wrap it, just picked it up in the last room. It just felt like the right time and place to put something from the bag.'

While she munched a custard cream, wondering if it was part of this religion to transport small boxes from one place to another, which made as much sense as everything else here, Brother Nobody poured her a cup of tea.

Once he sat down and had a sip of his own tea, he started his explanation. 'In the beginning was the Word, but nobody knew what the Word was, because no one was around to hear it right at the beginning. Nobody and nothing were all there was back then.

'Religions were built on this fundamental truth of getting something from nothing, and churches and cathedrals were built on those foundations. Magnificent cathedrals, each grander and *taller* than the next, striving to get ever closer to the heavens, and overflowing with ever more exquisite works of art. But even with all of this, few people were happy, and none actually understood their gods or their intentions.'

Itty took another biscuit. Although she'd grown up among Ethynite nuns, she'd never paid much attention to the fiddly details of religion, but she felt it was only polite to listen to Brother Nobody's tale.

'The original Humble Monks realized that trying to approach their celestials was the wrong way to go about things. They determined, instead, that it would be better to create sacred buildings which stretched farther *from* the heavens, and to honour the Great Lo-La by *not* creating works of art.' He put his hands together and briefly glanced upward, then bowed his head. 'Lo-La is so far beyond the bounds of human comprehension that creating works in His or Her or Their honour would be presumptuous. We strive to know as little as we can about our god or gods. None of us is worthy of notice by Lo-La, so we take no names, have no ambitions and do—well— nothing outstanding, safe in the knowledge that Lo-La will bestow upon us what we deserve. If He or She or They deem that we deserve anything.'

Itty stared at him. She could scarcely fathom that people like Brother Nobody had created many thousands of monasteries, hidden below ground—there were nowhere near that many on the surface. She blinked and picked up her teacup to take a sip. It was a thirst-quenching, refreshing brew—something with a citrus tang and the hint of meadowlands. The flavours mingled very nicely with those of the biscuits.

'Not glorifying one's gods is a very popular religion,' concluded the monk. 'Lots of people do it all the time.'

'How strange I've never heard of Lo-La. I've read almost all the books in Hyrhia's libraries, and I've never come across the Humble Monks.'

'Ooo, that's because we haven't written any books. What we do, or do not, is not worthy of recording on paper.'

'But you built all the tunnels and the monasteries.'

'Many we found, some we made, but we only constructed them because it felt right to take ourselves farther from our god. Or gods. We do not build to impress Him or Her or Them.'

Itty gestured around the room with her hand, holding the final biscuit from the plate—a vanilla bourbon—and scattering crumbs on the floor. 'But you made this room, right? And who brewed the tea, so that it was ready just as we arrived?'

Brother Nobody smiled. 'The ways of Lo-La are inexplicable, and the nature of the tunnels is mysterious.' He moved his hands in a complex, twisting shape. 'And how they intersect is beyond human comprehension. What Lo-La does, Lo-La does, at the time when Lo-La does it. Things are what they are.'

She stared at him a second time, once again trying to formulate a question. Eventually, she gave up, figuring that his answer would make little sense, anyway. She munched the last of her vanilla bourbon and wiped her fingers on the napkin. *Things happen in the tunnels*, she supposed, *and we may as well accept them, whoever or whatever is causing them.*

Explanation, tea, and biscuits finished, Brother Nobody led her out of the room, and they continued on their way, though Itty wasn't sure to where. The citrusy tea had revitalized her, and she was eager to see the sky, to hear something other than their echoing footsteps, to breathe fresh air, but there seemed to be no polite way to speed up the monk's relaxed amble.

She settled for asking him if there were many tea rooms in the tunnels and monasteries ('It depends what *many* is—there are as many as we need. Though we don't need many, I suppose.'), what the monasteries were like ('They're just monasteries—places to rest and meet. But not to pray, so as to avoid annoying Lo-La.'), and so on.

After a while, the flickering patterns of light cast by Brother Nobody's torch on the tunnel walls vanished, and the air became much cooler. The darkness beyond the torch's range gave the impression of deadening the sound of their footsteps. A sudden breeze made the flame flicker and brought a chill to Itty's neck. They were in some large space; an unbounded, achingly empty, painfully lonely space. She swallowed and whispered, 'Where are we?'

Brother Nobody looked around. 'I believe we're on the crossing between Monasteries 1,195 and 2,933.'

He grabbed Itty's arm just as she was about to take a step. 'Careful!'

She jerked back. 'What?'

'You almost walked off the bridge, look.' He held his torch near the ground.

Itty gasped. The path on which they stood ended abruptly just where she'd been about to step. There was nothing but impenetrable inky-blackness beyond the edge, just inches from her toes.

The monk called out a loud 'Halloooo' and listened for its echo, then rummaged on the ground for a small pebble, which he dropped over the edge. He and Itty peered into the darkness, waiting for any indication of its landing.

'I don't know why I bother doing that,' Brother Nobody muttered. 'No one's ever heard a sound from down there. We don't know how deep it is; nobody's ever come back.'

Itty kept a tight grip on his arm as they continued their journey.

After a few moments, the lack of conversation got to Itty and she asked, 'Where are the other monks?'

'Ooo, there are plenty of us here, but it's a big place—the monastery network. Loads of tunnels and bridges, and more are being discovered all the time. There's one faction among the Humble Monks, the *Extremely* Humble Monks, who try to explore deeper and deeper parts of creation—they can't pass up a pothole if they come across one, in the hope that it will take them farther down. Most of us just wander and our paths seldom cross. You can get from anywhere to anywhere in the world via the monasteries, not that we ever need to. Some of us, the Esoteric Humble Monks, believe that you can also get to places not of this Earth via the monastery network.' He leaned in conspiratorially. 'Between you and me, though, I think those monks are a bit strange.'

'Don't you ever get lost?'

'How could we get lost if we don't have anywhere we need to go?'

'I'd like to get to the surface,' she said drily. 'I don't suppose we're getting closer, are we?'

A few more minutes passed.

'Are there just, er, men here?'

'Our sisters are the Perfectly Reasonable Nuns, though they tend to remain closer to the surface. They don't see the point of digging as deep as we do; the sisters say they can easily pay Lo-La no attention no matter where they happen to be.'

They lapsed into silence again, and a few minutes later—or was it hours, she couldn't tell—Itty sensed walls enclosing them once more. They must have reached Monastery 2,933, she guessed. Her earlier tension had faded away, and she felt quite relaxed. *It might not be so bad to be a Humble Monk—or a Perfectly Reasonable Nun, I suppose I would have to be,* she thought, *but I don't think I could spend the rest of my life underground.*

'It's very, er, pleasant here, but I *really* would like to get above ground.'

'Ooo yes, you did say that earlier, didn't you? Here.' He stopped beside a pair of doors, one on either side of the tunnel. As he opened the first one, he said, 'It can be a little chilly up on the surface, so you might need a jumper.'

The door belonged to a clothes cupboard containing a dozen sweaters, cardigans, jackets and the like. Itty's eyes were instantly drawn to a scarlet and gold waistcoat.

'You're sure I can just take this?' she asked.

Brother Nobody nodded, while tucking the carpetbag into an exactly right-sized space on the bottom shelf.

'Where do the clothes come from?'

'Lo-La guides and Lo-La provides.' The monk shrugged, which she conjectured to be his standard reaction to any question that might touch upon the topic of his religion.

'Just through here and keep going.' He opened the other door and gestured for Itty to enter.

'Is that it? Could I have asked for a door anytime?'

Brother Nobody looked shocked. 'No, that would be bizarre, wouldn't it? It had to be the *right* time! Lo-La guides us all.'

Itty smiled and joked, 'And the right place, too.'

The monk paled, eyes bugging, and looked so mortified that she regretted saying it.

'Sorry,' she mumbled, not quite knowing what she was apologizing for.

He raised his eyes to the ceiling. 'Great Lord or Lady for We Do Not Know, forgive this girl.' Looking back at Itty, he said, tension in his voice, 'The monasteries link all places, letting us be at one with the entire world—maybe spaces beyond that, if you listen to the Esoterics. From here we can reach anywhere Lo-La wants us to be without needing to be in any particular location. One does not joke about place; it is only a short step from that to mocking Lo-La.'

He took a shuddering breath. 'Sorry, forgive me, my child. I should not have become angry at your innocent lack of knowledge. Were I a member of a different religion, I would have you flogged or, worse, indoctrinated. I so seldom speak with outsiders that I forget, but that's no excuse. I'm a Humble Monk, and things—and people—are what they are.'

Just as a chastened Itty stepped through the doorway, a thought struck her. 'What about Brother Nobody 35 and, er, 180?'

'What about them?'

'You said they might want to ask me about the underworld.'

'Did I? Ooo, no matter, they probably wouldn't ask anything—that might get them too close to learning something about Lo-La, which could be risky. If Lo-La had wanted us to talk, we would have met them as we travelled, so obviously that was not what Lo-La desired, and who are we to question it? Take care and do come back sometime, child.'

'Will this take me home?'

Brother Nobody shrugged. 'Lo-La will lead you to where you need to be.'

He handed her the torch. 'Here, you might need this.'

'Aren't you coming with me?' Itty asked as she peered into the darkness on the other side of the doorway. Hearing no reply, she turned to look back, but Brother Nobody had already disappeared along the passage. She stepped through the door into another featureless tunnel.

While she walked along the tunnel beyond the doorway, she considered Brother Nobody's attitude towards life—just wandering aimlessly, thinking about nothing and no one, no difficult choices to make. No, that wasn't right; he had been there right when she needed him and was pleasant company while she made her way from Karrin's door to the one she'd just passed through. It would have been a lonely trek without him, if she could have found her way at all. In fact, without him to guide her, she might still be groping in the darkness.

Perhaps the world did need people whose role in life was to provide assistance, and maybe Lo-La existed to ensure they'd always be where they needed to be.

I'm not sure where I need to be, but I want to be home. Itty blew out a long breath and trudged onward.

The floor sloped steadily upwards, getting steeper and steeper. After a while, the smooth floor became steps, then stopped at a ladder consisting of individual metal rungs hammered into the stone. She placed the torch in a holder beside the ladder and peered upwards. Light glimmered far above. As she climbed, the light grew brighter.

Just as her arms were about to give out, she found herself at the top, with no more rungs to reach for. Dripping with sweat and legs aching, Itty pushed open a metal grate, hauled herself into a dimly lit shallow cave and flopped onto the ground beside the hole from which she'd emerged.

She lay there until her panting subsided, then, groaning, pulled herself to her feet and made her way outside the cave. It was moonlit night-time, and the skies were clear. The Hippopotamus and the Rhododendron were visible, but tilted at different angles compared to when Captain Smart had shown her the constellations. She couldn't find the North West Star. All she could surmise from the patterns in the stars was that her current location must be far from anywhere else she'd ever been in her life.

But she was back on the surface! Lost and alone, it was true, but above ground again. With sky and stars and fresh air and a pleasant breeze. She took several long, deep breaths. She didn't know what continent she might be on, but her journey home could start now. Despite her weariness and aches, she could feel her cheeks pull her face into a smile.

She lay down on the grass, closed her eyes and promptly fell asleep.

Chapter 9: Village Life

No right-minded person believes in the existence of dragons.

They are, without argument, a physical impossibility. Calculations of weight to power ratios indicate that no winged creature larger than an Azelian condor can possibly fly. Renowned aeronautical engineer Sir Oscar de Montford states that wings alone would not keep a dragon in the air. He estimates that a beast with gaseous bladders operating in the same manner as modern dirigibles would have to be the size of a house to be able to carry even just one cow. How could such a flying animal remain hidden from all of humanity?

I won't even start on the ridiculous idea of a biological creature capable of generating fire.

The very notion of dragons is patently ludicrous.

Letter to the Ishterbian Times, P.N. Lunethral,
Col. (retired).

The sun was shining. Itty lay on the grass for a moment, smiling in the heat, until she remembered the last time she'd seen the sun—when she and poor Captain Smart had been cast adrift in the empty sea. Despite the warmth of the morning, she shivered at the thought. Yet, somehow, she was still alive—unlike the captain. *Things will never turn out as bad as that again… I hope. Now, how do I get home?*

As she stood up and took a deep breath of clean, fresh air, she glanced back at the cave, wondering if she'd ever meet Brother Nobody 231 again. The cave entrance was almost rectangular, with shrubs growing out of clusters of rocks on either side, giving the impression of a child's approximation of a door.

She became aware of a muted grumbling rising above the whisper of the breeze gently wafting through the long grass. Puzzled, she looked around for its source, before realizing the sound was coming from her pocket. She stuck her hand in, rummaging past her notebook, the captain's compass, something smooth, a pencil… *Wait! Something smooth?* She felt for the strange object again, but her fingers seemed to slide off its surface. She dug deeper into her pocket. Something stung her, and pulling her hand out rapidly, she caused the smooth thing to tumble out. A grubby old oil lamp.

Where did that come from? She picked it up and wiped off some of the grime.

Itty dropped the lamp as vanilla and cardamom-scented smoke surged from it, coalescing into the hazy shape of a tall man. The body solidified, and as the smoke dissipated, her memories snapped into place. A suddenly familiar voice spoke. 'What is your– Wait, am I allowed out again? Ah, we're not in that awful place with that bossy woman anymore. Thank goodness. What is your second wish, O mistress?'

'Nothing yet,' Itty said drily. Recalling how the djinn had tricked her when she'd asked to travel the seas, she didn't want to be rushed into another wish, even if what she wanted was to return to Hyrhia—how many ways could he maliciously misinterpret that? She'd take him to task about her first wish and think about the second later, but she had more pressing things on her mind at the moment. 'Do you know where we are?'

The djinn looked around. He squinted at the sun. He scratched his head. Kneeling, he sniffed the ground. He picked a stalk of grass and rubbed it between his fingers, muttering to himself. He tasted the grass, then spat it out, stood up again.

Nodding slowly, he said with absolute confidence, 'No.'

He pointed behind her. 'But perhaps someone in that village could tell you.' With that, he vanished back into the lamp.

Itty contemplated rubbing it again, but shook her head and returned the lamp to her pocket. *Is nothing ever going to be easy?*

As she strode across the field, her stomach noisily informed her that she was hungry. Tea and biscuits with Brother Nobody had been a long time ago, and she hoped the village had a tavern or a bakery. It had been ages since she'd last enjoyed an apricot or raspberry croissant from *Pierre's Patisserie* back in central Hyrhia.

The village was small but pretty, consisting of little more than a couple of dozen buildings along each side of a single street. An ornate orange and gold sign above the door of a timber-clad two-storey building read 'First and Last Chance Saloon.' A combined barber's shop and doctor's surgery huddled in its shade on the left, with a poster in its window reading 'We cut, and we put back together again. Best rates in town.' On the inn's other side was a three-storey affair, its brightly coloured stained-glass windows and elaborate wood carvings putting Itty in mind of a church. The sign above the door proclaimed it to be a shoe shop. Opposite stood a general store with a window display of canned food and other preserves, working clothes, tools and crockery.

Itty scratched her head at the sight of two more shoe shops on the street, equally ornate as the first and only slightly smaller. The rest of the village's buildings appeared to be private residences, quaint and tidy, some with neatly fenced gardens and others with prettily fashioned porches.

What was missing was people.

'Hello,' Itty called. 'Is anyone here?'

'Go away!'

Itty spun around. 'Where are you?'

'Go away. Keep walking. Leave us alone.'

'Why?' She stamped her foot and tried again. 'Listen, whoever you are, I don't know what's going on. I don't even know where I am. I've been walking for miles. I'm tired and I'm hungry. I just want somewhere to rest for a while, then I'll be on my way. Something to eat would be nice too, if you don't mind.'

Silence.

Where was everyone? The town obviously wasn't deserted—she'd heard that voice, hadn't she? Or had it been her imagination?

'Hello,' she called again, as she pushed open the door to the saloon and peered in. No one inside. She crossed the road to enter the store. The tinkling of the bell above its door was the only sound she'd heard in the village apart from the mysterious voice, but she found no one there either, though its shelves looked well-stocked. She even tried the barber's shop: empty.

She was tempted to go back and take something from the store's shelves. She could leave a few dinari, but she wasn't sure if whoever lived here used Estalian money; in any case, it felt rude to just take things. Sitting down on the step outside the inn, she called out, 'I'm not going anywhere. I'm going to stay right here until you show your faces.'

Despite the confidence in her voice, Itty's heart thudded in her chest. Had something happened to her while she was in the Down-Underworld?

Was she… dead? She didn't know how the underworld worked, and it was possible, she thought, that she'd died there but hadn't realized it. Perhaps Karrin hadn't wanted to admit that Itty's door had been a normal soul door instead of a route back to the surface. Was she now in the *next place*?

Clonk!

Something smacked her on the back of the head, and the world went dark.

She groaned, her stomach churning and her head throbbing. 'What happened? Where am I?'

'Take it easy, dear,' a kindly voice said. 'You're fine. You just had a nasty bump on the head.'

Itty's eyes snapped open. 'Someone hit me!' She tried to sit up but found herself strapped to a bed in a small room.

The room was empty save for the bed, and the monotony of the plain wooden panel walls, floorboards and bare plank ceiling was broken only by a door and a curtainless window. It was like being inside a large wooden box.

'Now, now, dear, don't strain yourself.' A black-haired woman in a long brown dress with a white apron stood at the door. Despite the tone of her voice, she had one of those faces that looked permanently angry, as if life were one long series of irritations to be endured only with the utmost effort. She scurried around the bed, checking the straps that restrained Itty's wrists, ankles and waist by giving each a quick tug.

'What's going on? Lemme go, lemme go! I want out,' Itty shouted as she struggled against her restraints.

'Stop it! Now, be a good girl and relax,' the woman said and left the room. She returned moments later with eight other men and women. They ranged from middle-aged to verging on ancient, and all wore serious expressions.

Itty opened her mouth, but before she could make a sound, the first woman spoke. 'If you keep quiet and behave, dear, we could bring you something to eat and drink. Does that seem like a good idea?'

Itty's thoughts of screaming vanished at the mention of food. Her stomach gurgled, and she nodded, setting off a jangle of pain inside her skull.

The woman called over her shoulder, 'Nathan, bring some broth please, and a cup of water.' Turning back to Itty, she demanded, 'Who are you spying for?'

'Spying? What?' Itty could only stare back at the woman.

'Who do you intend to give our secrets to? Is it those schemers at Rille, or the Tweezlins?'

'Are they other countries? I've never heard of Rille or Tweezlinia. I've only just got here, wherever here is.'

'It's Tweezle, not Tweezlinia, but you're lying. You must've come through one or other of those villages to reach Yossburg. There's no other route from outside the valley.'

'No, no, I came through the monastery, the Humble Monks' monastery.'

Murmuring from the others filled the room. A rotund, florid-faced woman with grey hair in a tight bun and wearing a sober grey suit, stepped forward. 'Where is this monastery you claim to have come from? I've never heard of such a thing.'

'There's a cave in a field. The monastery's underground, you see. I can take you there,' Itty said eagerly. 'It has an entrance that looks a bit like a door. There's a metal grating in the floor near the back leading to the Monks' tunnel.'

A knock sounded and a fair-haired young man of about Itty's age entered, carrying a bowl of soup and a mug. Freckles dotted his cheeks and nose, and when he smiled at Itty, she saw that one of his front teeth was missing.

But it was the first smile she'd seen in the village, so she smiled back.

'Thank you, Nathan,' the angry-faced woman said as she took the bowl and mug. 'I wonder, would you be so kind as to fetch a map? You'll find one upstairs in the office.'

Nathan rushed out of the room and soon returned with the map. The grey-haired woman held it in front of Itty and asked her for the location of the cave.

'This would be easier if you untied me,' Itty said through gritted teeth.

'That's not going to happen, dear. Just point with your nose.'

Once the cave's location had been indicated after a lot of eye-crossing and assorted facial contortions, Itty let her head drop back. Her neck ached, as did her face from the squinting and nose wiggling. Nathan was instructed to hurry out to look for the cave with the grating at the back.

The angry-faced woman fed Itty some broth while they waited for him to complete his task. The others remained at the walls of the room, arms folded and glowering at Itty.

This isn't fair! What have I done to these people? Itty sighed. *Oh well, it'll be over soon.*

'My nose is itchy. Could someone scratch it?' she said.

No one moved.

'Please.'

The angry-faced woman muttered something and poked at Itty's nose with the handle of the spoon. After that, everything was still and silent for several more minutes.

'I found the cave, ma'am, right where the girl said it was,' Nathan panted on his return, obviously having run all the way there and back. 'It's got a grating like she said, but I couldn't open it.'

'Harrumph,' the grey-haired woman grunted. 'Our village of Yossburg, of which I am the mayor, is a small one, and currently sorely oppressed by our larger neighbours, Rille and Tweezle. If anything, the presence of this hidden passage confirms you're a spy.'

'No! I'm not, I'm not. You must believe me.' *I'm getting really fed up with all of this. It was better back on the ship!*

The mayor smiled, but it was not a friendly expression. 'Unfortunately, I'm afraid it's not as simple as that…' She paused for a moment as if collecting her thoughts. 'We've got a second problem, one which you might be able to help with. You see, there's a dragon—'

Itty spluttered. 'You're joking, right? Everybody knows dragons don't exist.' No one else in the room was laughing, or even smiling, and she began to struggle against her restraints once again. 'I don't know what you get out of tying up visitors, accusing them of being spies and then making up ridiculous stories, but enough is enough. Let me go!'

The mayor scowled at her. '*As I was saying!* There's a dragon. It arrived about three months ago, probably lured in by those swine in Rille. The beast has been terrorizing our farms ever since, carrying off livestock. It can't be long before it starts on people.

'Now, before you suggest it, we have tried to track down the beast, but we can't locate its lair. Oh, I know, we could pay some roving warrior-knight to kill it, but this is a small village, and we can't afford the expense.'

Itty couldn't decide whether to laugh at the idea of dragons or to cry at the indignity of remaining a prisoner.

The mayor gestured towards the others in the room. 'Our village elders have consulted the books of lore and have established… They're pretty certain…' She cleared her throat. 'They think that sacrificing a maiden will satisfy the foul creature and send it on its way. I want to offer my sincerest apologies for the inconvenience—we all do—but your arrival here was quite fortuitous.'

'You mean…? Me? No, no, no, no. You can't do that!' Itty shouted.

'We'll provide you with a final dinner, the best the village can offer. Then we'll take you to a place we know the dragon frequents.'

Itty continued to shout as everyone else shuffled out of the room, a few with chins held high but most looking sheepish and embarrassed.

Late that afternoon, the angry-faced woman brought in a tray with a sumptuous feast: buttered potatoes, garlic-fried pork and beef, steaming vegetables, a bed of peppered quails' eggs, spiced breads, sugary pastries, apples and pears, and many other dishes Itty didn't recognize.

'Let me go, please. You don't have to do this.'

'I'm afraid we do, dear,' the woman said with a sad smile. 'Now, be a good girl and open wide for this first bite.'

Itty stubbornly kept her mouth closed, trying to ignore the heavenly aroma of the food.

The woman threw down the fork. 'Well, if you're going to be like that, you ungrateful… You don't deserve the effort we put into making you comfortable! This food doesn't grow on trees, you know.'

Itty thought about snarkily asking where the apples and pears came from then, but decided that arguing with the woman wouldn't help her situation.

A few minutes later, still hungry, she found herself dangling over the shoulder of a large man as a small party of villagers marched into the woods. She wriggled and slapped at him, getting no reaction. She kicked and yelled, and the permanently angry woman grabbed her chin and pulled her head up so that they were face-to-face. 'Be quiet, girl, or we'll cut out your tongue,' she hissed.

Itty shut up.

After an hourlong march, twisting and turning so often that Itty was totally befuddled, they reached a clearing in the woods. She thought it looked quite picturesque, apart from the charring on the surrounding bushes and trees, not to mention the blackened stake standing in the middle. She didn't know what had caused the damage, but she felt certain it was no dragon.

The villagers tied Itty to the stake and draped a musty sheep's fleece over her shoulders. 'We want to make you look and smell mutton-y, miss. We hope you don't mind,' a ruddy-faced man said as he smeared some sheep's dung on her trouser legs.

Itty thought for a moment. 'Why?'

'Why what?' the man on sheep dung duty asked.

'Why do you want me to be a sheep? Your mayor said you wanted to sacrifice a maiden.'

The man scratched his head, causing sheep pellets to lodge in his hair. 'Well, you see… The elders, they… 'Ere, Bert, why're we making this young woman up to be a sheep?'

'Ah, now, you see,' said Bert, a fat, balding man who possessed the air of someone considering himself the village expert on everything. 'We need to sacrifice a maiden, right, to satisfy the dragon? But the dragon, y'see, he only comes for sheep, not maidens. We need to, like, lure him here with a tasty sheep, and then when he gets here, *vwa-la*, there's a maiden, and Bob's yer uncle.'

Itty blinked at him.

Just before they left, the mayor stepped forward. 'Your sacrifice will not be forgotten. It is a great thing you do for our humble village.'

Itty yelled, 'You can't do this. Let me go.'

The villagers left, Itty's shouts and screams echoing behind them.

Eventually, she became tired and slumped against the stake, sobbing. Back in Hyrhia, her imagination provided dragons who would easily be discouraged by a croissant thrust in their direction. But here, in the darkness, alone and with no croissants, these imaginary dragons came closer and showed her their teeth. She pictured them biting and tearing, and…

After a while, her tears dried up, and her churning thoughts became calm. In the quiet, without the villagers fussing around her, she realized she had let herself get caught up in a farce. Dragons didn't exist; she knew that. Fiction section, that's where to find all the dragon books. The villagers were going to return the following day to check that the dragon had taken her, and when they saw her still here, they'd come to their senses and release her.

She had to make it through one night. Just one night. How hard could that be? She'd survived the Estalian Navy and lived in the

Down-Underworld with a three-headed dog. A single night in the woods would be nothing compared to those.

However, only a few minutes later, her shoulders began to ache. She shuffled her bottom and wiggled her arms until she was a bit more comfortable. Then, her legs and back started to twinge. She shuffled and wriggled some more, until she was sitting at the base of the stake, leaning against it.

She looked upwards and imagined pictures in the clouds. Most of them twisted to take on the shape of dragons, so she stopped studying them. She knew dragons didn't exist; they appeared only in storybooks and her imagination. But she was struggling to keep her imagination under control.

Her stomach rumbled; she wished she'd had some of that dinner after all. It was going to be a long time until she would have a chance to eat.

To distract herself, she sang some popular songs and made-up rhymes:

There was a young woman from Hyrhia,
Who was an inveterate worrier.
With no one to save her,
She had to be braver,
And so, she became a great warrior.

Not my best effort, she thought. *And who am I kidding? I'm not much of a warrior.*

'Oh gods, I'm so bored!' she yelled into the emptiness, wondering if Lo-La might be listening.

Finally, the sun edged its way below the treeline, and the sky darkened. As the air grew colder, Itty was thankful for the fleece, though she was less keen on the smell coming from her legs. Exhausted from the stresses of her day, she drifted off to sleep but jerked awake at every animal noise. She had no idea what they were, but they seemed exceptionally shrill in the hushed stillness of the night.

The animal noises faded and stopped, and the sudden quiet made Itty feel more uneasy than the sounds had. Before she could react, the silence was broken by a sound louder than anything she'd heard so far that night: the flapping of an enormous flag or cloak… Or wings…

Itty's imagination whispered that, yes, there is such a thing as a dragon, while the rest of her brain argued that they existed only in stories.

Her imagination asked, *How sure of that are you, precisely?*

As her heart thumped and her mind raced in circles, Itty forced herself to breathe in and out slowly and calmly, straining her ears for the sound to come again.

She screamed as a huge shape dropped out of the sky and landed right in front of her with a ground-shaking thud. She couldn't tell what it was in the dim light of the night's sliver of moon, only that it was gigantic.

The shape roared back at her.

She screamed again.

Chapter 10: Dragon

A famous philosopher once trapped a dragon in a box—a very big box. Within this dragon trap, he had already placed a bottle containing a poisonous gas, along with a device which would cause the bottle to open by random chance. He proclaimed that the dragon was simultaneously both dead and alive, because no one could tell from outside the box whether the poison had been released or not.

His neighbours told one another that the dragon was most certainly alive. 'Look at how the box shakes,' they said, 'and listen to the roaring that comes from within.'

The great thinker dismissed this babble as unscientific nonsense, because he absolutely and categorically knew that the dragon's condition depended only upon the operation of the device. And that would be determined solely by the fickle whims of fate. 'However,' he conceded, 'when I open the box, logic dictates that the state of unknowing will collapse, and the dragon will cease to be both dead and alive. As I will now demonstrate.'

His ignorant and unscientific neighbours stood well back as the great and wise philosopher unlocked the dragon trap.

They later told anyone who would listen that the dragon had indeed been alive, and definitely not dead. However, not enough of the philosopher could be found afterwards for anyone to ask him precisely what his experiment was intended to prove.

Never, ever, ever put a dragon in a box, from Shrewd Inga's Big Book of Fables.

'Oh, do be a creature who is not making a racket that is an infernal one,' boomed an immensely deep voice from somewhere in front of Imperceptibility.

She inhaled again, preparing to let loose another scream.

'No, please don't be a thing which is screaming. You're a creature who is very noisy for a person that is a sheep, and you're a creature that is giving me a headache.'

'I'm not a sheep!' she snapped.

'Well, you look like a thing that is one.' A large head loomed right in front of Itty; its long snout huffed warm, moist air at her, causing her to pull her legs back and scrabble upright. 'And you smell like a being that is a sheep.'

'I'm a person!' she squeaked.

The head gave a deep rumbling chuckle. 'A person? And what is it that makes a person? Is it a thing that talks? I talk. You talk. Cattle talk, and sheep are creatures who talk. Trees talk, though the speech that is theirs is very slow. But not as slow as that of the stars, and I know about things that are stars. Are we all persons? Who is it that decides what thing is a person and what's not?' Another gust of hot air wafted towards her. 'Do persons eat things that are persons?'

Itty swallowed, thought about screaming, and swallowed again. 'Please don't eat me.'

'Ha, ha, ha!' the voice boomed. 'Don't worry, little thing—little *person*—I'm not a thing that is hungry. Yet. Perhaps I'll play with the thing that is you for a while. Or perhaps, I'll be a person that talks, because that's what persons do, and we are things that are persons, did you not say?'

Relief flooded Itty. An instant later, a lump settled in her stomach as she imagined what the monster might consider 'play.' For the moment, she decided, talking should be her preferred option.

'Excuse me,' she said tentatively. 'Are you a dragon?'

'Am I a dragon or am I not, that is a question. Is a dragon one thing or another, that is a second question. What is it that makes a thing a dragon?'

Itty's terror faded away as her impatience grew. *Whatever this thing is, it's certainly long-winded.*

'Is it these wings?'

A gust of wind tousled Itty's hair, and something briefly obscured the moon.

'Is it these claws?'

She heard the hard ground near her feet being torn up by what must have been enormous claws. Grit and pebbles hit her ankles.

'Is it this tail?'

Itty winced when there came a swish and a mighty crack, as if from a giant whip, followed by the sound of collapsing trees.

'Or… Is it this fire?'

Flames jetted above Itty's head: first red, then yellow, through white, to eye-searing blue. In the light of the roaring flare, Itty's jaw dropped at the sight of the monster. A real, living, breathing dragon, right in front of her. She marvelled at the iridescence of the crimson scales and imprinted in her mind every detail of the long head pointing at the sky, the huge mouth belching fire and full of enormous sharp teeth, the sinuous neck leading to a body as tall as she was. The wings on either side dwarfed the body and were covered with shimmering crystalline feathers. A long, gently swishing tail elegantly completed the creature's perfection.

All of a sudden, the dragon jolted, coughed, and collapsed. The flames vanished.

'Owwwww!'

'What's wrong?' Itty asked, wondering what could hurt such a majestic creature.

'My haunch is the thing that is wrong, darling sheep-person. The wrong is a thing that is stuck in it.'

Before Itty could ask what the thing was or if she could help, the dragon continued, 'I'll be a creature who is all right after a rest.'

With that, he curled up beside her and promptly went to sleep, enveloping her in the damp, warm air of his snoring.

Despite her perilous situation, Itty must have dozed off too, because the next thing she knew, the sun was peeking over the trees.

Where am I? Then her body stiffened as memories crept back. *The dragon!*

She looked around.

He was still there, still asleep, still snoring. Still huge.

She had to get away before he woke up.

Pins and needles in her extremities reminded her that she was tied to the stake in the middle of the clearing. Without making a sound, she stretched her legs and arms as far as she could, easing their aches and trying to get some feeling back into them. Once her legs had stopped wobbling, she struggled to her feet and threw her weight against the stake, pulling and pushing, until it started to give way.

Ten minutes later, panting and sweating, Itty toppled the stake, tumbling with it and banging her elbow on the ground. She stifled a cry of pain and shuffled her arms off the end of the stake. *Why didn't I think of doing this last night instead of waiting for the villagers to return?* she thought, angry with herself. *Serves me right for being smug and for thinking there're no such things as dragons. Wow! Dragons actually exist. This is amazing. As long as I remain alive.*

Her wrists were still bound behind her back, but at least she could move. She wriggled her legs through the loop of her arms so that her hands were in front of her, and worried at the knot with her teeth until it loosened. Finally, she was free.

Just as she was about to run, a large green eye flicked open and stared at her.

The dragon rumbled. 'Where do you think that it is you are going, little person-sheep?'

'I–'

'Were you thinking, or were you not, of trying to escape, dear creature?' Looking away as if she barely mattered, the dragon reached out a long talon and casually gouged a line in the hard ground in front of her.

Itty gulped. Short of some miracle, death was inevitable. Perhaps she'd see Karrin again, sooner than both had expected. *Maybe I can stay in the Down-Underworld for a while, instead of going through my afterlife door immediately.*

A sudden thought struck her: did she have any coins to give Karrin, to pay for crossing the Sticks? She stuck her hands in her pockets and rummaged: that lump was Captain Smart's compass, that was a box of matches, here was a handkerchief she didn't want to investigate too closely, and a book. Her fingers grazed something smooth and metallic, sliding over it as quickly as her mind did, then she found her purse. Emptying it into her hand, she found half a dozen coins and some fluff.

At the clink of the coins, the dragon's massive head snapped around. She looked up to see him staring at her hand and licking his lips.

This was it: the end. However, she wasn't going to cower, not after everything she'd been through to end up here. Clutching her coins tightly, she stood up and puffed out her chest.

'Before you kill and eat me, I want to say one thing.'

'What? Eat you, funny little person-thing that you are?'

Oblivious to the dragon's blink of surprise, Itty continued, 'You are the most majestic creature I have ever seen.'

The dragon's jaw dropped open. 'What did you say?'

Itty cleared her throat and spoke again. 'I said you are the most handsome being I have ever met. You're nothing at all like the scary monsters I've read about. If my life ends here, it's worth it to have seen you with my own eyes.'

The skin on the dragon's face became slightly redder—was he blushing? 'It's, that is... I– I– I've never had that reaction before. Normally you little persons are all persons who are screaming or shouting.' He turned his whole body towards Itty.

'Owwww!' He flinched and closed his eyes.

Itty peered at him. 'You did that last night, too. Where does it hurt?'

The dragon pointed a claw towards the middle of his left haunch and groaned. 'Dear person-sheep being, it is a thing that is the tip of a spear, and I just can't get it to be a thing that is not in me.' A tear appeared in his eye. 'How's a dragon meant to be a person looking his best with what is an ugly spear tip stuck in his rear?'

He shook his head, almost bashing her with the end of his snout. 'Knights! I keep being attacked by creatures that are knights, or is it knights that are creatures? There I am, minding the business that is my own, *not* eating a sheep. Then some knight-person comes along on his white creature that is a horse—why is it always that they are horses that are white? Do knights not like horses that are creatures of other colours?'

The dragon looked at Itty for a moment, then his eyes welled up. 'He's all "Have at thee" or "Die, foul creature" when he shouts, and his shouting is so loud. It's enough of a thing to make you cry, and no choice do I have but to defend myself.' He blinked away a shimmer of tears. 'A knight is not a good thing for eating. The armour is an alluring thing of temptation, but the contents are far too sinewy things, and gristly. The armour is a thing that I like, but the knight-creature inside…' The dragon pulled a face, and a shudder rippled all the way from his snout to the tip of his tail.

His long neck bobbed and twisted as his gaze followed Itty's walk around his body.

She examined the spear stuck in his rear end. It was embedded underneath one scale and pressed on surrounding scales when the dragon moved his leg, reminding her of a story she once read about Anne Drockles and an injured lion.

'You poor thing. Here, let me see if I can help. Just lean over this way.'

The dragon lowered itself so Itty could reach, and she grasped the spearhead and wiggled it. The dragon hissed, and Itty froze.

'Sorry, sorry. I didn't mean to hurt you. It's stuck really tight.' She braced a foot against the dragon's side. 'Just… a… little… more…' With a pop, the fragment of spear pulled loose, lightly spattering the ground with a few droplets of purple blood. 'There you go. The scale's a bit of a mess, though. There's a crack that seems to go all the way through.'

The dragon wriggled in delight. 'Ahhh, that is a feeling that feels so much better.' He surveyed the damaged scale. 'I'll be a creature of teeth and bite the end of the scale off and then a creature of fire to cauterize the rest that remains. Be a person standing back.'

A hand-sized piece of scale fell to the ground as the dragon blasted his side with scorching fire. Itty picked up the fragment and traced her finger across the cool, smooth surface.

The dragon shivered and yelped, 'Don't do that!'

Itty jumped.

'Sorry,' said the dragon. 'I didn't mean to be a creature who frightens you, but that is a thing that tickles when you stroke it.'

'You can feel me touching this scale, even though it's not attached to you?' She stared at it—shiny crimson on one side, a darker maroon on the other.

'Yes, of course, that I can. Action at a distance, distance and action. Doesn't that work for you, dear sheep-person that you are?'

'No, I don't think so. But I do try very hard not to become detached from bits of my body.'

'No matter. Keep the scale if you want what it is; I know it's pretty—after all, it came from me. But, please, try not to touch the part that is the back; it's very sensitive. Well, I suppose we should introduce the persons who are ourselves to each other. I'm a dragon who is called Schankenkrausloftenisburg. Who is it that you are?'

Itty stared at him, rolling the name around in her head, before saying, 'Pleased to meet you, Schanken… Schankenkr… Oh, sorry, is it OK if I call you Shanks? I'm Imperceptibility Happenstance, Itty.'

The dragon blinked his huge eyes. 'Have we met before? Your name is a name that sounds familiar, though it is an unusual name for a sheep.'

'I'm pretty sure I'd remember if we'd met.' Itty said.

'Perhaps,' he mused, 'it is from a time that is different to this one. Ripples in the quantum.'

Itty puzzled over this for a moment, then pulled the conversation back to more solid ground. 'Anyway, I'm not a sheep!'

'You look like one, person who appears to be a sheep.' The dragon inhaled. 'And a sheep is a creature, too, you have the odour of.'

'This is just a fleece to keep me warm, and the villagers smeared sheep you-know-what on my legs to make me smell.' Itty brushed at her legs and took off the fleece. 'See.'

Shanks poked at the sheepskin beside her, then brought his head down close to Itty, squinting as he peered at her. 'It is still a bit like a sheep that you look. Are you trying to be a person who is a trickster? Are you a very small knight?'

'Can't you see I have no armour?' she said, tapping her chest to demonstrate the lack of metal.

Shanks tilted his head one way and the other as if trying to see her properly.

Itty thought for a moment, then asked, 'I hope you don't mind me asking, Shanks, but are you long-sighted?'

The dragon blinked. 'It is a thing that all dragons are. We can spot things that are down here from places that are way up there.' He gestured with a wing. 'But close on the ground, everything that's a thing is a blur, it is. It is this way that things are.'

Itty thought for a bit, then asked, 'How well can you control your fire? I have an idea that will help you see. Something I read about in a book.'

She dug two shallow circular pits into which she placed several rocks. 'The ground here is sandstone, and if you can make it hot enough, it'll melt and form glass. Then I need you to focus your flame on the centres and gradually, ever so gradually, reduce the heat. The more slowly you can let the glass cool, the clearer it'll be.'

An hour later, the dragon was exhausted after all his concentrated flaming. Itty was tired and hot, not to mention singed in several places. In front of them were two convex discs of clearish glass.

Itty held one up at arm's length. 'Take a look at me through this. It's not going to be perfect by a long stretch, but it'll have to do.'

Shanks leaned close and oriented his head so that Itty was visible through the lens. 'Oh my!' he said. 'That's a thing that is astonishing. It's not a sheep that you are, dear… *person*.'

Itty rolled her eyes. 'Now we need to make a frame so that we can attach these to your head. Metal, I think…' She looked around. 'Metal. We could do with some metal.'

The dragon coughed, gagged, and coughed again, then regurgitated a shiny pool of molten metal. 'Iron, that it is. Will that do?'

'You store iron inside your body?'

'It's what we eat. Heavy metal is what we prefer—gold, silver, or uranium when we can find it. But iron is a metal that is common in this world, and it must do. It is the iron that's the best part of those knights that are otherwise things that are irritating.'

Itty shivered at the thought that the pool of metal might be all that was left of a bold knight in shining armour, and perhaps his white horse too.

'Right,' she said shakily. 'We need to make something to hold the glass discs with hooks to go around your ears.'

She drew two circles in the ground and a line connecting them, then two more lines to act as the glasses legs—very long lines, because of the length of the dragon's head— and asked him to use his claw to make them deep gouges.

As he dribbled molten iron into the mould, she said, 'Now, we just have to wait for this to cool, then we can put the lenses in.'

'I wonder, Itty creature, if I might nibble on those coins in the purse that is yours. They are things that smell like very nice things, and I am a person who is hungry after all that smelting.'

It wasn't very long before Itty was able to wedge a pair of glasses on Shanks' snout.

'They're not the greatest, but they ought to help a bit,' she said. 'You can probably get better ones next time you're in a big city.'

The dragon looked so far up and down and all around that he almost knotted his neck. He peered into the trees; he lifted rocks and examined insects scurrying underneath; he squinted at flowers. 'My, my! I never knew all this that I can see now was in the world.' He cried tears of joy. Huge drops gathered under the rim of his glasses and trickled along his cheeks to splash to the ground. 'My dear Imperceptibility Happenstance, Itty shee—*person*, I am forever in the debt that is yours.'

Just then, Imperceptibility detected a hint of spices—cardamom and vanilla—and sulphur. She was sure she could hear muttered swearing and 'Can't trust a dragon to eat anybody.'

Chapter 11: Flight

Left or right, what a fright.
Up or down, smile or frown.
Strange or charm, bet the farm.
Here or there, when or where?
This or that, who or what?
My cat barks.
My duck quarks.
Left and right, it's a sight.
Up and down, like a clown.
Strange and charm, what's the harm?
Here and there, it's everywhere.
This and that, with my cat.
Woof.

The Quantum Polka (Trad.)

Several minutes later, Shanks was still examining the patterns of veins on leaves and flowers. He kept taking his spectacles off and putting them on again, marvelling at all the details he could see. He inspected his claws, then grabbed Imperceptibility's hand, taking care not to squeeze too hard, and peered at the creases of skin at her knuckles.

'My, my,' he chuckled. 'I didn't know you person-creatures were things that are so wrinkly. I am a person liking my glashes. I will need to be a person showing them to other dragon-persons.'

'Glasses,' Itty corrected.

'Glasses! Glasses,' he murmured as he poked gently at her skin. 'It looks like some of your wrinkles are things that have more wrinkles on them—are there more wrinkles on the wrinkles that you have on your finger wrinkles? Can I be a person who can see more sights that are small?'

'There's something called a small-thing-seer, a bit like a complicated pair of glasses. Well, half a pair of glasses. Actually, more like a telescope, if you've come across those. I've never actually used one myself, but you can use them to look at very tiny objects right up close. There are books showing how to make and use small-thing-seers in the science and magic section of the library. Perhaps I can borrow one when I next visit Hyrhia.'

When I next visit… I want to go home. I want to go home now. *How can I get there?* she wondered. *I don't even know where I am now.* 'Shanks, can you tell me where we are?'

He let go of her hand and settled back on his haunches. 'Ah, dear person-creature of the *glasses*, that is a difficult concept for a person who is a dragon, for we exist as a probabilistic distribution across space.'

Brow furrowed, Itty turned to the dragon. 'Huh? A what?'

'You creatures, persons and sheep, even knights and horses, exist in one place at one time within your dimensions that number three and no more. We creatures who are dragons are persons born in higher dimensions, birthed from our syres into the spaces between your dimensions, where we exist as probabilities, as energy potentialities, as *quantum*. Distance is a thing that doesn't matter; we can be persons who are everywhere at the same time, and we choose which place to actualize.'

How can you be everywhere at the same time? Confusion galloped through Itty's mind. *Actualize? Choose…*

Her eyes widened. 'Do you mean you can go anywhere just by thinking it?'

Shanks nodded. 'As long as the place is a place I recognize.'

Another idea entered the tangle of her thoughts, and she ventured, 'Does this have anything to do with the Humble Monks' tunnels? Brother Nobody told me they connect everywhere to everywhere else.'

'Who do you think were the persons who built them? And created the spaces in between, where the tunnels are not there? Places that do not exist and that have nothing in them.' The dragon sounded smug.

'If you're everywhere, how come we almost never see dragons?'

'I didn't say we are persons who *are* everywhere, I said we *could be* everywhere, which are two things not the same. The universe is a thing that is a large thing, larger even than potentiality. Gaps are plentiful in spaces that exist behind and between your dimensions for us to hide within and to travel through, unseen.' Shanks looked up at the sky. 'However, that you never see persons who are dragons is a statement that is not a true statement. It is the time that is daytime now, is it not? But, small creature-person, what things do you see above in the time that is night?'

'Stars?' Itty tentatively answered after a short think, not entirely sure where the dragon might be going with this.

'Those stars are things that are ancient dragons, persons who are beings of my race who have chosen to leave their worlds and contemplate the universe. You are surrounded by venerable dragon-persons, young Itty-person! Some ancients become syres to create new persons that will become dragons, an event that happens at a time perhaps once every hundred centuries. They are syres who send out their knowledge in a burst that is a massive outpouring of energy.'

Itty interrupted: 'I think I might have read about that—are you talking about sky-brighteners? What astronomers try to tell us are exploding stars?'

'Yes, yes. Exploding *syres*. Have you seen a star that is a shooting star? That is a creature who is a newly-syred dragon. Infants that are ours are creatures who digest the knowledge of their syres, so that they may grow into persons who are dragons. And young dragons, such as the person that is me, are beings who choose a world to study and be part of. I chose this one because you small creatures that are also persons are so intriguing—even more interesting thanks to these things that you made that are my new glasses.'

Itty stared at him. *Dragons are complicated! None of the books I've ever read about dragons said anything about them being stars.*

She put her hands on her hips. 'Getting back to this—what did you call it?—*quantum*, you say that you're sort of everywhere at once. But you don't actually know where we're standing right now…'

Shanks frowned at her as if he were frustrated at her inability to understand something that comes second nature to dragons. It crossed Itty's mind that he probably didn't have many conversations with humans; she imagined that his interactions with knights were somewhat limited.

He thought for a moment, then said, 'I see what is nearby—especially well now—but not how this location that is nearby sits within the dimensions of everywhere that I know. I am a person in a place that is here, and I can be a person in a different place that is far away, without going through the places that are in between.'

'You can recognize different places,' Itty said carefully, 'but you don't know how they join to each other, because you don't travel the same way we do?'

The dragon smiled and nodded.

Her stomach rumbled, reminding her that she'd last eaten the morning before. There was no food here, at least not for humans, but she knew somewhere to try.

'There's a village near here—Yossburg, it's called. It was an hour's walk to get here yesterday, but I don't know what direction we came from. I kind of had other things on my mind. Do you know the village?' She looked up at him. 'Lots of shoe shops and an inn called the *First and Last Chance Saloon*. The people from there are the ones who tied me up as a sacrifice to you.'

'I know this place that is a village called Yossberg. The person-creatures who live there are noisy beings, and shout and throw things that hurt when I am a dragon who is flying over this place that is Yossburg.'

'Why do you fly over the village if they cause you so much trouble?'

'There is something about this place that is a familiar thing, but I do not know what thing it is. It is as if I have been a dragon in it before, except that I know that Yossburg is a place I have never been a creature visiting.' He scratched his head with a claw. 'I am a person who has a puzzle, and I must become a person who solves the puzzle that is Yossburg.'

The dragon slagged a rock with a burst of flame.

'Do you want me to raze to the ground this place that is Yossburg for making you a person who is a tied-up person?' He looked at Itty with wide, earnest eyes—eyes that appeared even larger than normal through the glasses' lenses. 'My kind has observed that this behaviour that is retaliation is an activity you who are beings trapped within the lower dimensions do quite a lot. I confess it is not a thing that I comprehend, but it is a thing that

I know of. Perhaps, if I do this for you, I will come to understand more about you person-creatures.'

'No! No, don't do that!' Itty put a hand on his knee.

The dragon's ears drooped, and he looked slightly disappointed.

She continued, 'I just want to go there for something to eat, and then figure out how to get home. Besides, we'd never have met if it wasn't for them. You can come with me. Meet the villagers and show them you're not scary. You can learn more about people, too.'

'I am a person who likes to learn.' Shanks' ears perked up as he smiled and nodded. 'Maybe I can see more wrinkles there. Let us be going then to this place that is called Yossburg of which I am a dragon who knows the location. Please become a passenger-person that is seated upon my back.'

Itty wasn't completely convinced about the wisdom of flying on a dragon, remembering her humbling experience of heights on the

Invigilator's rigging, but realized she had little choice. She clambered up the foreleg Shanks offered and settled herself across his shoulders. Squeezing her eyes shut, she clung on tight as he thundered along the ground, wings stretched out. With two mighty flaps of the huge wings, they were airborne.

Being thrown around with her eyes closed felt worse than seeing where she was going, and Itty opened her eyes again before her stomach could do something unpleasant—she guessed the dragon wouldn't be particularly pleased to be thrown up on. She swallowed and tried hard to focus on the horizon and not think about the vanishing ground below.

When they were high above the ground, Shanks' crystalline wing feathers extended delicate tendrils upwards, growing and curving around. The expanding crystals spread like frost on a windowpane and merged with each other, until the pair were encased in a bright-faceted bubble of sparkling red translucency.

'What's happening?' Itty shouted, the sound of her voice causing some of the wing crystals to tinkle and chime in response. When she realized there was no sensation of flight or the expected loud buffeting of air as they soared, she added, 'Sorry,' more quietly.

The crimson shell of the dragon's feathers thickened, and some regions became opaque, forming smooth surfaces joined by sharp edges, making it seem that Itty sat inside a giant ruby. Images took shape on the opaque areas, gradually becoming clearer, as if the surfaces were windows to other places.

'Where are we, Shanks?'

'This is the space that is in the gaps between your dimensions; this is the *quantum*, the place that is the domain of the dragon. All the places you can be are visible through the crystal panes that are quantum windows.'

'Everywhere?'

'Yes, everywhere that can be and everywhere that is. You just need to find it in the quantum. It needs to be found, one place among the many, and we can be persons going there.'

'So, you could take me home? To Hyrhia?' Itty asked.

'I am a person who is sorry that I don't know this place that is a place called Hyrhia. You will have to be a person who finds the place that is Hyrhia in the views that you see.'

Itty eagerly scanned the crystal windows, searching for something familiar. There were arid deserts and tangled forests; wide fields and bustling towns; snow-peaked mountains and fetid swamps and storm-tossed seas. One window showed empty darkness, and another a fiery sphere; one view was so bright it hurt to look at it; something that looked like a vast, empty greenhouse could be seen through a window near her shoulder. Some facets showed distant vistas from a great height; some were so close that she could make out faces. In a few, people stared back at her with expressions of surprise, and in others, the faces were most definitely not human. But there were too many windows for her to peer through them all. She didn't spot Hyrhia in any that her eyes darted between.

Just as her wonder started to descend into frustration, the dragon oriented towards one window, through which Itty could make out a village. As it drew closer, she recognized Yossburg. The multi-storey shoe shops were certainly distinctive.

'We have arrived,' the dragon said. 'Our location is the one that is concurrent with the village that is Yossburg.'

As the window grew larger, they flew through it, and the crystal sphere split apart, retracting back into the dragon's wings. Itty could once again feel the wind on her face, though there was no sign of her earlier queasiness—she thought she must be getting used to flying. Shanks' massive wings beat twice more, and he landed with a thud just outside the village.

Itty dismounted, took a deep breath, and marched into the village.

'Come out,' she shouted. 'Come and see your dragon! He's not a danger.'

As on her first visit, there was no response.

'Stop being silly! I know you're here. We went through all this yesterday. Before, need I remind you, you tried to kill me!'

She paced up and down the street.

'We're not going away, you know, so you might as well come out. I'm doing this for your own good.'

After a few minutes, the door to the *First and Last Chance Saloon* opened. Hands shoved the mayor out, and a short stick with a white cloth attached came flying out after her. Trembling, she picked up the flag and waved it.

'We're sorry,' she said in a shaky voice. Muttering came from somewhere within the saloon, but Itty couldn't make it out. The mayor nodded, then stood straighter and looked Itty in the eye. 'Please don't kill us. Don't destroy our village.'

'Destroy… Kill… What are you talking about? You think…?' Itty replayed what she'd said up to now, and realized that maybe it had been misinterpreted. She resisted the urge to laugh and pointed back at the dragon, who was nonchalantly grooming himself, tidying his wings after the short flight. 'I brought Shanks here to show you that he's *not* a monster to be feared. He's not going to kill anyone, and he's definitely not going to destroy any village.' She pivoted in a circle and shouted, 'Everybody, come out. I promise you're safe.'

Chapter 12: Yossburg

In southern Erigonia, not more than a month's journey by mule train from Khaleshka, the enthusiastic traveller will come upon the picturesque valley of Esmiya. Nestled within the snow-topped Karrigs, thickly-forested Esmiya contains a surprise for the unsuspecting visitor. Three surprises, to be precise! The villages of Rille, Tweezle and Yossburg are home to Erigonia's finest shoe designers and manufacturaries. Each village, quaint and friendly, specializes in footwear of various forms, all exquisite—and, tourists will be pleased to learn, all at truly affordable prices. Visit one, or all three, and return with an extra bounce in your step. While you're there, why not spend some time in Rille's world-famous museum, where you can learn much more about the history of the region and, naturally, shoemaking?

Of course, there's more to Esmiya than just shoes; modern industry has, as one resident put it, a *foothold* here too, in the form of one of Sir Oscar de Montford's aeronautical research facilities. Alas, fans of mechanized flight will not be able to visit the site itself, but if you're lucky, you can sometimes catch sight of test flights of the latest prototype dirigibles.

Excerpt from the *Esmiya Tourist and Visitors' Guide.*

Gradually, doors opened, and villagers cautiously stepped into the daylight. They stared at the unusual and very large creature in their midst, who peered back. Shanks commented to Itty that he'd never seen so many people up close before, at least, not who weren't screaming and running away. He asked her about the ones who seemed to mainly comprise wrinkles. When she explained that these were the elderly, his eyes widened.

'There are many things that are things for me to learn about you persons,' he said. 'Old dragons become stars that are very smooth things and very bright, not creatures that are slow and full of creases. I must talk with your old persons who are wrinkled.'

'Just one thing,' Itty said quickly. 'Most of them won't like their wrinkles being pointed out.'

One young man approached, fair-haired and freckled, whom Itty recognized as Nathan.

'Begging your pardon, miss, but is that a real dragon?'

She considered a rude response—after all, these people hadn't been particularly nice to her when she was last here. Then she sighed inwardly. Her foster parents always told her that politeness cost little effort but paid back handsomely.

She forced a smile and said, 'Yes. He's a real dragon, and he's called Shanks. Would you like me to introduce you to him?'

Nathan looked at the dragon and back at Itty, swallowed and nodded.

She grabbed his hand and pulled him the few steps to the dragon. Behind them, she heard gasps from the other villagers. 'Shanks, meet Nathan. Nathan, meet Shanks.'

The dragon slid his glasses down from his forehead and inspected the boy.

Nathan's hand tightened on Itty's. She gave it an encouraging squeeze back.

'Hello, small creature that is a Nathan. I am a person pleased to be meeting you,' rumbled Shanks. 'Do you have any things that are metal, for peckish is what I am?' He smiled, displaying his huge white fangs, which probably wasn't the most reassuring thing for a dragon to do directly after saying he was hungry.

The colour drained from Nathan's face. Villagers behind them gasped again.

'It's okay. He doesn't eat people,' Itty said quickly. 'Well, apart from knights, but that's for the metal. And anyway, it's only because they attack him first.'

Nathan, mouth hanging open, released her hand and reached to touch Shank's hide.

'Ma'am,' Itty called to the mayor, 'if your village has any spare metal—the heavier, the better—Shanks might appreciate a small snack.' She added, 'I'm a little hungry myself, too, though not for metal. Normal food for me, please.'

The mayor conferred with a couple of the other villagers, who scurried away. Shortly after, the blacksmith returned, pushing a wheelbarrow containing some rusted horseshoes and other bits of metal, and a waiter emerged from the saloon with a tray of pastries and tea. He also carried a small folding table tucked underneath his arm. He set it up in front of Itty and the mayor and placed the tray on top. No one else moved.

The villagers stared as Shanks melted the iron with a brief blast of fire and slurped up the resultant puddle. One small child squeaked and ducked behind her mother's skirt, immediately peeking back out at the dragon, wide-eyed. As the blacksmith walked away, he muttered that Mr Johansenn would have to go without new wheel rims for his wagon for a little longer.

Itty thought she would keep the villagers waiting as she nibbled at one of the cakes and sipped the tea, something aromatic with a hint of honey—it was the least they deserved for their treatment of her. As she selected a second cake with her chin held high, she surveyed her audience.

She was a little disappointed to find they weren't looking at her, but at Shanks.

'Mmmm.' She set down the empty cup with a deliberate clink of china and dusted a few crumbs off her clothes. 'That was delicious. Thank you. Does everyone here bake as well as this?'

No one paid her any heed, as all eyes remained anxiously glued to the dragon.

She clapped her hands to get the villagers' attention. 'I will admit that I was somewhat offended by your earlier behaviour.'

The mayor and the others looked sheepish. Many found something interesting to study at their feet.

'But I'm willing to let bygones be bygones,' Itty continued. 'Now, tell me why you thought a dragon was attacking the village.'

The mayor cleared her throat. 'Perhaps we can discuss this inside; it'll be more comfortable. Will—ah—your dragon be okay out here?'

'He's not *my* dragon. Shanks is his own being. But he'll be fine out here.' She called, 'Nathan, could you keep an eye on Shanks, please? Make sure the others don't pester him too much. He won't be able to resist because he really likes people.'

Nathan's eyebrows rose.

'I mean, to talk to,' Itty hurriedly added, 'not to eat. I see some of the children are curious; you could take them to meet him.'

The mayor opened the door to the largest of the village's shoe shops and invited Itty to enter. 'This is what makes our village special.'

Footwear crowded shelves attached to every part of the walls that wasn't door or window. All around were heavy, no-nonsense brogues, sturdy but elegant riding boots, colourful children's galoshes, and robust-looking sandals.

'I'm sure you must have heard of Erigonian shoes,' the mayor said.

'No.' Itty gave a half smile. 'I'm afraid I don't pay much attention to clothes.'

Looking Itty up and down, the mayor muttered, 'I can see that.'

Itty picked up a pair of blue walking boots, surprised at their lightness. They looked very comfortable.

The mayor said, 'The shelf above is more your size. Go ahead, try them on.' She cast a glance at Itty's feet. 'Your own shoes do seem a bit worse for wear and covered in, well… Perhaps we can just throw them away. What do you say?'

Itty scowled, thinking that the mayor would be disappointed if she thought this was adequate recompense for being sacrificed to a dragon, but then she put the boots on and walked up and down the shop floor. They were even more comfortable than she imagined, and she said so, arguing with herself that the mayor had probably been doing what she thought was best, and anyway, Shanks was a welcome friend. She could perhaps do with a few more friends, so far from home.

'Footwear is what we're famous for,' the mayor said. 'I wonder, dear, if we might exchange your trousers too.' She wrinkled her nose. 'They're a little, shall we say, aromatic.'

Recalling who had smeared sheep dung on her legs just the day before, Itty gave the mayor a sharp look.

'Ah. Well. Yes.' The mayor coughed. 'I'm sure you can find something to fit in that storeroom over there.' She pointed to a door in the back of the shop.

Inside the small room, Itty found several boxes of neat black trousers and shirts, obviously apparel for the shop staff. She also found a box of much brighter clothes and returned wearing a pair of loose lemon trousers with turquoise spots.

'Erm, I see you found our holiday fancy dress costu–' the mayor said. She blinked twice and sighed. 'Oh, never mind, they somehow suit you. Have a seat, and I'll tell you our history.'

She opened the shop door and called to someone outside, 'Marjorie, would you be so kind as to bring us some fresh tea? Thank you so much.'

Once tea had been poured, the mayor started her tale. 'A very rich cobbler, famous throughout the province of Erigonia, had three children, Alphonse, Rathbone and Ferdinia. They were all skilled shoemakers, but never saw eye to eye and continually argued about who was best. In exasperation, their father established three villages in a secluded valley, this valley—Rille, Tweezle and Yossburg—and gave one to each of his children. He said, "The more skilled you are, the more your village will prosper. After a while, it will be obvious which of you is the best."'"

She paused for a sip of tea. 'The villages grew, and all three prospered. Ferdinia specialized in outdoor footwear here in Yossburg, like those fine boots you're wearing; Rathbone made Tweezle the pinnacle of finery; and Alphonse excelled in leisure shoes in the village of Rille. The rivalry between the three led to their work becoming truly outstanding, and people flooded into the valley from across all of Erigonia to buy fine Esmiyan footwear.'

The mayor lifted the hem of her dress to show Itty her boots: elegant embossed red leather button-ups with a moderate heel. 'Look at the tooling on the leather here, Tweezle's best work.

'Of course, initially, the equal success of all three didn't please any of the children, but their father thought it was amusing. Over the years, the people of the three villages began to work and play together, and there was soon as much trading among them as between the rest of Erigonia and the valley. Although we retained our own identities and favoured different types of footwear, the rivalry between the siblings had been all but forgotten.'

'That sounds idyllic, but what's–' Itty asked.

The mayor waved her silent. 'It was indeed idyllic, but recently our neighbours have simply cut us off. They've got armed roadblocks on all the routes from the village. We can't leave to sell our boots and shoes, and no visitors come. That's why we thought you were a spy, the first stranger to arrive here for ages. We need to protect our patterns and techniques, the source of our prosperity.

'We're attacked and forced back when we try to visit the other villages, too. It's not just happening within the village. Their people harass our farmers and, as you saw, they managed to convince us we were being attacked by a dragon. We'd find fire damage and singed remains, like at the clearing where we, um, left you.' The mayor's cheeks reddened. 'Let me say how sorry I am for that. We genuinely thought there was a dragon—I mean a dangerous one, not like your friend. The other villagers must be stealing our livestock themselves. Another of their despicable, underhanded tricks.'

Itty looked around the shoe shop while she thought for a moment.

'I know we got off on the wrong foot—ha, ha—but you seem to be nice people, and these are very comfortable boots.' She twirled her left foot, admiring the supple leather and the way the blue stood out against the turquoise and yellow of her bright new trousers. 'I'd like to help your village, Madame Mayor, if I can. Perhaps, in return, you can help me get home to Hyrhia.'

'I don't know how easy it is to travel to Estalia, but I'm sure we can help you get as far as one of the coastal cities, and you ought to be able to find a ship there.'

'Thanks, that'd be a great help.' Itty smiled. 'Anyway, as you said, I'm a stranger here, but that also means no one in the other villages will recognize me. I can visit them—just another outsider coming to do some shoe shopping—and find out what's going on.'

The mayor slowly nodded. 'That makes sense, but you can't just go traipsing along the roads to the other villages. They'll know you could only have come from here.'

'I have a plan... Do you recall the cave where I arrived? The Humble Monks claim that the monastery tunnels take you to where you need to be. I don't know how they work, but they do. The monks say it's the will of the Great Lo-La, though I'm not sure I believe in Him, er, Her, or possibly Them, but–'

'The great who?'

Itty waved a hand in dismissal. 'It doesn't matter. Anyway, whether or not I believe in Lo-La, I'm sure the tunnels will take me to Tweezle or Rille if that's where I need to go.

I'll take someone as a guide to the other villages, and we'll have a look.'

The mayor thought for a few seconds. 'Nathan's parents used to take him with them to the market at Rille every other week until the current problems started—he's got some cousins there. And he's been to Tweezle a few times. We can disguise him so he won't be recognized.'

The pair finished their cups of tea and went outside, where a dozen of the village children were clambering over Shanks, pulling his ears, ruffling his wing feathers or chasing his tail as he flicked it from side to side. A few of them had discovered that scratching under his chin would make him go cross-eyed and let puffs of smoke leak from his nostrils.

'Itty-person,' he called. 'These small person-creatures are very entertaining, are they not? And friendly, and not very wrinkly. I think I would like to remain in this place for a while.'

'Please do stay here and look after the village. The mayor told me that Yossburg's neighbours are victimizing the people here, and you can help protect them. Nathan and I will take a trip to the other villages to find out why.'

'Oh, do be persons that are careful, creature dear. Perhaps I should come and be a person that helps also.'

'No, not yet, Shanks. We want to be discreet, at least to begin with, and you would probably stand out a little. We might need your help later. It'd be better to keep you as a surprise.'

'Do you still have that piece of scale that was mine? If you touch the back, I will come.'

Itty snapped her fingers. 'I have an even better idea. Do you know Marsh code?'

The dragon shook his head. 'What is it that a Marsh code is?'

'It's something I read about in a library book. A code devised by tribes in the swamplands of northern Alutriea, where it's so foggy that it's impossible to see long distances. The natives bash out sequences of taps on their shields with long and short gaps between them to send signals across the marshes.'

She picked up a small stone and hit another one with it three times—a short pause between the first two, then a longer pause. 'That's Marsh code for the letter *a* and this'— she knocked four short taps, paused, one short tap, paused, short, long, short, short, pause, short, long, long, short—'is *help*. If you learn Marsh code, I can use your scale to send messages to you from wherever I am, and call for help if we need it.'

Itty spent the rest of the day teaching the dragon, along with most of Yossburg's children, Marsh code.

It was dark by the time she and Nathan—his fair hair dyed black—set off on their mission, striding across the field towards the Humble Monks' cave, to the fading sound of small children and a large dragon enthusiastically banging rocks together.

Chapter 13: Rille

The health-giving properties of water are not to be underestimated. When mixed with sweetened fruit and left to ferment, it forms substances that are greatly enjoyed by many people, bringing a healthy red glow to their cheeks.

Of course, not all waters are equal. You can't just take water from any old stream and add fruit to produce a hangover-free brew. No, you need to start with *Avian Water*, fresh, luxurious, flowing directly from the marshes of Alutriea into our transportable wells. We filter it seventeen times and add our own secret ingredients to make this *the* unique, truly rich water of choice.

Advertisement for Avian Water.

'Is it safe down there?' Nathan asked, cautiously peering through the metal grate in the floor of the cave.

'Of course. I've been through these tunnels before,' Itty replied with more confidence than she felt. 'They're how I got here from...' She hesitated, not wanting to dishearten him further with stories of the Down-Underworld and spirits of the dead. 'From somewhere far from here. Now, make sure your lantern's secure. This ladder goes down a long way.'

She slung the strap of her own lantern over her shoulder, placed one blue-booted foot on the top rung and started to climb down. It was certainly less tiring, and much quicker, climbing down than up. Within minutes, the pair reached the stone steps and, shortly after, they came to a door.

I don't remember this door being red. Is it the same door I came through, or have the tunnels changed? Itty stood in front of the faded and peeling red-painted door trying to picture the one she'd come through what felt like aeons ago, but it was a blank. She guessed she simply hadn't given it any attention on her way to the surface. *Well, I can't give up this soon.* She pulled the rust-covered handle and opened the door. They stepped into a dark tunnel.

'Which way?' Nathan asked as he held up his lantern, illuminating rough walls and a smooth, well-trodden floor.

Itty half-smiled, recalling how she'd asked Brother Nobody the same question when she first entered the tunnels. 'You might not believe me, but it really doesn't matter—our feet will take us where we need to go.'

She wasn't actually sure if *she* believed that herself, and a chill ran its fingers down her spine. She hoped she might bump into Brother Nobody 231 again. Or any of the other Humble Monks.

Nathan stared at Itty for a few moments as she started down the passageway, before coming to life and hurrying to catch up.

After an hour walking along the featureless tunnel, Nathan asked, 'Miss, are you sure this is the right direction?'

She murmured, 'Let's keep going for a bit longer.' It occurred to her that the tunnels might not work without a Humble Monk as a guide, but she didn't want to alarm Nathan by mentioning that.

A further ten minutes passed in a silence broken only by their plodding footsteps. Itty licked her lips. *Should it take this long? Did I spend this much time walking with Brother Nobody? Is this all a big mistake?* It had seemed a sensible idea up on the surface, but down here… If they turned around now and retraced their steps, could they even find their way back to Yossburg? They should have left a marker at the door. Better still, brought some coloured beads or string to leave a trail they could easily retrace, like in the story she recalled about Hansel and Gretel and the Minotaur.

Something glinted ahead—a shiny doorknob. Relief flooded through Itty, although there was no discernible door, just a plain brass knob at about waist-height in the otherwise unmarked wall.

She reached for the knob and twisted it. Nothing happened. She tugged on the doorknob, then threw her shoulder against where she imagined a door must be. Still nothing. She kicked at the wall. Her eyes started to fill with tears of frustration. The doors she and Brother Nobody found always opened, and always led to the right place. She'd been so sure this one would have worked the same. They'd come all this way for nothing.

'I'm sorry, Nathan,' she said, her voice trembling. 'We should give up and turn back. The tunnel's not working for me, and I don't know what to do.'

Nathan grasped the doorknob and jiggled it. 'Maybe it's just stuck. Our back door sometimes needs a good twist.' He wrenched sharply and, with a sudden crack, a door swung open in the wall. He stuck his head through the gap, peered around and then popped back out again.

'Wow—that's amazing! I know exactly where we are. The tunnel worked just like you said!' He stepped through the opening.

Itty followed, a wave of relief passing through her. She wondered if different doors in the Humble Monks' tunnels were for different people, like the spirit doors in the Down-Underworld. *Why would Lo-La do that?* She would have to find out more, though she reckoned she'd need to find a monk first. *Then again, he'll probably just smile enigmatically and say, 'Lo-La does what Lo-La does.'*

The door opened into a dusty alcove which turned out to be a gap behind a large stone statue of a seated warrior. The statue presided over a long room lined with suits of armour and weapons. Their polished metal gleamed in the moonlight streaming through the room's windows.

'We're in the Rille Imperial Museum,' Nathan said. 'I visited it once, quite a few years ago, on a school trip. This is the armour room. That statue's King Berenice, cut from a single piece of granite, you know?' He raced from exhibit to exhibit as if he were an excited youngster, grinning at everything he saw. 'Look here, this is what Sir Royce wore in the Thirty Years War. And here's the sword Prince Irkledon used at the Battle of Alemnia.'

Itty smiled at his enthusiasm, but whispered, 'Keep the noise down. We don't want to be caught. And dim your lantern—the windows.'

It was unlikely that anyone would be able to see their lantern light through the narrow latticed windows above each display alcove, but Itty didn't want to take any chances.

Nathan stopped and turned to her, face suddenly pale. He gulped and whispered, 'How did we get here—the armour room is on the top floor of the museum, and we were… We were underground, really far underground. Not to mention, Rille is at least two hours away from Yossburg, and that's on horseback at a good old trot—we got here a lot quicker than that.'

'I know.' She put a reassuring hand on his shoulder. 'Yep, the tunnels are weird. They're something the Humble Monks made, or maybe dragons. Something to do with quantum energy, Shanks said, whatever that is. It doesn't matter; we're here now. I'll send a message back to the others and then let's see what we can find out.' She extracted the dragon scale from one of her pockets and tapped out Marsh code on its sensitive reverse side, knowing Shanks would sense her message: 'Arrived Rille, stop. All quiet, stop.'

As they tiptoed across the armour room, Itty glanced at the sword Nathan had been excited about earlier, and at the knives and crossbows making up some of the other displays. Nathan pointed at a club and asked if it might be smart to arm themselves before they left the museum.

Itty shook her head. 'We're here just to see what's going on. If someone finds us, we can say we're lost. They might not believe us, but it would be a lot worse if it looks like we've been stealing.'

With a shock, she realized she was a spy, an actual spy—committing the very crime she'd been accused of when she first entered

Yossburg. She doubted her punishment could be as bad as being tied up and left as an appetizer for a dragon, but it wouldn't be good. She shivered. But there was little she could do about it now, she thought, apart from being careful.

They crept through the museum, taking care not to bump against any of the exhibits. Beyond the armour room was an even larger room, crowded with elegant clothing and footwear—more shoes, even, than Itty had seen in the shop back in Yossburg. They had to traverse the length of the room to reach the staircase down.

Unfortunately, the stairs only took them down one floor, and the pair were forced to creep back across the building to find the next flight down. It was like the back-and-forth crossing of the River Sticks in Karrin's boat.

This floor contained displays of local history, focussed on the development of various sorts of footwear, followed by yet another shoe room. There were many different types of sandals and slippers, but the shelves labelled farming boots and waterproof footwear were empty.

The next floor down housed the machine room: some agricultural devices and a lot of leatherworking gadgets and tools. They passed a room full of ancient books; Nathan had to drag Itty away from a particularly interesting history of shoemaking in the region.

Finally, after a transport chamber (various carts and carriages, and ingenious wheeled shelving which could be used to transport delicate shoes across bumpy roads without damaging them) and another shoe room, they reached the gift shop. The shop sold mainly tea-towels with pictures of shoes on them, and whimsical ornaments and soft toys shaped like shoes, not forgetting posters and postcards featuring well-known shoe designs.

Itty reached for one of the tea-towels. It showed a simplified map of the area, decorated with examples of the different footwear from the three villages. A meandering river cut through two sides of the triangle the villages made. Yossburg lay on one side of the river, while Tweezle and Rille were on the other. The only passable routes through the Karrig mountains led to the other two villages, which was why it had been so easy for them to cut Yossburg off from the world outside the valley.

On the far side of the gift shop, just beyond the cash desk, lay the building's exit: a pair of tall, sturdy oak doors. The doors were fastened by a heavy bolt with a lock plate, but the lock itself was open.

Itty slowly slid the bolt across, wincing at every squeak and hoping there was no one around to see the handle on the outside of the door move, then gently pushed one of the doors open. She looked left and right, and up to the windows of the houses across the street. Nothing moved. She stepped out and–

Splash!

She jolted at finding herself up to her ankle in cold water. Then, sliding on the slippery ground, she ended up flat on her back in an enormous puddle.

A window across the street illuminated in response to the noise, but luckily, the fall had extinguished her lantern. A head appeared in the window, looked up and down the street, muttered, 'Blasted drunkards,' and disappeared again.

When darkness was restored, Nathan crept through the museum door. He slowly waded through the water, making almost no sound, helped Itty to her feet and retrieved her lantern; they were relieved to discover it wasn't wet inside, merely extinguished. Nathan turned the wick on his lantern up slightly and held the light high.

They weren't standing in a puddle, but in an expanse of water covering the entire street.

'This isn't normal, is it?' Itty whispered.

Nathan shook his head. 'This should be Market Square, but it's a lake.' He doused his lantern, leaving just the light of the moon to make patterns on the ripples forming around their legs as they waded through the village.

They didn't find a dry street in the town. Sandbags blocked several buildings' doors, though people seemed to have given up on others, as if the water was just too much to contend with. Through a few uncurtained windows, Itty glimpsed reflections of the moon on flooded floors.

Nathan guided them through gradually deepening water towards what he said should have been a gentle stream on the village common. Instead, they found a torrential flow overwhelming the three footbridges which crossed the path of the stream.

Does this flooding have anything to do with hostilities between Rille and Yossburg? How? Could Yossburg's residents have done something to the river? Itty wondered. *No, surely they would have mentioned it. Nathan would know about it.*

After circling the entire village, they re-entered the museum and slid the door bolt across behind them. They stood in the foyer in soaked boots, puddles forming around them.

As Nathan relit his lantern, he asked, 'What next?' Now that they were inside again, he could speak without fear of being detected.

'When was the last time you were in Rille?' Itty asked.

'Months ago. We used to visit every fortnight, but then they blocked the roads.'

'And there was no flooding then?'

Nathan shook his head.

'So, this must be recent. I wonder what happened. We should have a party from Yossburg come visit. They could help to deal with the flooding.'

She tapped another message to Shanks: 'Village flooded, stop. No sign Rille behind attacks on Yossburg, stop. Returning now, stop.'

Itty surveyed the muddy footprints leading right to the door. There was no chance of their visit going undetected.

'Right, we'll go back into the Humble Monks' tunnel and return to Yossburg. Or…' Her eyes widened. 'Brother Nobody said the tunnels will take you wherever you need to go. Maybe we'll end up in Tweezle or somewhere else, and this was a detour just to show us what state Rille's in.'

'I'm not so sure. I don't trust those tunnels.' Nathan folded his arms. 'Who's to say we won't end up totally lost? I don't want to go into them again. I'm going to use the roads to get back to Yossburg.' He held up a hand to pre-empt Itty's response. 'Yes, it'll take longer. And I might run into guards, but it's still a safer bet than the tunnel. The guards on the roads will be paying more attention to people coming into the village than anyone leaving it.'

'You're right.' Itty let her shoulders drop. 'I've only been through the tunnels twice and I don't understand them. We were lucky we even found the door to the museum in the first place. Let's go back. Maybe Shanks can help—at least, he'll be able to clear the roads.'

'It's not that bad. We know Rille can't be the people behind Yossburg's problems, not with all this flooding. And, cheer up! You've brought us a dragon—who else could've done that?'

Itty thought, *Yeah, but finding nothing means the mayor might decide not to help me get to the coast.* She gave Nathan a weak smile. 'I guess. Well, come on. Let's start walking.'

When the pair turned towards the museum exit, she caught the scent of spices, cardamom and a hint of vanilla. She was sure she heard something, a muttering, then a scuttling. Suddenly, there was a tremendous crash, as if every shelf in the museum shop had collapsed at exactly the same moment. In the silence that followed, Itty could hear a throaty chuckle as the ringing in her ears faded.

Splashing and shouting came from outside—calls of 'The museum' and 'Robbers! Get 'em.'

The museum door rattled.

Chapter 14: Dark

Colour is a puzzling concept. Why do some hues, such as scarlet, come from animals, while others have a botanical basis—lavender, for example? Why do still others, like ochre, have mineral origins? A few colours are more perplexing: where does white come from? Snow is white, yet the water it becomes is colourless. And black: why is the sky black in a moonless night but a blue so pale it is almost white on a winter's day?

I propose a unifying theory in which there are three elemental colours, namely the purest of blood reds, a verdant green, and a royal blue of flawless simplicity, and that all other colours are composed of elements of these, entrapped within the nature of each entity, conferring upon the entity its characteristic colour.

I have, myself, invented an extruded triangular glass device, which can split any colour into its elemental constituents, thus establishing once and for all that all colours are combinations of these three and nothing more.

With my ingenious light prison, I can demonstrate that white is the perfection of all three in equal amounts, and black is what is left when light is absent.

From *Principia Naturae*, the collected knowledge of Sir Isaac Oldson.

Itty launched herself at the museum door, quickly twisting the latch on the lock plate.

The rattling outside stopped, and one of the voices grunted, 'That's odd—the door's locked. Who's got the key? Yonich?'

Itty and Nathan held their breath as another voice grumbled, 'Don't look at me. I thought you had it.'

'Trainee, have you got the key?' said the first voice.

'Nay, Officer Grigor,' a third voice whined. 'Nobody ever locks the museum, so we never need it. It's probably still on the hook back at the guardhouse.'

'Well, go and get it, then!' the first voice shouted. 'Do I have to do all the thinking around here?'

The voices argued outside the museum for a moment longer, then footsteps splashed off into the distance as someone—the trainee, no doubt—ran to get the key to the museum. The remaining voices muttered about the calibre of trainee constables these days, and how much standards had slipped since they'd signed up back in the day.

The two intruders gently let out their breath and tiptoed to the stairs, thankful for the incompetence of Rille's guards, especially trainee constable guards. As soon as they reached the top, they ran.

They hurtled past the machines and tools, up the next stairs, weaving around the shelves of books and shoes. Finally, they raced through the armour room, diving through the door behind the statue of King Berenice and closing it after them. They leaned against the back of the door, panting.

'Well, so much for taking the over-ground route home,' Itty whispered between gasps. She stood up straight. 'We'd better get moving. They might know about the secret door.' She shivered, not only because of a droplet of water from her earlier fall trickling down her back. 'And even if they don't, we've probably left a trail of wet footprints for them to follow.'

Fortunately, they still had their lanterns. They lit them and set off along the tunnel at a quick pace.

A warm breeze wafted from ahead, drying Itty's clothes. The pair paused to remove their boots and wet socks. As long as they avoided the occasional pebble, walking barefoot on the smooth tunnel floor was more pleasant than squelching along in sodden footwear and would prevent painful rubbing and blisters. It was also quieter, which she hoped would make it harder for the Rille guards to track them once they made it into the tunnel.

After a while of silent padding, Itty noticed the aroma of cooking drifting on the breeze. She wondered if a doorway to the Down-Underworld might be open, letting the odours from one of Karrin's barbeques waft through.

'Where's that weird smell coming from?' asked Nathan. 'Leather and pine trees.' He sniffed. 'And cheese.'

Itty stopped. 'What? Cheese and pine trees? I don't smell that. I smell…' She inhaled deeply and thought hard about what was tickling her nose, then sniffed again. 'I smell cooking. Meat—lamb, I think, because there's definitely a hint of mint.'

Nathan scratched his head. 'But how does–'

'I don't know!' Itty threw up her hands and snapped. 'I'm not an expert on these tunnels. Even the Humble Monks don't understand everything about them. Shanks knows a lot, but—I'm *really* sorry—I didn't think to ask him about smells before we set off, did I?'

Their shadows on the tunnel walls jumped about as she waved her arms, swinging the lantern with them. Nathan took a step backwards, bumping against the wall, shock at her outburst written on his face.

When she saw his expression, Itty stopped flailing. 'Sorry,' she mumbled. 'Sorry, I don't know what came over me. The smells, it's just… I dunno… tunnel magic. It's been a long day—night—whatever—and I just –'

'Hmmm…' He had stopped listening and was feeling the wall behind him. 'I think there's a door here. Do you think it's the one to Yossburg?'

'No, the door should look like…' She put a hand to her mouth. *What should the door look like?* 'Oh my! We didn't look when we came through, did we? And I wasn't paying much attention when I first came to Yossburg. Brother Nobody opened the door for me, so I didn't have much time to see it from this side. It was wooden, I think, and had a… a whatchamacallit.' She gestured with her thumb as if she were pressing down on something. 'A latch, like on a kitchen door.'

'This one has a latch—see here.' Nathan brushed the space around it then held up his hand, which came away covered in black. 'The door's covered in a lot of dust or soot or something; that's why we didn't see it.' He rubbed some more. 'And it's a wooden door. Is it the right one?'

Before Itty could reply, he added, 'You said doors appear when we need them.' He tapped on it. 'This must be the right door for us.' He pressed on the latch and pulled the door open.

Just then they heard running footsteps behind them and a shout of 'There they are!' It was the same gruff voice they'd heard at the museum. 'Get them!' The footsteps sped up.

Itty and Nathan jumped through the doorway, slamming the door behind them in the hope that their pursuers wouldn't spot it. They ran, shadows from the lanterns dancing on the tunnel walls.

The corridor didn't slope upwards, as she would have expected for the Yossburg entrance, but she was more concerned with evading the Rille guards for the moment.

The tunnel twisted left, then right, then left again. It zig-zagged so much Itty began to feel dizzy.

Eventually, the pair stopped. They dropped their lanterns and stood panting, hands on knees. Itty felt as if she would throw up.

'I can't hear anything,' Nathan gasped. 'Maybe they couldn't open the door, or maybe the tunnel took them somewhere else.'

He peered back but could see only as far as the last sharp corner. 'I guess we should continue. We might meet them if we go back.'

Itty nodded, still unable to speak. She took deep breaths, trying to keep the contents of her stomach under control, and they started marching again.

Her feet began to ache as the adrenaline left her system, and she called for a brief rest. Sitting on the floor, she brushed the dust off the reddened soles of her feet before massaging them for a few moments. After putting on their socks and almost dry boots, the pair set off, plodding along the tunnel.

The tunnel wasn't a uniform width or height, but got taller and shorter or wider and narrower as they walked. At one point, it was so small that they had to crawl single file on hands and knees to pass through. Nathan baulked at the idea, but Itty pointed out that they had to either go forwards or turn back to the guards—there were no other options. She crossed her fingers and raised her eyes, and said under her breath, 'Lo-La guides and Lo-La provides.' *I sure hope so!*

Thankfully, the tight section was a short one, and they were soon able to stand up and breathe easily again. Itty mouthed a 'Thank you' to Lo-La.

Nathan's lantern flickered. Just as he said, 'Maybe we should douse one light to save oil,' both lanterns' flames sputtered and went out.

He whimpered.

'OK, don't panic,' whispered Itty in the darkness. 'We've got a few matches, but let's save them until we really need them. I'm going to stand right here and stretch out my arms. Now, walk towards my voice. Come towards my—'

The pair bumped into each other, and each grabbed the other's hand.

'I'm already facing in the direction we need to go, so I'll step to my left until I find the wall, OK?' She took three small steps, and her hand brushed against the wall.

'Now, put your right hand on my shoulder and move around behind me; the wall's just to the left. Let's just keep walking until we find a way out. We'll feel the door on the wall.'

Nathan whispered, his voice so tight it was virtually a squeak, 'What if the door's on the other wall?'

Itty thought for a bit, then said, 'Change of plan. Move back to my right side and give me your left hand. OK, good. Now stretch as far to the right as you can. Can you touch the other wall?'

'Yes!' Nathan's relief was palpable.

'OK, let's walk along like this. One of us will feel when there's a door.' To herself she added, *I hope*, thinking about doorways that might be below the level where they were touching. At the same time, she tried hard not to imagine anything else living in the blackness of the tunnel. She reminded herself that she'd met nothing when she was walking with Brother Nobody, so the tunnels were probably empty. *Then again*, the anxious part of her mind told her, *you had a functioning torch then, didn't you?* That irritating little voice also unhelpfully brought up the memory of almost stepping off the side of a bridge into unfathomable depths.

'Um, Nathan, I don't want to worry you, but sometimes the tunnels give way to bridges between different monasteries. If you suddenly aren't touching the wall, or you feel a cool breeze, we're most likely on one of those bridges. Just stop. Don't walk any farther.'

'Why?'

She wanted to say, 'Because you'll fall off and die, you idiot,' but instead, chose to downplay the danger to avoid panicking him. 'The tunnels will get us where we need to be.' *I hope. Where's Brother Nobody 231 when I need him? Or any Humble Monk at all.* 'But we could get lost if we don't take care with the bridges and open spaces.'

'OK,' said Nathan amiably.

They continued along the corridor in this rather awkward fashion for what felt like hours, neither saying a word. Even though it was pitch black, Itty closed her eyes so that she could concentrate on her hearing. The only sounds beyond their breathing were the brushing of their fingers along the walls and the tap of their boots on the ground— sometimes sharp, when the tunnel had a hard floor, and sometimes soft, when they were walking on bare earth. She figured that their pursuers had given up the chase.

After some more time, to keep their spirits up, they shared stories about themselves in whispers. Nathan told her about growing up in the valley and how busy Yossburg got in summer when tourists flooded in. She thought it sounded nice, but wasn't sure she could live somewhere with no bookshops, let alone libraries. In return, Itty told Nathan about growing up in a bustling city and how hot it was for much of the year, which he didn't find so appealing.

Every so often she would squeeze his hand and the pair would stop, holding their breath and listening intently for any sign they were being followed. Peering back the way they had come, Itty thought she saw sparks of light in the distance, but they flickered away when she tried to focus on them. She could still see them when she closed her eyes, so concluded they must be figments of her imagination.

'I think I touched something metal,' Nathan exclaimed suddenly.

'Light a match and let's have a look,' Itty said as she released his hand, 'but cup it in your hands to hide the flame in case there's anyone else in the tunnels.'

Their optimism was dashed when all they saw was a brass holder for a torch—but, unfortunately, no torch. Not even any fragments of one on the ground. Nathan's shoulders slumped, and he sniffed.

The match extinguished.

'Now, Nathan, be brave. We'll get out. Here, take my hand again, and reach out for the wall. Let's keep going.'

Itty found herself losing concentration as they shuffled along. Pictures of Hyrhia floated through her mind: the library, her home, the men who'd kidnapped her, the busy market. Wait… The market. The tent! The man with the bright white smile and… Something… Something important… A lamp? *A lamp would be very useful right now.* The thought fluttered out of her mind. Images of Karrin appeared in her imagination and told her to keep going. Captain Smart joined in, and Shanks too, urging her on. A smile crept across her face at the memory of her recent friends as she continued along the zig-zagging dark space.

Nathan's hand felt comfortably warm in hers, and she blushed, glad they were in a dark tunnel.

Smack!

An 'oof' from Nathan indicated that he'd walked straight into the smooth wall, too.

'Nathan, are you OK? Strike a match, please, so we can see where we are.'

'Um, perhaps you could let go of my hand.'

Itty quickly dropped it and felt her face heat up.

Nathan lit a match, and they blinked in the sudden small light, which illuminated a large door in front of them.

This time, she studied every detail of the door before they opened it, just in case she needed to remember it were she to find herself here again. Double doors, about twice as tall as she was, and each wider still than that; they looked like barn doors, but what sort of barn would be here, in an underground tunnel? The large doors were made of vertical wooden slats, painted in sequences of red, green and blue, and every slat butted precisely against its neighbour, with no gaps to let through any hint of what might lie beyond. The wood was smooth to the touch and pleasantly cool.

The match flame reached Nathan's fingers, and he squeaked and blew it out.

'Come on,' Itty said. 'Let's get through here before we light another.'

There was no handle, so they leaned their shoulders against one of the doors and pushed hard. With a creak, the door opened slightly. When the gap was big enough, they squeezed through, into yet more darkness.

Behind them, the door eased shut with a gentle thud. Itty and Nathan jerked around and tried to reopen it, but the smoothness of the wood and lack of any handle made it more like a wall than a door.

'Well, I guess we don't get back into the tunnels through this door,' Nathan whispered.

'What's that smell?' Itty hissed. 'It's revolt–'

'Buck-caw!' something shrieked. More somethings echoed the noise.

Itty screamed, adding to the cacophony.

'It's OK, it's OK!' Nathan shouted. 'They're just chickens, I think.' More quietly, he added, 'I hope they're just chickens.'

The squawking and irritated grumbling continued as Itty, never having encountered annoyed chickens in great numbers before, clutched Nathan. She held on to him perhaps a little tighter than she needed to, but he didn't seem to object.

'If there are chickens here, there must be another way out,' he said hoarsely.

Chapter 15: Dam!

Botanology [BOT-'N-OL-UH-JEE]—
the scientific manipulation of flora to encourage unusual or abnormal growth patterns, often used to create impenetrable defences and protective, yet decorative undergrowth.

Botanomancy [BOT-'N-OH-MAN-SEE]—
the application of grey magic to encourage unearthly growth patterns among plant species, often used to create invasive flora and aggressive, yet decorative undergrowth.

Botanophobia [BOT-'N-OH-FOH-B'-YA]—
thoroughly rational fear of unusual or unearthly looking plants, particularly the aggressive, yet decorative ones.

The Curious Reader's Illustrated Dictionary of
Science and Magic.

A muffled high-pitched bark came from somewhere ahead of them, and a door opened, letting in daylight.

Itty and Nathan—and two dozen chickens—were standing in a shed of some sort, with a narrow, flat-capped head peering at them from the doorway.

'What be ye doing in my henhouse? Come out, come out!'

They tiptoed over disgruntled chickens and through the shed door. Itty blinked in early morning sunlight and breathed in fresh air unsullied by the odours of the henhouse.

She wondered if time did something odd in the tunnels—they couldn't have been walking all night, could they? *No, it must be the tunnel. My legs don't feel tired. I must remember to ask Shanks about it.*

The scrawny, flat-capped head was attached to an equally scrawny body, both belonging to a very old man who seemed to consist solely of bones, wrinkles, and badly fitting clothes. A rickety fence stood behind him with a wheelbarrow and a plough leaning against it. On the other side of the fence, a handful of sheep were nibbling at clumps of rather dry-looking grass.

Itty spat out a feather and asked, 'Excuse me, sir, where are we?'

The old man eyed her suspiciously. 'This be Barnes Farm.'

'And where be that? I mean, where's that? What's the nearest town?'

'That be Tweezle.'

Itty heaved a sigh of relief. *This isn't so bad. We're on the right track.* 'How do we get there, please?'

Pushing back his cap and scratching his almost bald head, he pointed with his other hand. 'Down t' end o' that thar lane, then you'm turn right on t' road, and Tweezle be about a mile thataway.'

'Do you visit Tweezle often? Have you noticed anything… odd… about the village?'

'Odd? Who are'n ye, and why be ye asking about Tweezle?' He squinted at her. 'And what were'n ye doing in my henhouse?'

Itty looked around, seeking inspiration. She got nothing from the fence posts behind the man, nor from the imprint of a horseshoe on the ground. The chickens who'd ventured out of the henhouse to peck at the dirt around her feet were no help, either.

Nathan had nothing to contribute as he'd been ignoring the conversation, instead kneeling by a small dog of indeterminate breed, stroking and cooing at it. Its eagerly wagging tail, energized by the young man's fussing, threatened to topple the animal.

After a moment, she said, 'Um, yes. It was a joke, yes, a trick played by my brother, er, cousin. When we were asleep, that's right. When we were asleep, he carried us from our beds and locked us in your henhouse. He's a right one, my cousin. Just wait 'til I get my hands on him, ho, ho, ho.' She cringed at what she was saying, hoping it might be enough to keep them from getting into trouble.

The man frowned at her.

Itty brushed her hands down her shirt. 'Well, we'll be on our way now, Mr…?'

'Barnes.'

'Oh yes, Barnes Farm, you said. Ha, ha, of course. Sorry. Thank you for your hospitality, Mr Barnes. Haveaniceday-bye.' She gave a quick wave, then she and Nathan set off down the lane.

Glancing back, she could see Mr Barnes scratching his head again and staring after them.

'Some folk be right strange, eh, Roscoe?' she heard, as he reached down to rub between his dog's ears. 'Right strange.'

Roscoe barked, and Nathan and Itty picked up their pace.

As soon as they turned the corner at the end of the lane and were obscured from Farmer Barnes by a row of trees, they slowed down. Their footsteps kicked up puffs of dust. Itty noticed that the grass by the side of the road was brown and shrivelled. Even the buzzing of insects sounded parched and dreary.

'Is this area usually so dry?' she asked Nathan. 'It's like the desert around Hyrhia.'

He knelt and picked up a handful of earth, letting the desiccated soil trickle through his fingers. 'I haven't been to Tweezle for ages but, no, I'd say this is not at all usual.' He straightened up and looked around pensively. 'Not usual at all.'

About half an hour later, they reached the village. Everything was quiet as they passed a row of quaint wooden houses, similar in style to those of the other villages in the valley. A repetitive squeaking came from somewhere ahead.

Around the next corner was the village's main square, where they found a long queue of people silently waiting at a water pump. After four squeaky pulls of the handle, one person would leave with a full bucket, and the queue would shift forward one position. Two or three villagers gave the newcomers an indifferent glance before returning their despondent gaze to the ground.

Itty approached the woman at the end of the queue and asked, 'Excuse me, why's it so dry here?'

The slump-shouldered woman seemed not to notice at first, then turned towards them tiredly. 'Water's gone. It be Yossburg's doing, it be.'

Nathan blurted, 'Yossburg? But it's Rille that's got all the water.'

'It be Yossburg what done it. Them been switchin' our water t' Rille. Them stole our river. Them be jealous of our prosperity. Them says the three villages be equal, them do, but we know we'm better, and Yossburg be jealous. That mayor o' them, she'm ambitious. She bain't tolerate rivals and she'm attackin' both villages, that be the truth of it.'

Itty itched to ask Nathan about the rivalry and about the mayor, but didn't dare say anything in front of the Tweezlins.

'How could they steal a river?' she asked. 'Do you mean there's a blockage or something upstream? Has anyone looked?'

By now, a few other people in the queue had turned to gaze at the newcomers.

The woman frowned. 'Why you'm so interested? Be ye from Yossburg?'

Itty and Nathan glanced at each other.

'No, no, not at all. We're just'—Itty chuckled nervously—'tourists, hiking across the valley. We've heard so much about Esmiya and its villages. We're, you know, interested in finding out what life here is really like. I can see you're all very busy, so we'll, um, carry on. On our hike, I mean. The river's this way, right?'

She pointed along the direction they'd been walking.

The woman stretched an arm at right angles to where Itty was indicating. 'No, river be that way.' She squinted at Itty and Nathan. 'If you'm be hikers, where be you'm rucksacks?'

'Ah. Ha, ha. Now that's a funny thing,' said Itty, feeling a blush rise on her cheeks. 'People keep asking us about that.'

Nathan added, 'Wherever we go, we try to live off nature. You see, we eat plants and, um, catch and kill small animals.'

Itty shuddered. 'Mainly the plants. And we sleep under the stars.' She patted her sides. 'Everything we need, we can carry in our pockets. Well, bye-haveaniceday.'

Itty and Nathan once again found themselves scurrying off quickly.

The villagers returned to their stoic wait for water, staring at the ground, as the pump handle continued to squeak plaintively.

When the pair reached the river, it was dry, no more than a trickle to show which way was upstream and which was downstream.

'Do you think your mayor could have caused this? Could Yossburg have anything at all to do with what's happening here?'

Nathan shook his head. 'No, that makes no sense. We wouldn't steal a village's water— look at those poor folk.' He swung an arm in Tweezle's direction. 'How could we do anything like that?'

'What if there were just a few people in the village who didn't like Tweezle, or Rille, for that matter?'

'To divert a whole river, that'd need lots of people—they couldn't have kept it secret. No, I'm sure it's nothing to do with us. Someone else is doing this to all the villages.'

The pair followed the trickle up its slight slope.

As they walked, Nathan pointed out different kinds of trees and the tracks of various small animals. Itty wasn't paying a lot of attention to what he was saying, but now and then, she caught herself staring at his profile and smiling at his enthusiasm. Each time he turned towards her, she looked away before he could notice and felt her cheeks redden.

The trail on the riverbank grew narrower, and the pair had to walk closer together. Their arms bumped against each other, and hand occasionally brushed hand, sending a tingle up Itty's arm. Her imagination had the accidental brush turn into holding hands, and she blushed again as her insides flip-flopped.

Farther from Tweezle, the greenery was lusher, and it became difficult to push through the long grass. After a while, Itty said, 'This is no good; let's call Shanks. He can look for the blockage much more easily.'

She pulled the dragon's scale out of her pocket and tapped a message: 'Tweezle dry, stop. River blocked, stop. Please come, stop.' He was still connected to this broken-off fragment of scale and would know precisely where it was, no matter the distance—not that distance meant anything to a quantum dragon. He would be able to follow the signal here.

They found a rock and sat down to wait, leaning against each other companionably.

A few minutes later, a pinprick appeared in the sky, expanding into a pinkish dot. It grew—not getting closer, but somehow becoming bigger at a fixed point in the distance. It resolved into a red sharp-sided polyhedron. *So that's what it looks like from the outside.* The shape rushed closer and became translucent, then the dragon burst through it. The ruby crystal shrank behind him and vanished, and the downdraught from his wings almost toppled Itty and Nathan. They coughed and spluttered from the dust blown up from the ground and had to shield their eyes.

'Dear person-sheep, Itty, I am a creature glad to see your person, and you, too, Nathan-person,' Shanks said as he landed. 'You are beings having many adventures, are you not?'

Itty explained in some detail about finding Rille flooded and Tweezle parched. 'There must be something farther upstream that's diverting the flow. It'll take us ages to climb uphill to find it—but you can fly ahead and check things out quickly. Please, Shanks.'

'Fly, I can, small person-sheep. And fly I will.'

He began to run, huge body lurching from side to side; then, with two flaps of his enormous wings, he was airborne again.

A few minutes later, he returned, looking pale, with eyes darting in all directions, and tail flicking left and right.

'There is a thing there that blocks the river, a dense wall of plants, not natural. I could not be a person crossing it; it hurts—it is a thing I have not come across before, not a thing that I know. It is a thing that glows a light that is invisible, and the light hurts, and I cannot see through it. It is a light that interferes with the quantum, and I know not the thing that it is.'

Itty didn't understand what he meant by an invisible light, but asked how far away the wall of trees was.

'Too far for persons to walk quickly. I can be a dragon carrying you closer, but not too close. It is a thing that hurts. I will take you so that you can see.'

Apart from the minor issue with the spear tip, Itty had never seen the dragon flustered and upset before and paled at the idea of something strong enough to hurt the mighty creature. She was determined that whatever was causing this needed to be stopped.

She said, 'Perhaps we should walk. I don't want you to be hurt.'

He stood up straighter. 'It is a thing that is bad; a thing that should not be a thing that exists, and the sooner that it does not exist, the better. I will take your persons.'

It took a few moments for Itty and Nathan to climb onto Shanks. Itty hopped on first, but Nathan couldn't work out the best way to get himself seated on a dragon's back, so she had to dismount to help him get on.

He mumbled something about saddles.

'Pardon. What was that?' she asked as she gave him cupped hands to use to step up.

'I said this would be so much easier with a proper saddle and harness. Mr Iverson could make a nice one—he does all the horses in the village. He's the blacksmith.'

Itty stared at him for a moment, wondering why she hadn't thought of that. A cushioned seat wouldn't be as painful as the dragon's knobbly shoulder bones and all those other parts that moved under his skin. But still, she couldn't put a harness on her friend.

'Nathan, Shanks isn't some animal that needs a saddle. He's a person—a large, dragon-shaped one—and lets us ride him because he wants to. Now, no more complaining—let's get you up.'

Once Nathan was seated, she climbed on again and had to wriggle her way around Nathan's knees to get into position in front of him.

When the dragon started moving, Nathan tightened his arms around her waist, giving her an unexpectedly warm fuzzy feeling that ran from her stomach to her fingertips. He shouted with joy as they took off and flew upstream. Itty's ears were glad the flight was only a short one.

'Wow! That was awesome. Can we do it again?' he said as they dismounted.

'Maybe later,' Itty murmured as she looked at the dragon. He was breathing quickly and trembling, and his wings were held tense around his body. 'Shanks, back off far enough that it stops hurting, but not too far away. We might need you.'

As the dragon flew off again, she turned to look uphill. Some distance away, a wall of green and brown blocked the bed of the river, spanning the entire width of the hillside.

As she and Nathan got closer, Itty saw it was made of plants. Trees and bushes and grasses grew so close together that they formed a tangled, impenetrable barrier. It was taller than a house and ran as far as she could see. Every so often, the wall bulged outwards to form buttresses like on a castle.

'What could have made a wall grow like this?' Nathan asked.

Itty rested a hand on one of the twisted branches forming the wall, then immediately jerked back. The wall was warm to the touch and seemed to be vibrating. She prodded it with a stick, and when nothing happened, she pressed an ear against it. There was a periodic shushing sound, as if the plant had a pulse. 'I don't know, but it's not natural.' Stepping back and looking up, she said, 'There's no way we can climb it here. We'll need to find a break in the plants or look for a way over it farther around. Let's walk this way.' She set off to the right.

Only the sound of their feet swishing and crunching through the undergrowth broke the silence. Goosebumps prickled Itty's arms as she realized that there was no birdsong or chirping of insects. She glanced at Nathan, who gave her a weak smile in return.

They'd passed several buttresses, seeing no break in the wall, when six heavily armed soldiers stepped out from behind the next one.

'Halt! What are you doing here? Don't you know this is private property?'

Itty was almost relieved to find some life in the woods, but then noticed a series of steps climbing the wall behind the soldiers. She groaned inwardly. *To get so close…*

'Oh, hello, sirs.' She tried the same explanation as she'd used in the village. 'We're tourists, hiking across the valley. We thought this fine wall of trees was an interesting phenomenon and we wanted to take a look. We mean no harm and didn't realize we were trespassing—we saw no signs. We do apologize, don't we, Nathan? And we'll turn around and leave right away.'

She got ready to walk away quickly—again.

'Oh no, you don't!' the leader of the guards snapped, as the other soldiers tensed, ready to attack. 'We're taking you to Mr de Montford.'

Itty smiled sweetly and asked, 'Excuse me, kind sirs, but is your Mr de Montford related to the famous businessman, Sir Oscar?'

The lead guard narrowed his eyes. 'How do you know about Sir Oscar?'

Itty continued, 'Would such an important person really want to waste his time with two harmless tourists? Are we even worth *your* valuable time?'

Instead of replying, the guards pointed their weapons at her and Nathan. They were long metal pipes, connected via a flexible tube to rectangular packs the soldiers carried on their backs. Itty had no idea what they could do and didn't especially want to find out. They obviously didn't get many tourists in these parts.

Nathan stuck his hands in the air.

'Come with us,' the leader barked.

The soldiers took them up the fragile-looking stairs to the top of the plant wall. The springy steps weren't carved out of the wall or attached to it; they appeared to be a natural— or at least, no more unnatural than the rest— part of the wall's oddly deliberate growth pattern. Itty had to grab Nathan's arm for support when she stumbled as the branches making up the stair she had just stepped on twisted together, tightening and becoming stronger in order to take her weight. She glanced behind to see the step relax again, and decided to keep her eyes fixed straight ahead and try to ignore what she was climbing on.

On the other side of the wall was a lake with a large island in the middle, or perhaps it was an island with a wide moat; the wall was behaving as a dam, preventing the water from flowing into Tweezle. *There must be a runoff on the other side, funnelling excess water towards Rille,* Itty thought. To fix both villages' problems, she needed to persuade whoever built this— de Montford, she surmised—to return the river to its normal course.

'This way.' The leader of the soldiers pointed towards a small red-brick building farther along the lake's shoreline.

'I see by the crests on your breastplates that you are religious men, Itty said. 'I don't recognize all the symbols, though aspects of them remind me of several religions,' It helped to know more about your potential enemies, she remembered from a strange little book about warfare and baking she'd once read: *The Tart of War* by Sunny Sue. 'I wonder, kind sirs, if you could tell me who you are.'

The lead soldier turned to her and said, 'We are of the Order of the Lapsed Atheist.'

She breathed in sharply. They were in trouble now. According to the stories she'd read about them, the Lapsed Atheists were probably the most vicious mercenaries in the whole world. Because of their unconditional belief in any and all gods, the sect historically had fought many battles with other, more narrow-minded religions. Over time, they became the fiercest and most fanatical of all the orders of warrior-priests. Worshipping so many gods was an expensive endeavour—all the offerings and sacrifices—thus they had to sell their skills and were well paid for it.

Trying to build rapport, Itty continued, though in a weaker voice, 'I met someone called Brother Nobody recently, a very nice man. You must have a lot in common with the Humble Monks. Your and their outlooks on the ineffability of the gods must be quite similar.'

The soldier's face went red, and his knuckles, wrapped around his strange weapon, turned white. He spat on the ground. 'Never mention those subterranean defilers again. They seek to hide from the glories of the heavens, whereas we honour and worship all.'

Itty decided to remain silent for the rest of their march.

Chapter 16: Fuel

Human flight has been a dream since before the invention of the word 'flying.' Leonard the Winkle, so-named for his love of shellfish, sketched blueprints for flying devices over six hundred years ago, but the first machine capable of carrying a person over a distance of more than a few feet (and not just straight down) was designed and built by Mildred de Montford only a short century ago.

It is said, perhaps apocryphally, that she was inspired by the flatulence of her husband, who after a strong Khaleshkan curry, would raise the bedclothes several inches into the air. Nonetheless, she fashioned the world's first hot-air balloon out of silk bedsheets, generating hot gasses from a small fire behaving as a substitute for her husband's digestive tract. After several disasters, less flammable alternatives to silk were developed, along with safer and not as pungent heat sources as the dried manure she initially used as fuel.

Nowadays, the family has a de facto monopoly on artificial flying machines, ranging from small balloons capable of holding four people to vast dirigibles carrying hundreds of passengers across the world's oceans.

Rumours abound that the current CEO of de Montford Aeronautical Engineering, Sir Oscar de Montford, is funding the development of more advanced fuels in a research base secluded within the Karrig mountain range in southern Arcania. The company has been contacted for comments but, as yet, no reply has been received.

Article from *The Estalian Economist*, world-wide trade and manufacturing special edition.

The soldiers stopped at a small wooden guardhouse on the water's edge. A sign by its door read:

DE MONTFORD AERONAUTICAL ENGINEERING
ADVANCED FUEL RESEARCH
TOP SECRET
NO VISITORS PERMITTED

An official in a blue uniform with a peaked cap opened the door.

'Reverend Major Smite And Ye Shall Receive reporting, sah!' bellowed the lead soldier, saluting the official. 'Trespassers captured, sah!'

'Thank you, Reverend Major.' The official, wearing a shiny badge with 'Mr Naimliss' inscribed on it, eyed the pair of captives, who were doing their best to look insignificant and harmless. 'I'll take them from here.'

'Yes, sah!'

The soldiers handed Itty and Nathan over. Reverend Major Smite gave another snappy salute, metal glove clanging against his helmet, before the troop spun on their heels and marched off.

'The Reverend Major's ever so keen, you know. Nothing gets past him—he arrested two deer and a ferret only last week. Bit single-minded, though—considers everyone a trespasser.' said the official with a smile, leading the way into the hut. Inside, two other officials were playing cards at a small table. They glanced at the newcomers, then returned to studying the cards in their hands.

'Now, let's get down to business. Name?'

'Imperceptibility Happenstance. Why have we been–?'

'And you?'

'Er, Nathan Rubenstein, sir.'

Mr Naimliss scanned through several pages on his clipboard, before flicking them back. He stared at it for a moment, as if assembling his thoughts, then regarded the pair with narrowed eyes. 'You're not on the list... Perhaps the Reverend Major was right after all, and we have caught some trespassers. What are you doing here? This is private property. Didn't you see the signs?'

Itty wondered if she should try the lost tourists story again. She decided that directness was probably safer, since Mr Naimliss didn't look as if he would be easy to fool.

'Did you know that this'—she waved her arms to indicate her surroundings—'this lake, or facility, or whatever it is you have here has dammed the river running through the valley, starving Tweezle of water and flooding Rille?'

'Waterways don't fall within my jurisdiction, I'm afraid.'

'Well, is there someone in here who can help us?'

Mr Naimliss' mouth twitched down at the edges, and he gave a palm-up shrug. 'My job is to ensure that the entry and exit regulations are applied correctly and with the appropriate paperwork. I'm sorry, I'd love to help you, but there's nothing I can do. If your name isn't here'—he tapped his clipboard—'you don't get in.'

Itty stared at him for a moment, then glanced at Nathan. *It's worth a try.* She burst into tears. 'Buh-buh-but,' she wailed, 'the vill-vill-villages.'

Nathan blinked, then seemed to work out what she was doing. He patted her on the shoulder and sighed. 'There, there, we'll just have to give them the bad news.' He frowned at the official. 'And Mr Naimliss looked so kind. I really would have expected someone so important and caring to help us. Just goes to show.'

As they turned to leave, they could see the official's face drop.

He called, 'Wait!' and looked at his notes. 'What did you say your names are?'

After writing them down, he said, 'Tell you what; it's a nice sunny day and I could do with a break. As a special treat, I'll take you to Mr de Montford. Perhaps he can help, eh? There's no need to cry, young lady. Come on, follow me.'

He hurried through a door at the back of the building as if to escape from the flood of tears, and onto a timber roadway which led to the island in the sparkling blue lake they'd seen before.

Itty stopped crying immediately and wiped her tears on her sleeve, then she and Nathan ran to catch up with Mr Naimliss.

She was surprised to find the road bouncing up and down with the impact of each step she took. Unbalanced, she stumbled and fell. While she was down at road level, she took the opportunity to peer over the edge. The road surface rested on half-barrel floats in the water, not in any way anchored to the lake floor. Small ripples radiated from the floats as Mr Naimliss and Nathan returned to assist her, vibrating the road.

'We get so few visitors that I keep forgetting new people aren't used to our pontoon bridge,' Mr Naimliss said, as he and Nathan helped her to her feet. He puffed out his chest with obvious pride. 'It's only temporary, because Mr de Montford built this place so quickly. The bridge was his idea—ingenious, isn't it? Sir Oscar's a very clever man. Did you know this entire facility only took three months to construct?' He uttered a little half-laugh. 'Or should I say grow? Impressive, eh? After Mr de Montford's seismomancers had dug out the central laboratories and offices—that's where we're going—the world's best botanologists and botanomancers were hired to create the walls of this lake to protect the core facility.'

'Why does it need protection?' Itty asked.

The man leaned in close, allowing Itty to deduce that he'd recently eaten something containing an eye-watering amount of garlic. He tapped the side of his rather long and narrow nose and whispered, 'Secrets.'

Itty kept a hand on Nathan's arm to steady herself as the trio continued along the undulating road. The island was roughly circular, bisected by a dead straight road running, as far as Itty could see, from nothing in particular to nowhere else. The road's surface looked incredibly smooth and was painted with long white lines. Black skid marks showed that something large and fast must have driven along it for short distances. An enormous barn-like building stood off to one side of the road. One end of it was open, offering a view of three oceanic dirigibles with workers scurrying over them like ants on a sugar loaf. On the other side of the road were two smaller buildings, and it was towards one of these that the official led Itty and Nathan.

'Here we are, Hangar Number Two.' He opened a door, and the sounds of hammering, sawing and shouting burst through. 'We won't actually be entering the main manufacturing and research space—secrets, as I said. But we can take the shaft down to Mr de Montford's office. Just through here, come along.'

He ushered the pair past a room containing a donkey harnessed to a large horizontal spindle. A chain was wound around the spindle and disappeared into the ceiling, such that it would be pulled up or down as the donkey walked in circles. They entered an even stranger narrow room with mirrors on its walls, split by handrails at waist-height, and no chairs—the room was too small for furniture. Mr Naimliss closed the door behind them.

Before Itty could work out what the room might be, where de Montford was, what Mr Naimliss had meant when he said 'shaft,' and—most important of all—how her reflection in the mirror had accumulated so much dirt, the official pressed a button on a wall panel. The donkey brayed, and the room started to vibrate. Then the floor dropped. Itty emitted a slight squeak and reached for Nathan's arm; she felt as if she was floating. The sensation continued for just over a minute, which was almost too much for the stability of her stomach, as she and Nathan stared wide-eyed at the calm official. Then a bell rang, and a faint donkey bray echoed from far above. After the room jerked to a halt, she felt her normal weight again and managed to persuade her stomach to retain its contents.

The official opened the door, but rather than the outer door of Hangar Two and the island beyond meeting her eyes, a green-carpeted windowless corridor was revealed, lit by several small, smokeless oil lamps in niches along grey walls. She wondered if this was another of the Humble Monks' tunnels. If it was, it was very different indeed to any she'd been in so far, but she had to admit she hadn't been in many tunnels. Perhaps some of the monks' tunnels had carpets, maybe even thicker than these.

Nathan scratched his head and squinted at the gap between the door and the wall. 'Mr Naimliss, sir, what just happened?'

'Oh, that? It's just our upper-downer. A clever piece of technology invented by Sir Oscar; much better than old-fashioned stairs. They'll have them in all the cities soon. Marvellous devices, absolutely marvellous.'

Itty wondered if the Humble Monks knew about upper-downers—one would have saved her some time on the way up to the cave near Yossburg. Then again, what would the monks fill their freed-up time with but with more walking?

Mr Naimliss made shooing motions with his hands. 'This way. Come along, come along.' He all but pushed them along the passageway until they reached a door with a plaque that read 'Sir Oscar de Montford, CEO.' The official knocked and entered a room containing a desk behind which sat a stern-faced woman with her dark hair tied up in a no-nonsense bun.

He took off his cap, revealing a straggly and greasy combover. 'Ms Stone, these two young people…' He paused to look at his clipboard. 'Ms Imperceptibility Happenstance and Mr Nathan Rubenstein have raised some concerns about the impact of our facility on the local area. Specifically, the situation regarding water flows towards, let me see,

Tweezle and Rille. Is that right?' He raised his eyebrows and looked towards Itty, who nodded.

'I wonder, Ms Stone, if Mr de Montford might possibly have a few minutes to perhaps meet with our visitors to assure them that he—that is, we—are taking the utmost care of the environment, and that they have nothing to be worried about?' By the end of his speech, his head was bobbing as if his neck were unable to support its weight.

Before the woman could reply, a door at the other end of the room banged open, making everyone apart from Ms Stone jump. A fat, bald man in an expensive-looking but badly fitting pinstripe suit entered. 'Clara, where are the notes from my – Who are you? Clara, what are these people doing down here?'

Ms Stone opened her mouth to reply, but Mr Naimliss spoke first, fumbling with his clipboard and hat and nodding even more frenetically than before. 'Mr de Montford, if you may, sorry to bother you, sir, please excuse the intrusion. These young people have expressed some concerns about the effect the facility is having on the local environment and—'

'Why in blithering blazes are you wasting my time bringing them here?' the fat man bellowed, face blooming into redness.

As he took another breath in preparation for blasting the unfortunate official again, Itty stepped forward and spoke up. 'Mr de Montford—Sir Oscar—may I say what a privilege it is to meet you. I've followed your work in the national newspapers back home in Hyrhia. I think what you're doing in the aeronautical industry is truly amazing.'

Oscar de Montford's anger evaporated, and his face returned to a more normal colour. 'Erm, harrumph. Thank you, young lady.' He smiled, showing rather uneven and blackened teeth. 'What did you say your name was?'

'Imperceptibility Happenstance, sir.' She curtseyed, immediately feeling a little embarrassed when she remembered she was wearing dust-stained pantaloons and not a skirt.

'And why are you here?'

'I realise this is probably something far too trivial for someone as important as you, but…'

Oscar de Montford puffed his chest out.

Itty continued, 'Well, you see, sir, the people in the valley seem to be having problems with their water. Their villages, I mean. Problems with their river. It would appear that this—um, I mean your—impressive facility is redirecting all of Tweezle's water to Rille. And I—we, Nathan and I, that is—wondered if you might be able to do something about it?' She smiled her best simpering smile, all the time mentally crossing her fingers.

Thanks to Hyrhia's newspapers, she knew de Montford was a ruthless businessman who was suspected of using many underhanded tactics to eliminate his competitors and opponents. However, no concrete proof had ever been found; evidence and witnesses tended to simply vanish.

Sir Oscar scowled at Mr Naimliss. 'You, whatsyername, is this true?'

The official looked confused. 'Is what true? Oh, you mean the river. Ah, yes. Yes, sir, I'm afraid we may have grown part of the lake wall on top of the Suseene river, which I believe does—did—service the villages of Rille and Tweezle, respectively.' As Sir Oscar's scowl deepened, the official coughed and continued. 'Well, you see, sir, it was the most cost effective option. You, yourself, made the decision to have the facility built here, despite the potential negatives outlined in the regulatory risk assessment documents.' He cringed as if expecting de Montford to hit him.

'Hmph. If *I* made that decision, it must have been the right one.' He waved a dismissive hand. 'Take these people away. Pay them off. Or kill them. Whatever makes the problem go away.'

'But, Sir Oscar!' Itty cried, too focussed on the matter of the river to notice the threat to her life. 'You're making the lives of the villagers miserable. They've already lost their livelihoods; they'll soon be losing their lives.'

'Livelihoods? These villages, they're the little cobbler places, aren't they? Shoes and suchlike?'

Itty and Nathan nodded.

'What do I care about shoes, girl?' He gestured towards the sky, somewhere far above the office ceiling. 'I'm doing real work here, real world-changing work, building the future of fast, efficient and economical air travel. With my dirigibles opening up international trade, I can import all the footwear I could ever want from anywhere in the world at a fraction of the prices these Reel and Twiddle places charge.' He laughed coldly. 'In fact, it's better for me if these villages don't exist. No local competition, dontcha know? I'm a busy man. Too busy for this.' He directed his glare at Mr Naimliss.

'Get rid of these nuisances, whatsyername.' With that, he snatched the notes Ms Stone held out for him and returned to his office, slamming the door behind him.

'What an unpleasant man!' Itty said.

Clara Stone's wide eyes darted from Itty and Nathan to Mr Naimliss and back again.

Mr Naimliss looked uncomfortable. 'You two had better come with me.'

As they walked back along the corridor, he asked in a hushed tone, 'You seem like very nice young people. I would prefer not to, er, kill you. I don't suppose you might be willing to accept a bribe? Or just go away? Already, the paperwork's going to be a mess.'

'Most certainly not!' Itty replied.

'What? Wait!' said Nathan, eyes wide. 'Didn't you hear what he just said?'

Itty gritted her teeth, and whispered, 'He's bluffing.' Louder, she said, 'We want no more or less than the villages' river to be returned to normal.'

'Ah, I was afraid you might say that. This way, please.'

He opened another door along the passageway, leading them onto a gallery partway up the side of a tall, wide cavern, the ceiling of which was festooned with more of the smokeless oil lamps Itty had seen earlier. She wondered how they got up there, and how they were refilled when the oil ran out, if they were oil lamps at all, but then she became distracted by what she saw below.

Free-roaming pigs filled the floor of the cavern, each with a small bag attached to its rear quarters. Dozens of workers roamed among the pigs, detaching and reattaching bags to the animals, and piling up carts with the filled bags, before taking them to holes in the wall. A mixture of sounds assaulted Itty's ears—pigs squealing, workers shouting, the squeak of the carts, and the chugging of machinery behind the walls.

There was something odd about the carts and the workers' uniforms, and it took her a moment to realize what it was. She probably wouldn't have noticed if she hadn't spent time with a dragon who ate the stuff—there was no exposed metal anywhere in the cavern. The carts and tools were wooden, the men's belts and pigs' harnesses had no metal buckles or buttons, and the doors and wall hatches had wooden handles and hinges. After a few seconds bathed in the smells from below, which weren't as overpowering as she'd expected from so many animals, she recalled one of Isaac Oldson's papers she'd once read, *On the Spontaneous Combustion of Gaseous Materials Under Varied Conditions*. With all of the flammable gas being produced by the pigs and trapped in here, a spark would trigger a disaster.

'This is the hub of our fuel production centre,' said Mr Naimliss proudly. 'We gather, um, waste from these pigs, and process it to provide the combustible fuel required for Mr de Montford's dirigibles. Very clever, it is. Did you know, this is the most efficient production system in the world, and the combustibles are totally odourless? All thanks to Mr de Montford's patented animal mash—that orange stuff the workers down there are feeding the pigs, do you see? I'm awfully sorry, but I'm going to have to ask you to become part of the mash now; it'll be painless, I promise. It's just down here.'

He was pointing a small hand-held weapon at them. 'If you could perhaps come with me to the feeding system on the floor below. Do you see it, yes?' He contorted his face into a quick smile. 'It'll all be over before you know it.'

Itty turned to him with her hands on her hips. 'You're not going to shoot that, are you, what with all the pig gas here?'

The smile on Mr Naimliss's face widened. 'This isn't a common-or-garden combusting weapon, Ms Happenstance. It's yet another of Mr de Montford's wonderful inventions. No metal, no flames; spring-powered, but it'll still do you a lot of damage. Now, come along.'

Nathan's eyes darted left and right.

Mr Naimliss's eyes narrowed. 'Please don't run. You won't get away.'

Itty carefully slipped her hand into a pocket, hoping the official wouldn't notice, and grasped the dragon scale. She tapped a sequence with three short gaps between, then three long gaps, then three short, paused, and repeated—tap-tap-tap, tap, tap, tap, tap-tap-tap. 'S.O.S.' in Marsh code, the signal she'd agreed with Shanks that meant *emergency, we're in danger, come immediately*.

Chapter 17: Nice Doggy

There are countless tales of the abilities and behaviours of mythical creatures—creatures such as unicorns, gryphons, multi-headed dogs, and the duck-billed platypus.

However, significantly less is written about matters relating to the well-being of these creatures. Do you know what a manticore eats? (Despite popular belief, it's not maidens!) Or what diseases harpies are susceptible to? Few are the experts who can deal with kraken scurvy or a phoenix with heartburn. Could you perform the Heimlich manoeuvre on a choking ouroboros? And who can tell when a duck-billed platypus is ill and not just looking for sympathy?

Over the next three years, our undergraduate degree course will teach you all the skills you'll need to deal with all sorts of mythical creatures, real or imagined. You'll learn what (or whom) they eat and how to diagnose and treat all known ailments, along with a few unknown ones.

The course blends formal lectures, small group tutorials, practical project work[1], and independent study.

Apply now and lay the foundations for your future thrilling career as a crypto-veterinarian.

1 Please note that the university accepts no liability for any disfavourable events which may occur during practical lessons, and students are advised to make provision for their own personal medical insurance.

Prospectus for Care of Mythical Creatures, School of Unreal Health, University of Dreadmond.

I tty wasn't sure what would happen as a result of her S.O.S., but hoped for more than nothing. And that it would happen soon.

Mr Naimliss continued to prod Nathan and her along corridors and down flights of stairs to get to the cavern floor, prattling all the time about Sir Oscar and the facility. He didn't seem at all concerned about adding a pair of intruders to the pigs' food supply. If it wasn't for being held at gunpoint, Itty would have felt like she was being taken on a guided tour of the place.

'This is one of the largest fuel generation plants in the world, did you know? Why, odourless fuel for 60% of Mr de Montford's fleet is provided by just this one facility. It's also one of the most efficient. We reclaim 96.3% of the energy released by our biological manufacturing units—BMUs, as we call the pigs. Isn't that amazing? Oh, it is a little niffy down on the floor, I must admit, but I imagine that you two detected no smell outside—not a fume is allowed to leak from the core of the building.'

Thirty seconds passed with still no indication of Shanks' arrival, then a minute, then two. *Come on, Shanks!* Itty tapped out her message again, while the oblivious Mr Naimliss prattled on.

'That's because we power our machinery from the waste products of Mr de Montford's wonderful airship fuel production process.

Why, even those gaseous vapours you can smell rise to the ceiling where they automatically provide fuel for the lights. No human intervention required at all. Mr de Montford likes to say the only smell that escapes the building is that of folding money.' He chuckled.

Itty wondered if Mr Naimliss disposed of unwelcome visitors often, possibly by boring them to death. *Perhaps that's why the facility is such a secret in the valley—no one ever had a chance to come back with news of what they'd found, and it's looking like we won't either.*

As the group wound their way downwards, the sounds of pigs and engines increased, as did the stench of hot machinery and animals squeezed into a confined space. Mr de Montford's smell-reducing formulation couldn't totally eradicate the reek of so many animals and their waste mixed in with the intrusive oiliness of rumbling machines.

She started to feel sick, and not just because of the smell and the noise. Unless Shanks came, there was no possibility of avoiding a horrible death.

Nathan shot her a look. 'We need to do something,' he hissed. 'Create a distraction, and I'll grab his gun.'

Itty whispered back, 'I've tried signalling Shanks, but he's not coming. Something's wrong.'

Nathan blinked and his mouth made an 'o' shape. 'The invisible light, that's it. The shield that hurts him. He can't get through it.'

She paled and stopped walking. No help was coming.

Mr Naimliss poked her in the back with his firearm. 'Keep moving.'

Itty rummaged in her pockets as she started walking again, searching for something that could help them. After touching a notebook, a pencil and a handkerchief, her fingers grazed something smooth and round, a jug perhaps. Mystified, she tried to work out what it was by touch alone. An image of a smiling mouth with bright white teeth came to mind, along with the smell of vanilla and cardamom. Then the half memory vanished as her hand slipped past the shape to grasp something sticklike—Karrin's flute from the River Sticks, her parting gift. 'Blow this, and Krispy will come,' Karrin had said.

Ignored by pig and worker alike, the three stepped onto the floor of the vast cavern.

Itty nudged Nathan and murmured, 'Pretend to stumble.'

He tangled his feet, almost falling, and while Mr Naimliss was distracted, she pulled the flute from her pocket, put it to her lips, and blew.

The flute made no sound, but the pigs nearby fell silent and stared at her, eyes unblinking and ears twitching.

Itty waited. Nothing else happened. *Where's the dog? Did Karrin just make up the flute's power to make me feel better? Maybe I didn't use it properly.*

Itty blew again, as hard as she could, and now all the pigs in the hall—hundreds of them—ceased their snuffling and silently turned towards her. The workers moving among the pigs stopped what they were doing and stared at the pigs.

'What's happening?' one of the labourers called from across the chamber.

Another removed his helmet and mask, revealing a face streaked with sweat. 'No idea. Something on the steps over there.' He pointed with a gloved hand. 'The pigs're all looking at the woman in the bright clothes.'

All the human eyes joined those of the pigs to stare at Itty.

Mr Naimliss turned to her as well, a mixture of anger and worry on his face. 'What did you do?'

Itty didn't know exactly what she had done, but before she could answer, the pigs clustered in the centre of the large floor started to squeal, then ran in all directions, clambering over other pigs, trampling workers, and overturning wagons filled with bags of pig dung.

The panic spread to the humans too, and workers ran for the exits, throwing down masks and gloves. Some dove through the waste hatches in their desperation to get away.

From the edge of the chamber, Mr Naimliss, Nathan and Itty stared open-mouthed at the chaos.

Did I do that? Itty wondered, simmering unease threatening to boil over into panic. She looked at the flute in her hand. *Just by blowing this?*

As she watched, a black spot appeared on the floor space deserted by pigs and workers. It grew, covering the floor in matt black smoothness until it was several feet across. *No*, she realized, *not a spot, but a hole.*

There was a breeze as air was sucked into the opening, then a rumble, followed by a belch as warm barbeque-scented air was blown back out, mixing unpleasantly with the smell of pig waste.

Mr Naimliss waved his firearm at Itty. 'Did you do that?' he shouted. 'Make it stop!'

She glanced at him, then returned her attention to the black space. She murmured, 'I don't know how to. I don't know what it is.'

The air rushing out of the hole grew to a gale, its roar filling the whole cavern. As it increased in volume, Itty thought it sounded like an animal.

Of course! she thought. *The flute worked.*

Kerr-Russ-Bey erupted from the hole. All three heads bellowed as he scanned the cavern. Russ spotted Itty and barked. The other two heads snapped around and yipped excitedly. Hyperventilating pigs and screaming humans scattered as the enormous dog bounded across the room. He skidded to a halt right in front of her, and all three tongues smothered her in slobbery licks.

She pointed a finger at Mr Naimliss. 'Now you're for it.'

He groaned and fainted. Nathan, frozen and gape-mouthed, looked like he might collapse too. Itty pushed Krispy away and poked

Nathan in the shoulder. 'Snap out of it. This is no time for a snooze.'

Nathan closed his mouth, but still looked rather unsteady

One of Krispy's heads looked at a nearby pig and licked its lips. The terrified animal cowered.

Itty tapped Bey's snout and said, 'No time for that, either!'

'Nathan, this is Krispy. Krispy, this is Nathan; he's a friend. Don't eat him. Or the pigs.' She nudged a very pale Nathan and pointed to Mr Naimliss's hand. 'Grab his weapon; it might come in handy. Now, let's get out of here.'

'Not so fast!' a voice called down from the gallery.

Itty looked up to see Mr de Montford, who was accompanied by a dozen soldiers all pointing their cylindrical weapons—the same as Reverend Major Smite's soldiers had carried—at her, Nathan and Krispy. She turned to dive into the hole through which the dog had appeared, but it had closed up.

'This way!' Nathan grabbed her arm and ran to the closest exit.

Itty followed him along a corridor with Krispy bringing up the rear. Behind them came the rattle of wooden armour as the soldiers pursued.

'Wait,' she called to the others and pulled back to a solid-looking door marked 'Security.' 'We can hide in here. It'll have been built to withstand attacks… I hope.'

They dove into the security room and barred the heavy door. As they heaved deep breaths, fists thudded on the outside, but the door held.

A desk sat in the middle of the room with two chairs beside it. Krispy was worrying at a paper bag at the foot of one of the chairs. The bag split open, and sandwiches and a sausage tumbled out, to be quickly gulped down by the dog. *Someone's not getting their lunch today*, Itty thought, a laugh bubbling up as hysteria threatened to overtake her. She closed her eyes and concentrated on breathing slowly. Calmer, she opened her eyes. Telling Nathan to look for anything useful, she set about investigating the room.

A crumpled piece of paper lay on the desk with the words 'BMU food supplement and processing' printed at the top. She picked it up and glanced at it—it seemed to be a list of herbs and minerals, along with instructions for mixing and heating them.

She was more intrigued by the control panels of some sort that covered two walls, and a bank of assorted keys festooning another. She found a key marked 'Armoury' and shoved it and the recipe sheet into her pocket.

A panel marked 'Perimeter' was affixed to one wall, showing a map of the lake with the island in the middle and semi-circular red lines emanating from several dots on the shore of the lake. Itty guessed these were the buttresses she had seen when they were outside. They were labelled with 'Force field west 13,' 'Force field east 7,' and so on; correspondingly identified switches occupied the space below the map.

Nathan scratched his head and said, 'Force field? Could that be the invisible light that hurt Shanks?'

'Dunno,' said Itty, slapping all the switches. 'Let's find out.' She smiled grimly.

An eerie silence fell as a pervasive background hum they hadn't been consciously aware of suddenly ceased.

She pulled out the dragon scale and tapped 'S.O.S.' again. She added, 'Trapped inside, stop. Come quickly, stop.'

Sir Oscar's voice blasted from somewhere overhead. 'We know you're in there. There's no way out except through the door. Open up. If we have to break in, well…'

Itty ignored him and examined the panels on the other wall. Switches and levers covered it, with labels that mentioned external exits and animal pens. She smacked them all open:

anything that could add to the chaos beyond the door was bound to help.

An enormous explosion shook the walls, and the screams outside, from human and pig alike, became louder. She jumped, wondering what she'd done this time.

'Dear Itty sheep-person, where is it that you are?' boomed a deep voice from somewhere outside the room.

'My dragon's here; you'd better let us go,' Itty yelled at the ceiling, not quite knowing where to address the unseen Mr de Montford. 'Now!'

'Ha! You think that we can't deal with a pathetic little dragon?' Sir Oscar laughed. 'A mere youngling at that. Open up if you want him to live.'

Shanks' howl of pain sent lumps of ice plummeting in Itty's stomach. Her knees buckled, and only Nathan's quick reactions prevented her from collapsing to the floor.

The dragon wailed again.

'Don't hurt him,' she pleaded. 'Please don't hurt Shanks. We're coming out.'

With trembling hands, she unlocked the door. As soon as she opened it, two soldiers seized her arms. Two more took hold of Nathan, retrieving Naimliss's gun from him, and a phalanx surrounded Krispy, poking him with spears when he moved in their direction.

They were manhandled back to the cavern floor, the only sign of its previous activities being the abandoned food and waste wagons. One had tipped on its side, with a single wheel still turning and squeaking plaintively. A dozen soldiers with the strange cylindrical weapons attached to their backpacks stood in a circle around a cowering Shanks. The weapons were humming, and the dragon was whimpering. Mr Naimliss had recovered from his earlier fainting spell and was standing next to Mr de Montford, though he still looked a little groggy; one of the guards handed him back the weapon Nathan had taken.

Itty's shoulders slumped.

The soldiers shoved her, Nathan and Krispy towards Shanks, then stepped back and joined the unsmiling guards circling them.

Shanks looked at her with a forlorn expression, tears smearing his spectacles. He groaned, and a tremble ran through his body. 'I am a person who is powerless, Itty-person. This is a thing that hurts.'

Itty didn't stop to consider what these weapons could do to her; she rushed to the dragon's side and threw her arms around his neck. 'I'm sorry. This is all my fault. I'm so sorry,' she wailed.

Krispy growled, and a soldier threw a spear at him, grazing his flank. The dog yelped.

'No! Stop it!' Itty cried, fingers clenching in sympathy.

Nathan bent to pick up the spear, but one of the other soldiers called out, 'Leave it, sonny, or you'll get another coming your way.'

Sir Oscar glared at them and gestured around the chamber. 'Look at this mess. You've caused me a lot of trouble, but we'll recover.' He extracted a fat cigar from his jacket's inside pocket and placed it between his lips. 'Still, I have your pretty dragon, girl, and a rather unusual puppy dog—they'll make me a tidy sum on the mythical creatures black market, so the day's not been a total loss.' Rubbing his hands together, he laughed. 'Not a loss, by any means.'

Shanks moaned, and Itty yelled, 'You're killing him. Stop it!'

Sir Oscar flicked a glance at the dragon. He took the cigar from his mouth and pointed it at the men with the strange weapons. 'You, with the radionizers, reduce the amplitude. I don't want to see my profits go up in smoke.'

The weapons' hum decreased slightly, and Shanks relaxed a little, sinking to the floor.

Sir Oscar returned the cigar to his smirking lips. He fumbled in another pocket for his lighter and brought it to the end of the cigar.

Mr Naimliss shouted, 'No! Mr de Montford. Sir Oscar. Don't!'

Sir Oscar flicked the lighter.

Then everything went red.

Chapter 18: An Old Friend

Many religions posit the existence of a Heaven or Nirvana, or one of a thousand other names, as the destination for those who have lived a good life, and a corresponding Hell or nightmarish purgatory for those who have not.

The scholar of comparative religion, however, will discover that there is as little agreement on precisely what constitutes a 'good life' as there is about what to call the hereafter. As such, it is evident that a person consigned to purgatory in one creed might be permitted to enter paradise in another. This is a confusing matter for people, not to mention gods.

The conclusion reached by many naïve thinkers is that the afterlife cannot possibly exist, but considerable work by the Order of the Lapsed Atheist has resulted in a sophisticated theological proof that one experiences all these afterlives simultaneously, a truth which will be defended to the death by Lapsed Atheists everywhere.

From *The One True Truth Amongst Many*,
Apocrypha of the Order of the Lapsed
Atheist.

There was nothing but whiteness in every direction. Itty could only tell where the ground was because the whiteness on which she stood was more or less solid. She waved her hand in front of her face, and tendrils of mist eddied around it like ethereal snakes.

'Halloo,' she shouted. 'Is anyone there?'

The fog swallowed the sound of her voice, but she heard a muffled shout of 'Over here' in the distance and started to walk in its direction. The ground was spongy, like thick, loamy soil, but with a smooth and impervious surface. Her feet sank slightly into it, and she felt like she was walking in a dream.

She continued to call out and the voice gradually became louder—Nathan! After a few moments, Itty saw a human-shaped darker patch of fog and ran towards it.

'Are you all right?' she and Nathan asked at the same time. Then they replied in unison, 'Yes, what about you?' Laughing and embracing, they held each other tight for a long time.

Itty pulled back. Holding on to Nathan's arms, she looked into his eyes. 'I thought you were gone.'

On the spur of the moment, she stood on tiptoes and quickly kissed him on the cheek.

His eyes grew wide, then he smiled. Itty blushed and smiled back.

While they stared at each other, not quite knowing what to say next, Krispy bounded out of the fog, barking happily, and licked their faces as they fussed him in return.

'Where are we?' Nathan asked.

'I have no idea. All I can remember is Sir Oscar and his soldiers, and Mr Naimliss shouting.'

Nathan scratched his head. 'Maybe they shot us with those strange weapons and we're in some weird prison waiting to be made into pig food.'

Itty jerked her head up and grabbed his hand. 'Did you hear that? Another voice, over that way.' She pointed.

The pair hurried towards the other voice, with Krispy running ahead and back excitedly, looming out of the mist each time he returned. Before long, they encountered Mr Naimliss accompanied by several pigs. The pigs looked confused and more than a little anxious at the sight of the three-headed dog, even though Itty made sure he understood they weren't food.

Mr Naimliss had retrieved his handgun, and shakily pointing it at Itty, barked, 'What have you people done? Where are we?'

All three of Krispy's heads lowered and snarled at him, and the official stepped backwards.

Itty put her hands on her hips and snapped, 'We didn't do anything. This is all your fault, you know. You and Mr High-and-Mighty de

Montford. And, no, we don't know where we are.'

Mr Naimliss thrust his gun in her direction again. 'Well, get us home.'

'How do you think we'll do that, you idiot? Just put that stupid thing away and help us figure out what we *can* do!'

He gritted his teeth but holstered the gun.

She looked around. 'Shanks!' she cried. 'Where is he? Has anyone heard his voice?'

Nathan and Mr Naimliss both shook their heads.

Itty called the dragon's name, and the others joined in. Krispy added his booming barks.

There was nothing but silence in return.

The fog cleared, blown away by a gust of wind which brought the briny scent of the sea. As the breeze died down, the top of a mast appeared in the distance, then the ship itself hove into view. It was a gleaming, completely grey, three-master with billowing sails and an Estalian Navy flag fluttering from the topmast. The vessel came closer, gliding through the smooth, white ground as if it were water, leaving a rolling wake behind. As the ship moved forward, the waves gradually subsided, sinking away to become the same featureless ground as that Itty and her companions stood on.

The group huddled together as the mysterious ship drew to a halt about twenty feet in front of them, sails still flapping and cracking in a wind that couldn't be felt from where they stood. Although the surface on which they were standing was solid, waves lapped against the gently rolling hull of the ship. The splashing sounds mixed with the creaking of the ship's timbers and the snap of the sails. Droplets of spray chilled Itty's cheeks before falling to the ground as white grit, to be absorbed back into the smooth surface.

They were looking at the ship from what amounted to sea-level rather than from the more usual viewpoint of a dockside, so they had to crane their necks back to see the rails on the upper deck.

A face looked over the railing and shouted, 'Ahoy! Who's down there?'

Itty squinted in the brightness and shaded her eyes from whatever it was that passed as sunlight here.

It can't be!

'Captain Smart, is that you?' she shouted.

'Happenstance?   Imperceptibility Happenstance!' His voice cracked. 'What are you doing here?'

'We don't know. We don't even know where *here* is!'

'Wait,' said Nathan. 'You two know each other?'

'Yes,' Itty replied. 'I spent several months on his ship before we were cast adrift and Captain Smart...' She swallowed. 'And Captain Smart died...'

She turned to look up at the captain and called, 'How— What...? You died! You're supposed to be dead!'

'This, my dear Ms Happenstance, is the afterlife. Well, *an* afterlife. My afterlife. Wait a moment. Come aboard, and we can talk without the necessity of raising our voices.' Captain Smart called something over his shoulder, and, with a rattling of chains, the gangplank eased out from the side of the ship and gently lowered. It slowed, then juddered to a halt about ten feet above their heads.

'Oh bother,' said the captain. He disappeared, and the gangplank rose again. Seconds later, he returned. 'Sorry about that. Should have realized you were too far below.' He threw a long rope ladder over the side of the ship. 'Try this.'

Leaving Krispy and the half dozen pigs on the ground, everyone scrambled up the ladder onto the deck of the ship.

'Welcome aboard the *Invigilator*,' the captain said, spreading his arms wide before embracing Itty in a warm hug.

She introduced the captain to the others and vice versa, and the captain continued his story.

'After I stepped through my door in the Down-Underworld, I walked up a gloomy, steep tunnel for hours, then popped out in a locker in the underdeck of this ship. It's a normal cupboard now—every now and then I open it to take a look, but it's still just an ordinary locker, not an entrance to a tunnel anymore.' His brow furrowed. 'No idea where the ship came from. Is this the ghost of the real *Invigilator*, or is it merely an excellent copy created just for me? The afterlife is supposed to be everything you ever wanted.' He raised his eyebrows. 'Or perhaps everything you deserve, which isn't necessarily the same thing.'

He rubbed his forehead. 'I'm not sure which this is.'

Itty said, 'Sometime after you left the Down-Underworld, Mr Ansif and the rest of the crew showed up. The *Invigilator* had sunk—maybe that's death for a ship, and that's how it got here. Have you seen any of your old crew?'

'I've come across no one else at all, and I've been here for—I don't know—months or perhaps years. Time doesn't seem to pass here. I haven't even seen the current crew of this ship. I know somebody's here: I can hear them moving around, and someone takes care of trimming the sails and cleaning and cooking. I can shout an order, and it gets acted on, but I see nobody. I've tried ordering them to show themselves, but that's the only command they never carry out.'

Everyone fell silent for a while, deep in their own thoughts.

Nathan stammered, 'Are we dead too?'

'No… No, I don't think so,' Itty muttered. 'We'd have to cross the River Sticks, and I'd see Karrin again.' Her brow creased. 'No, we can't be dead. I hope.' After a moment, she continued, 'So, anyway… what happens here? What do you do, captain?'

'The *Invigilator* sails the… well, seas, I suppose,' the captain said, looking at the strange white ground holding his ship. 'We catch sight of pirate vessels—those are the only other ships I've seen. Naturally, we pursue them. I direct my ship to come alongside and we exchange fire. The pirates never hit the *Invigilator*, but we hole their hulls without fail. Then their wreckage simply sinks into the ground—the sea or whatever it is— and vanishes. I've never seen any of the crew of those ships either, not a single body, alive or dead.

'I can't decide if this is someone's idea of my eternal reward, ridding the seas of evildoers, or an endless punishment of repeating the same pointless cycle of destruction.' He put his hand to his forehead again. 'Whichever it is, it's insufferably boring, and I'm really glad to see you again, and your friends.'

Itty suddenly remembered. 'Oh! One of us is missing. Shanks. I don't suppose you've seen a dragon?'

Captain Smart's eye widened. 'A dragon?' He shook his head. 'No, no dragons here.'

'Could you help us find him?'

'Certainly, young Happenstance.' He smiled, and his eyes twinkled. 'It'll make a pleasant change from chasing pirates.'

'Nathan,' Itty said, 'could you climb to the crow's nest and look out for any sign of Shanks?'

As Nathan climbed the rigging, Captain Smart said, 'We might be able to do better than that. Have you still got the compass I gave you?'

Itty stuck her hand in her pocket, brushing against something smooth and cool that she didn't recognize, but then she forgot about it as her fingers clasped the compass case. She pulled the compass out and handed it to the captain.

He held it fondly and, satisfied that it was undamaged, passed it back to her.

'If the legend of Smarrette's compass is true, this ought to work. And, if it doesn't, we haven't lost anything. Hold it tight, my dear, and think about your friend.'

She did as he instructed, repeating in her mind, *Please be safe, Shanks. Please be safe.*

The compass needle spun a few times, then settled down to point in one direction, quivering as if it was excited to be doing something important.

The captain glanced at it, then called towards the top deck, 'Hard a-starboard. Nor'-nor'-east, full speed.'

The ship's wheel spun under invisible hands, and the ship groaned and turned until it faced the same direction as the needle. The unfelt breeze became a strong wind and, sails billowing and thrashing, the *Invigilator* launched itself forward so suddenly that everyone stumbled. Only the captain retained his footing, obviously used to the behaviour of his ship.

'That's another thing,' he said as he pulled the rope ladder back onto the deck. 'The wind always blows in the right direction and with the perfect strength for whatever's needed.' He shrugged.

Krispy loped after the ship, followed by a cluster of indignantly oinking pigs.

After a few minutes, Nathan shouted from the top of the mid-mast, 'I see something.' He pointed. 'Red. I think it might be Shanks.'

Shanks lay sprawled on the ground and looked more like tattered rags than the magnificent creature Itty had first met. His skin was pale, and his scales dull. The spines on his neck had wilted, and fragments of his crystalline wing feathers dusted the white ground around him. His spectacles lay a few feet away, one lens cracked.

The captain threw down the ladder again, and Itty scurried down and ran to the dragon. 'Shanks! Shanks, are you all right?'

There was no reaction when she touched him, and his skin was cold. She pressed her ear against his side and heard wheezing and a faint thump-thud.

'Shanks!' she shouted again.

One eye blearily opened, and the dragon groaned. He tried to raise his head, but his trembling neck couldn't lift it off the ground. 'So weak,' he croaked.

'What happened to you?' Her eyes welled up at the sight of her injured friend.

'When the loud person-thing who was a fat person activated his ignitor, the gas of the pig-creatures became a thing that is an explosion. I gathered all you person-creatures in my wings and was a creature who jumped into the quantum.' The dragon groaned again. 'It hurt so much because of suddenness and because of the weapons of invisible light. I was not a person with the time or the ability to consider direction and distance, but just a person who wrapped creatures I could reach in a dragon shell and quantum jumped. Anything to be in a place that was somewhere that was not where the explosion was going to be.'

'You saved us!' Itty said. 'We're all alive, thanks to you.'

The others, including Krispy and the pigs, had joined them near Shanks by now. Krispy sniffed at the dragon, and the pigs collapsed on the ground, worn out by their run. Mr Naimliss said, 'Saving us is all very well, but what are you going to do about getting us home?'

Nathan eyed him and muttered, 'Why'd Shanks bother to save *him*?'

Shanks quivered and heaved a laborious breath, before whispering, 'I reached out quickly for a place, and was not a person with time to choose. But you might as well all be creatures as dead as the persons I left behind. I do not have any knowledge of where we are in existence right now, just that it is far from Esmiya. It is far from Earth. I used up so much of the energy that is mine that I have little that is remaining.' Itty had to strain to hear him. 'I am a thing who is weak now. I am a creature who is in much pain.'

She had a thought. 'Do you need iron? Would that help?' She turned to the others. 'Captain, can you spare some cannonballs?'

He shrugged. 'You can have as many as you want. The ship has a never-ending supply.'

Nathan and Mr Naimliss ran back to the ship, dropped half a dozen cannonballs over the side, then hurried down the ladder to pile them in front of Shanks.

The dragon was too feeble to melt the metal in order to drink the molten liquid, so had to settle for swallowing them whole to dissolve slowly in his stomach.

Itty could see the lumps squeeze down his neck.

As they waited for the dragon to recover, she caught him up on their situation. 'And so, we seem to be in the captain's afterlife, now.'

Shanks nodded. He had regained a little of his strength and colour, but his voice was still weak. 'That is a premise consistent with the probability wave that is mine. We are now creatures existing in a different plane to the one in which we normally are existing creatures.' His brow furrowed. 'That must be why I am not a person able to sense other dragon-kind probability waves.' His sides heaved. 'I have never been a creature so alone. I am always a person knowing where other dragons are, but their probability peaks are not perceptible here.'

He let his head slump to the ground again. 'I do not think, Itty-creature, that I can get us back to the place that is home. My knowledge does not include what dimension to move within, nor what direction to choose. I am a dragon with no other dragons to orient against.' He flicked his gaze from person to person. 'We are creatures who are all stuck in this place.'

Chapter 19: Escape

Déjà vu—

the sensation of having travelled back in time but not remembering it.

Encore vu—

the sense that you will do something in the future, whether you want to or not.

Déjà entendu—

the sensation of having heard a bad joke before, but not remembering until after the punchline has been uttered.

Déjà ne vu pas—

not being able to do something, time after time, often caused by the consumption of too much alcohol.

The Dictionary of Temporal Displacement,
Professor Marian Gesenhalter, DTemp.

Shanks' admission that they were stuck here sparked immediate panic. Everyone started talking at the same time, voices getting louder as they tried to make themselves heard over each other.

'How will we get home?'

'What do we do now?'

'Listen, everybody, now is not the time for hysteria.'

'I can't stay here!'

Frightened by the shouting, the pigs started to squeal, too.

But by then, no one was listening to anyone else.

Mr Naimliss drew his pistol and fired a single shot into the air. Everyone fell silent.

'That's better,' he said. 'Now, I know you don't like me because, well, let's not go into that right now. But I do know from years of working with the de Montfords that panicking solves nothing. We need to take stock of what we know and what we have, and maybe we can figure out what to do. Calmly and quietly.'

'Mr Naimliss is right,' conceded Itty, grudgingly. 'We don't know where we are, but we've got a ship. We can go places. Captain, do you know how big this sea is?'

Captain Smart shook his head. 'In the time I've been here, all I've seen are pirate clippers and the occasional… I presume they must be dolphins or the like, in the distance. The sea, or whatever it is, is featureless—no islands, no land. Though I suppose it actually is land of a sort.' Lifting his face to the sky, he continued, 'And the light never changes, just this permanently overcast grey; no sun ever breaks through. Night never happens either, so there are no stars to navigate by.'

He smiled. 'Do you recall me showing you the constellations just before I… you know?' The smile vanished. 'I miss the stars.'

Shanks had told her that ancient dragons became stars. The lack of stars made her feel even more sorry for the dragon, remembering when she'd been torn from everything she knew and forced onto the *Invigilator*.

'Anyway,' the captain continued, 'the only navigational instrument that I have at my disposal is the ship's compass, and I've travelled in all four directions as far as I can bear it, and nothing changes.' He sighed. 'Just the same flat, white nothingness, everywhere.'

Itty thought for a bit, shoving her hands into her pockets. 'Is there anything we could make use of on your ship?'

'I doubt it, I'm afraid. Yes, the ship's got cannon, but they're not much use for anything other than sinking pirates. And feeding dragons, I suppose. There are the usual maritime supplies: rope, netting, tar, weapons, food…'

At the mention of food, Itty's stomach rumbled. 'Is anyone else feeling peckish?'

The others nodded.

Captain Smart called back to the ship, 'Cook, dinner for four, if you please. My cabin. And some fresh meat for the dog—er, dogs—and slop for the pigs.' He looked at the dragon. 'Anything more we can get for you, old chap?'

Shanks shook his head and curled up to go to sleep again. The red of his skin had deepened a little, and some of his neck spines were upright again, but he still didn't look at all well. His wings were still trembling, and his breathing was uneven.

'It'll take a little time for my invisible crew to prepare dinner, and we have to stay out of their way, otherwise nothing will get done.' Pointing at Itty's hands still in her pockets, the captain chuckled. 'We could take a look at what we find in our pockets. You never know, something might help.'

The captain went first; his naval uniform had few pockets to mar its elegant lines, and all he had in them was a white silk handkerchief and his portable sextant.

'What about you, young man? Nathan, is it?' he asked as he folded the handkerchief and replaced it in his pocket.

Nathan stepped forward. 'This'll be quick.' He produced two bits of frayed string, a penknife, three coins, a small greenish-blue rock shaped like an egg, a matchbox with only two matches in it, and half a biscuit. 'None of that's going to help,' he said as he put it all back into his pockets, except the stale biscuit, which he offered to one of the pigs.

The pig gulped it down and oinked in appreciation, then butted its head against Nathan's legs in the hope of getting another morsel.

Mr Naimliss said, 'Apart from the gun, all I have is a cloth, some spare ammunition, a notepad and two pencils—both HB and in need of sharpening. Sorry.'

Just then, a bell rang from the ship's deck high above.

'Ah, dinner is served,' Captain Smart said, rubbing his hands together. 'Let's go back aboard.'

On deck were two buckets of mash for the pigs and three huge rare-cooked steaks for Krispy. As Nathan and Mr Naimliss carried them down to the animals, Itty wondered where the food came from. If stuff like fresh meat was to be found, it must have come in from somewhere.

'Captain, food presumably enters the ship in the galley. Maybe we can find a way out via the same route.'

Captain Smart shook his head. 'If I wait in the galley for food to appear, all that happens is that I go hungry. If I wait in my cabin, the meal never arrives, though I can smell it as if someone's waiting just outside the door. But when I open it, however, there's no one there. I've been all over the ship and have found no hidden way in or out.'

The captain's cabin was large enough to accommodate a six-seat table and had doors leading to a private water closet and sleeping quarters. The carpet was the same blue and red seaweed pattern as she remembered, but without the toast, bacon and eggs that had been spilled on it last time she was here. A dozen flickering oil lamps on the mahogany-panelled walls filled the room with a warm glow. Elaborate candlesticks on the massive table added to the light, but everyone had eyes only for the mountain of food sitting in front of them. Although only four places had been set, there appeared to be enough food for ten times as many.

Platters of roast pork and gammon (Itty was glad the pigs were eating outside) jostled for attention with two roast chickens and three different kinds of fish. Bowls of buttered carrots, broccoli, garlic peas, sweet potatoes and honey-roasted parsnip threatened to collapse the table, and jugs of gravy and sauces exuded mouth-watering aromas that enticed people to their places.

On a smaller table off to the side sat bottles of wine and fruit juices along with elaborate desserts, fruit confections, and chilled urns of several flavours of ice cream.

Itty couldn't recall when she last ate, but she was certain she'd never seen so much wonderful food in one place before. It certainly beat the mundane ship's rations which were all that had been on offer when she'd first found herself on the *Invigilator*.

For the next twenty-three minutes by the brass clock in the captain's cabin, the only sounds were crunching, chewing and slurping. Along with the occasional satisfied burp.

When stomachs were fully stretched and little more than bones and scraps remained on the table, Nathan said, 'Captain, if you always eat like this, it might not be so bad to stay.'

Everyone raised their glasses and laughed, but after the second sip, they all went quiet. Itty wondered if the others were also thinking about distant homes and loved ones.

Captain Smart broke the silence. 'Well, friends, I have to stay here—my life is done—but we should see what we can do to get you back to where you belong. Young Happenstance, it must be your turn to empty your pockets.'

She dug deep into her pockets and fished out item after item. 'Here's your compass, of course, and Karrin's flute.' Itty placed both objects on the table and rummaged some more. 'Here's the scale Shanks gave me. What's this?' Her hand seemed to touch something and then shy away from it, to land on something else. 'A notebook. Not much use without... Oh, a pencil as well. A storybook—*The Flight of the Ostrich*—I liked that one, it's about a flightless bird trying to... Oh, never mind, there's time for that later.' She stuck her hand in again. 'Purse; empty, thanks to Shanks. A handkerchief. The key for de Montford's armoury and a piece of paper I picked up there—something about food for the pigs.'

As she read it, Mr Naimliss jumped up. 'That's top secret. You can't have that; give it here. It's the recipe for Sir Oscar's fuel.'

The captain growled, 'Sit down, sir. None of these secrets matter while you're all trapped here. Is there anything else in your astonishing number of pockets, my dear?'

'A library card. Some sweets. That's all, I think.' Her fingers brushed against something smooth and, with nothing else to reach for, they clamped around it. 'Oh, wait. What on Earth is this?'

She pulled out a battered old oil lamp. 'Where did this come from? I don't recognize it.' As she held it up, a scent of cardamom and vanilla wafted through the cabin. Her fingers tingled where they touched its surface, conjuring up teasing half-memories: a smile with bright white teeth, promises—no, not promises… wishes!

'My magic lamp! How could I forget that? The djinn—he can get us home!'

A faint grumbling noise emanated from the lamp.

Mr Naimliss goggled at her and shouted, 'You have a magic lamp, and you didn't think to tell us?' He pulled at his rather sparse and greasy hair. 'You could've rescued us at any time.'

'Steady on, sirrah,' said the captain. 'Remain calm, please. Remember we are civilized people here.'

Itty rubbed her forehead. 'I– I don't know. I just… forgot.' She studied the lamp in her hand as memories seeped back, then noticed everyone staring at her. 'Ah, now I remember. The djinn makes me forget about the lamp.'

The staring eyes widened further.

'Yes, djinn. Well, um, I guess I should…'

Taking a deep breath, she picked up her dinner napkin, flicked off some crumbs, and rubbed the lamp.

'Wow!' said Nathan, as a cloud of smoke filled the cabin, bringing with it a strong smell of exotic spices.

As everyone waved the smoke away, a face appeared in the haze. Itty was sure she noticed a sour expression on the djinn's face before it transformed into a broad smile.

The djinn said, 'O mistress, how pleased I am to see you after such a long time. What is your desire, your second wish?'

'My second… Did I wish for something already?'

'Why certainly, most illustrious mistress. You wished for travel. Your very words, if I recall correctly, and I most undoubtedly do, were "My wish is to travel the seas." And, lo, you went on a sea journey, on a very fine ship. On this particular ship, I do believe, and under the command of this very captain, as it happens.' The djinn gestured expansively, waving a hand towards Captain Smart. 'What an astonishing coincidence it is that we find ourselves once again aboard his ship, and among so many friends.' He squinted at Itty and smiled again, showing far too many teeth. 'Surely, mistress, there can be no better evidence of the fulfilment of your first wish. A very fine and well-thought-out wish, if I may say so.' He bowed deeply towards the young woman.

Everyone tore their eyes from the djinn and stared at Itty, who blushed.

'I see. Um. Yes. Thank you. I guess.' Her mind went blank.

Then memories came tumbling back. 'Hang on! Lemme see that contract again. There was something about… endangering the life of the… Second? That's me, right?'

The djinn rolled his hands. 'I'm sure there's no need to read that stuffy old document again.'

Itty glared at him. 'You've been trying to kill me.'

'Ah. Ha. Now, there's a funny story.'

'So, your plan here is to let us die here…'

The djinn drew himself up tall. 'No, definitely not. If you die here, I'll be stuck here too.'

He smiled and bowed again. 'Now, what is your second wish, O mistress?'

She pulled herself upright. 'Yes, the wish. We need to get out of here. I wish we could all get home.'

The djinn put a hand to his cheek and pouted. 'Oh, mistress so fine, I'm sure you can understand that this is, how can I put it, a little…' His hand made circles in the air, dissipating the last of the smoke that remained from his entrance. 'Vague… Perhaps you would like to think a little more deeply and construct a more, shall we say, actionable wish? I'll adjourn to my lamp until you're ready, my mistress.'

With that, the lower half of the djinn's body transformed into smoke and started to drift towards the lamp.

'Wait!' Itty cried. 'Can we ask you a few questions first, to establish the limit of your powers?'

The djinn let his legs solidify again. He placed his hand on his chest. 'The limit of my powers! How could you think there is such a thing?'

'Well then, can you take us all back to the living world?'

The djinn pouted again. 'Well, yes, technically. But it might take a very long time—we are a great distance from your Earth, you know.'

Four pairs of eyes blinked at him.

He waved his arms in agitation. 'Okay, very well then, I might have some small limits to my powers,' he growled, then blustered, 'I *can* get you back, but it'll take one thousand, three hundred and… let me think… two years. And a few days.'

'Well, that's not going to work very well for any of us, is it now?' grumbled Mr Naimliss.

'You're not helping, Mr Naimliss,' muttered Itty. 'There must be something else we can do.'

'I know, I know,' said Nathan, leaping up. 'Why don't we get your djinn to cure Shanks, and then Shanks can take us back.'

Everyone brightened up, until Mr Naimliss reminded them that the dragon had said he didn't know where they were and thus couldn't orient himself for a journey back.

'So, we can use another wish to reveal the right direction?' Nathan asked.

'Let me interrupt you there, young sir. No, I'm afraid you can't do that. Awfully sorry,' the djinn smarmed. His eyes flicked left and right. 'You see, well, the thing is… Ah, yes, that's it. We djinn have to recharge between wishes, and we can't carry them out willy-nilly, one right after another.'

Itty's eyes narrowed. 'I've never heard of that. How long, exactly, does it take for this recharge of yours?'

'Oh, you know, a long time.' His hand languidly circled again. 'It depends upon the effort expended in carrying out the previous wish, of course. If, for example, I were to cure the dragon… Well, look at the state of him. Fixing that would use an awful lot of my energy.' The djinn puffed out his cheeks and blustered, 'Weeks. We're talking weeks of recovery time here. Months maybe, before you could wish for directions home. Big magic takes time, you know.'

'Time…' Itty murmured. 'Djinn, can you wind back time?'

The djinn stared at her, eyes widening. 'Oooh… I suppose… I've never done that before. Let me consult the rule book.'

He reached into the lamp, his hand shrinking until it would fit, and withdrew a tiny book. As he pulled his hand back, the book grew until it was a massive leather-bound tome about three inches thick. He pushed aside empty serving plates and bowls and, folding his legs underneath himself, sat down in the centre of the table with the book balanced on his knees. Licking a thumb, the djinn started to leaf through the book, scanning the pages from top to bottom. His reading sped up, and sheets of paper blurred past. After a few moments, he stopped and pointed to a section in the middle of a page.

'Aha, there it is. Well, what do you know? Yes, reversing time is possible.' He fell silent as he read the text to himself, lips moving. 'Yes, yes. No problem at all. There are a few trivial conditions and…' He stuck out his lower lip. 'Yes, and a few limits too—I can't go back very far.' He looked at Itty.

'Could you take us back to a time before I got the lamp?'

The djinn laughed. 'Are you serious? That'd create a paradox, a bit like your granddaughter going back in time to kill your father before he met your aunt.' He stopped, brow furrowing. 'Or something like that. Anyway, a paradox. If you never had the lamp, I wouldn't be here to grant you a wish. The universe would implode. Or turn inside out. Or something. I'm not sure exactly what; no one's been stupid enough to try it. A seriously bad thing.'

'Okay, how about when I was on the ship with Captain Smart.'

The djinn raised a finger and opened his mouth as if about to speak, but Itty continued, 'The first time, I mean. Before he was killed. Not now, here in his afterlife.'

The djinn let his finger drop. 'No paradox there, true, but it's a bit too far back. Sorry.'

'What about when I met Karrin?'

'Nope, too far.'

'Before I left the Down-Underworld?'

The djinn shook his head.

'Brother Nobody?'

The djinn looked up and smiled, then his face dropped. 'No.'

'When I arrived in Yossburg?'

The djinn thought about it, tilting his head up to the left and right, then a smile touched his lips. 'Yes! Yes, I can do that.'

Nathan had been listening closely to the exchange. 'But the captain will still be dead,' he whispered.

'What do you expect me to do about that?' huffed the djinn.

Captain Smart shrugged his shoulders, 'Ah well, I've lived my life. I've got used to this afterlife. It's a bit dull, true, but I'll have this meeting to think back on when you're gone.'

The djinn raised his finger again and coughed. 'Ah, perhaps not. If I rewind time, it'll be as if none of this happened for anyone apart from the wish maker and wish granter and… This meeting won't have happened either, so I would guess that there's nothing for the captain to remember. That's what the book says anyway. Maybe my mistress and I should ask you all when we next see you to check that's how it works.' He smiled broadly. 'Still, none of you will be any worse off than you were before arriving here.'

'That doesn't seem particularly fair,' said Itty.

The djinn shrugged. 'What's fairness got to do with it, O mistress? I'm a djinn. My job is to grant wishes. No more, no less. Now, do you want to get home or not?'

Itty looked at the captain, lip trembling.

Captain Smart returned her look and smiled. 'Come, child, it's not that bad. Normally people only get to say goodbye once. This is our third time and, who knows, maybe we'll meet again. Go back to the land of the living, girl.' He gestured towards the others. 'Help your friends. Help those villages. Don't fret about me. I'll be fine here.'

Itty sniffed and wiped her nose and then her eyes with her sleeve.

'Djinn, my wish is—'

'Wait!' Nathan called. He squeezed Itty's shoulder gently. 'Be brave.' He leaned in and kissed her. 'Be safe.'

She put a hand on his cheek and smiled. 'We'll meet again in Yossburg.'

Turning to the djinn, she enunciated clearly, 'Djinn, my wish is for you to rewind time until the point at which I arrived in Yossburg.'

The djinn bowed. 'Your wish is my command, O mistress,' he said in a deep voice. He clapped his hands together, and everything went dark.

Chapter 20: Second Chance

As a chrononaut, you are likely to find that it's really quite difficult to convince people that you've travelled back in time. Sure, you can predict their speech and tell them word for word what they're about to say before they utter it, but all that happens is that they will think you're a witch and then they'll run you out of town. Certainly, you can pick winners at sports events, the stock market, or other games where chance is involved; people will still think you consort with supernatural evil, as well as stupid for just telling people instead of quietly placing a bet and earning a fortune, and then they'll run you out of town. You might consider showing them objects you've brought from the future, but that won't work, because only items you possessed before your destination time will be available.

Notes for the Novice Time Traveller, Annette 'Dot' Brown and Martha McFlie.

Imperceptibility picked herself up from the ground just outside the village of Yossburg.

Have I actually travelled in time? Or was that just a weird dream? she thought.

Her stomach noisily informed her that she was hungry, so she started to walk towards the village. She recognized the layout and the shop windows—it wasn't a dream after all.

She'd forgotten how small the pretty little village was: not much more than a dozen buildings on either side of a single street. But devoid of life, with everyone hiding from visitors. She glanced at the *First and Last Chance Saloon*, and her stomach rumbled again. What had happened to that huge dinner she'd eaten aboard the *Invigilator*? Had it not come back in time with her—or perhaps rewinding time just had that effect on people. She wondered if Hyrhia's library had any books about time rewinding; maybe they'd tell her how it worked.

If she ever managed to return to Hyrhia, that is.

She paused for an instant, considering what might lie ahead: capture, being threatened with death—twice—and being blown up. She could walk away and avoid all that; forget about Shanks and Nathan and Sir Oscar, and save herself a lot of trouble.

No! That wouldn't be fair. The Humble Monks believed people ended up where they were needed. She had a duty to make things right, and she wanted to see Nathan again. Besides, she didn't know how to get home from here.

Looking around at the three enormous shoe shops, the hardware store and the barbershop, she scratched her forehead. *Where was I when I was bashed on the head last time?* It came to her: *Ah yes, sitting on the steps leading up to the saloon.*

Itty took up a position on the bottom step and called into the building, 'Hello. I know you're in there, waiting to bash me on the head. I'm not a spy, you know. I just want to talk to you.'

Silence.

'I know about your dragon problem. He's friendly, really. I can take you to him.'

Sharp gasps came from the surrounding buildings.

'Sorry,' Itty said, holding her hands up in a placating manner. 'That didn't come out the way I intended. Shanks—that's his name—doesn't eat people and he isn't terrorising your village. It's Oscar de Montford, who's not a dragon, just a nasty businessman—he's got it in for all of the villages in your valley. Actually, no, that's not quite right. He doesn't care about you one way or another. Compared to money, he doesn't think you're important at all. I'm here to make him change his mind, and I need your help.'

Still, no one replied.

'Madame Mayor, people of Yossburg, I know you suspect I'm a spy from Tweezle or Rille, but I promise you I'm not. The other villages are in as much trouble as you—worse, even. You think I came from one of those villages, don't you? I didn't; I used the Humble Monks' tunnels. Last time you sent Nathan to find the entrance in the field over there.' She pointed. 'And I can show you on the map again.'

A voice called out, 'What do you mean *last time*? We've never seen you before. You must be a spy.'

'She's a witch!' another voice shouted.

Itty slapped herself on the forehead. She needed to be more careful. 'No, sorry, Madame Mayor, that's not what I meant to say. I… um… was here once as a child, with my… um… parents.' *Yes, that's right.* 'I was so impressed with your village that I promised I'd return when I was older. And, yes, I've been… hitch-hiking. I've been using the monastery tunnels as shortcuts. Listen, I can show you, really, I can. There's even a shortcut to Tweezle in the tunnels.' She mentally kicked herself even before the mayor spoke.

'A shortcut to Tweezle? Spy!'

'They don't know about it!' Itty yelled, exasperated. Then, in a quieter voice, she said, 'I know you don't trust me, but can you come out, please? It'll be easier to have a conversation if we're not shouting at each other.' She lifted her arms above her head and turned all the way round. 'You can see I'm not armed. Anyway, there's just one of me and many more of you. Please come out.'

Ready to give up and leave the villagers to their fate, she flopped back down on the step, then she remembered Shanks and Nathan. She couldn't fail them. Her gaze dropped to her legs, which weren't covered in turquoise polka dots—the clothes she'd got after now hadn't come back either—and from there, on down to her feet.

Itty jumped up. 'I have proof. Look!' Balancing on one foot, she pulled off a tatty boot and twirled it in the air—as with her shipboard dinner and her new trousers, the nice Yossburg boots hadn't come back through time with her. 'When I was here before, you took one look at the state of my footwear and decided I could do better, Madame Mayor. I imagine you already have something in mind… Perhaps blue, similar to the style you wear yourself, third shelf from the left, second floor of that shop.' She pointed. 'If I meant your village harm, would I admit to you that I know something like that?'

The saloon door opened, and the mayor walked out. Nathan followed her, holding a poker.

'Nathan, you're alive!' Itty cried and rushed towards him.

He levelled the poker at her, stopping her in her tracks. 'How do you know my name? Keep back!'

'You don't remember us walking through the tunnels? Being captured? Krispy? Captain Smart?'

Nathan shook his head, looking very confused. 'I've no idea who you are or what you're talking about.'

'Oh.' Itty's eyes prickled. Even Nathan had forgotten all they'd been through together. No, not forgotten, she corrected herself, but never knew in the first place. With everything else going on, she was finding it difficult to keep in mind that she was the only one who could remember.

By this time, about twenty villagers surrounded her, all narrow-eyed and scowling. Some held pitchforks and axes, while others brandished pokers like Nathan had in his hand.

The mayor scowled at her. 'You'd better tell us what's going on, young lady.'

Itty cleared her throat. 'It's going to be a long story and hard to believe.' She dusted off her clothes. 'I wonder, Madame Mayor, if perhaps we could adjourn to the saloon and talk over some of that honey tea I remember from my last visit.'

The mayor stared at her.

Itty sighed. 'If you don't like my story, you can feed me to the dragon after. I won't complain; you won't even have to tie me up. But I'm ravenous at the moment, and would love some of your wonderful baked goods.'

The mayor called to another woman, 'Marjorie, could you arrange for some tea and cakes, please?'

Marjorie disappeared into the saloon.

Itty looked at the crowd surrounding her.

'Do none of you remember me? I saw you last time.' She pointed at one of the villagers, and then another. 'You, as well. Do you recognize me?'

The two women shook their heads and tightened their grip on their makeshift weapons.

Marjorie popped her head out of the saloon door and waved.

The mayor gestured towards the building and said, 'Shall we?'

She and Itty entered and sat at a table set for two. Half a dozen other people stood quietly a short distance away; Itty recognized some of them as the village elders who'd stood and watched when she'd been captured on her first visit to the village. The mayor poured two cups of tea and arched an eyebrow at her, inviting her to begin.

It was mid-afternoon by the time she'd finished telling them about the flood in one village and the drought in the other, confronting Sir Oscar, the explosion, and ending up in the afterlife. She left the details about Shanks and Krispy's participation out of her story—that might be a bit too much for the villagers to think about right now. She'd tell them more about the dragon soon, but some of them already showed signs of confusion, not that she really blamed them.

The mayor swallowed a bit of cake and asked, 'If there was such an enormous explosion, wouldn't we have heard it?' She stared at the girl. 'And how did you get back here?'

'Ah, well, you see, it hasn't happened yet. Not to you, I mean. The explosion's in your future, but I've experienced it.' She looked across to Nathan. 'And Nathan, too, but he doesn't remember. We were stranded in the afterlife, and then we…' A frown settled on her face.

Itty knew something had happened, but there was a gap in her memory about what the something was. The harder she concentrated, the blurrier the gap became. 'We… I… Time?'

She scratched her head. 'Something happened which wound back time, to bring me back here to stop the explosion. I can't remember what it was.' Hazy thoughts of a tooth-filled grin and smoke crossed Itty's mind, but she could make no sense of them.

Still, there wasn't time to delve into her memories right now. Smiling at the villagers with more confidence than she felt, she stood up. 'Listen, it doesn't matter how I got here. What matters is stopping de Montford before he destroys the whole valley!'

Madame Mayor didn't look convinced, and nor did the rest of the villagers. Itty sagged back into the chair. Then she bolted upright and jumped to her feet. 'Your dragon! A dragon is plaguing your village, isn't it? Or so you think.'

The mayor nodded, and a few of the villagers inhaled sharply.

'Well, he's not really. The dragon—Shanks—is only a youngster, and he's lost.' That wasn't completely true, but she needed to win the villagers over. 'He doesn't eat people.' She thought about what she'd just said. 'Well, apart from knights, and that's only because he's defending himself. Listen, I know you're thinking of sacrificing me to Shanks. Don't deny it! How about we go to the clearing and wait for the dragon? I'll stay by the pole—there's no need to tie me up and please don't smear my legs with… ick. You can hide in the trees, close enough to watch but far enough away to be safe. If the dragon attacks me, you've lost nothing, and if I can show you he's safe—which I will—you'll have gained a valuable friend.'

'Stay here, young lady,' the mayor said, chewing her lip. 'I need to consult the village council. Nathan, keep an eye on her.' She and several of the other villagers adjourned to another room.

Nathan stood to attention and held his poker at the ready.

Itty smiled and took another sip of the honey tea—it was just as good as she remembered. 'We were good friends on our journey. I trust we will be again.'

'Don't go trying to confuse me, girl–'

'My name's Imperceptibility. Imperceptibility Happenstance. Itty.'

'Don't go trying to confuse me, *Miss Happenstance*,' he growled, waving his poker in her direction. 'I don't know who you are or what you want, but this is my village, and I'll protect it.'

Itty's lip quivered, but before she could say anything more, the mayor returned.

'We're agreed,' she said. 'We'll take you to the clearing.'

'Oh, one other thing, Madame Mayor,' Itty said. 'I wonder if your blacksmith could spare some iron, or perhaps lead. Shanks likes metal, so it'll be a sort of welcome gift. I believe your smith is repairing some wheels for Mr Johansenn, and perhaps that can wait a little longer.' She thought for a moment more. 'Does your blacksmith also have some pincers I could borrow?'

The mayor's eyes narrowed. 'Are you sure you're not a witch?'

'No! I mean, yes, I'm not a witch.' Itty thought for a moment. 'Wait. What do you do to witches around here?'

It was the mayor's turn to consider things before replying. 'Well, it'd generally be sensible to treat them with respect.'

'OK, let's just say I'm a witch. Time traveller or witch, it's all the same to me, as long as we defeat Sir Oscar, and I can go home. Now, will you listen to me?'

She explained that, as the dragon comes at night, everyone should get some rest, and they'd all set off just after sunset.

'If you don't mind, young lady,' said the mayor, 'we'll escort you to one of the saloon's rooms and place a guard outside the door. You'll understand that we don't totally trust you yet.'

Itty's shoulders slumped. 'What choice do I have? Might I possibly make two more requests before I go with you?'

The mayor tilted her head.

'I'd like some more of those ginger cakes, please. And you may have noticed that my trousers are rather ragged and dirty. I know you have some nice lemon trousers with turquoise spots in a box in your largest shop's storerooms.'

Looking bemused, the mayor said, 'But that's our holiday fancy dress costu– Oh, never mind. Yes, we'll bring you the trousers and some more to eat. I'll even provide a pair of boots. Yes, from the shelf you specified. You were right; they're the ones I would have picked for you.' She narrowed her eyes. 'How come you know all this?'

'Madame Mayor, isn't this proof that I've done this already—been here before?'

Chapter 21: Interlude—The Adventurers' Guild

Top Three Most Amazing Places in the World

3: Friginal Falls. This glacier-fed waterfall in the far north of Kalderia is over a mile high, but the water is still frozen when it plunges into Lake Adovca. Vast festivals are held at the summer and winter solstices, when Kalderan Druids claim that the gods speak to them through the patterns of dawn light in the falling ice.

2: Waldo Dizzy Whirled. Ten square miles of white-knuckle rides and shows featuring your favourite storybook and pantomime characters, there's something for everyone in this, the theme park capital of Novistan.

1: The Adventurers' Guild. The Guild's museum in Khaleshka contains the rarest and most astonishing wonders in the world. The shelves of its library are filled with original works by the most incredible people who ever existed. Every visit is an education.

The Rough Guide to the World.

'Oh, come on! This is ridiculous.' Prince Ollipher's shout shattered the rapt silence in the hall.

'I beg your pardon,' Itty said.

'Madame Gatekeeper,' the prince called, 'can't you see that this is a tissue of lies and fabrications? This mere *girl* says she defeated a dragon and–'

'I didn't defeat him. He's my friend and travelling compan–'

'A dragon. A creature of myth and ignorant superstition. If that wasn't enough, she wants us to believe that she returned from the underworld *and* the afterlife. Even our most exceptional necromancers have never dared to make such bombastic claims.'

'Young man,' said an elderly, grey-bearded man. 'She did mention some interesting concepts relating to the quantum nature of dragons, which we should not dismiss without some investigation.'

Ollipher paused his rant to bow to the old man. 'Professor Arbitrage, I grant that may be the case, but this is undoubtedly something she overheard when listening to learned scholars such as yourself. I'm sure she has no understanding of the concepts herself.'

Itty put her hands on her hips. 'I know more than you do, and more importantly, my *friend* Shanks is an expert in dragons, seeing as he *is* one.'

The prince waved a dismissive hand. 'So you say.'

A smirk spread across his face. 'You said you met Sir Oscar de Montford. My family is well acquainted with his, and I can quickly establish the veracity of that meeting. Madame Gatekeeper, would you like me to make the appropriate enquiries?'

The gatekeeper blinked at him, obviously taken by surprise. 'Why, Master Ollipher, that would be very welcome indeed, but please don't go to any effort until her fate has been decided. There's little point in bothering Sir Oscar if Mistress Happenstance is unsuccessful in her bid to become a member of our guild.'

'As you wish, madam,' the prince said, making a small bow. Under his breath, but still loud enough to be heard across the chamber, he added, 'The only credible part of this flibbertigibbet's preposterous tale is that she annoyed Sir Oscar—I find her incredibly irritating and I've only known her for less than an hour.'

The gatekeeper had to call for order several times before the laughter in the chamber finally subsided.

Ollipher looked around smugly and asked, 'Ms Happydance, can you expand upon your pretence at travelling through time?'

The Gatekeeper tapped her glasses on her desk. 'Master Ollipher, I ask the questions here. Now, Mistress Happenstance, loathe though I am to agree with Master Ollipher, I must confess that I am intrigued by your temporal shift. I didn't catch how you achieved that—could you possibly elucidate?'

Itty pursed her lips and thought for a few seconds. 'I'm sorry, Madame Gatekeeper, but I cannot remember the specifics.'

'Hah!' said Ollipher.

'Silence, young man,' the Gatekeeper snapped.

'Well, Your Gatekeeperiness, I'm not sure what happened. I was on Captain Smart's ship, and we were talking about how to get back to Earth, and then… something happened, and I woke up near Yossburg.' She shrugged. 'Maybe time travel has affected my memory.'

'Well, something has,' Ollipher guffawed.

'Hmph. Well, Mistress Happenstance, perhaps you can continue your story, in the hope that things become clear later on. You were in the village, is that correct?'

Chapter 22:
Schankenkrausloftenisburg

It is a widespread fallacy that dragons *breathe* fire.

They do, however, generate immense heat internally, used to melt and digest the metals they eat. Impurities in the metals, which occasionally include the knight who was wearing the suit of armour just eaten, are compressed to form an ashy slag which is stored inside the dragon's body until such times as the creature can expel it. Dragon pellets are often so compacted that diamonds can be found within them, and dragon dung prospectors will spend lifetimes looking for that specimen of dragon waste which will make them rich.

Gases created by the digestion process are typically vented at the nether end of the dragon's alimentary canal or gradually through the skin, but they can also be propelled at great force through the mouth, producing the easily recognized jets of flame.

Dragonlore (Anon.)

Night had come, and the moon peeked above the surrounding trees, among which a dozen villagers hid. Itty stood by the pole in the centre of the clearing and inspected the sky, trying to remember which direction the dragon had come from last time.

'Shanks,' she called. 'Are you there? Halloo!' She repeated the call as she paced across the clearing. As time passed and still there was no sign of Shanks, her pacing sped up, and she tried to come up with a believable explanation for the dragon's non-appearance.

The flap of enormous wings spread a smile across her face, and she wondered what the villagers were thinking as Shanks dropped from the sky.

'Who is it who is making a noise that is annoying?' a familiar voice boomed.

'Shanks! It's so good to see you again. And you're well!' Itty called.

A huge snout oriented towards her and sniffed. 'Who are you who says you are a creature that knows the person who is me? Are you a knight come to be a person who is attacking? Why should I be a creature whose wellness is of concern to a being I have not met?'

'Shanks!' She concentrated on his full name: 'Schanken… krausloften… isburg, it's me, Itty Happenstance.'

The dragon's ears flattened. 'How is it that you are a stranger who knows the name that is mine?' He inhaled as if preparing a blast of fire.

Itty spoke rapidly. 'We met before and travelled together. We flew in your crystal wings.' Her voice wavered. 'You almost died, but we reversed time—somehow, I can't remember the details—and I'm back here to stop that from ever happening.'

Shanks pulled back in surprise. 'Reversed time?' He lowered himself to squint at her. 'A thing that is theoretically possible in a universe that is quantum.' He scratched his chin with a decidedly large claw. 'What was it like to travel in a time stream that reverses?'

'I, um, can't remember. It was dark. We were on the ship, talking about when to come back to, and we decided that my arrival at the village would be best. Then I did… something… and I was here. I mean, not here—I was at the edge of the village and I came here to meet you on the same night we, er, first met.'

'Ship? Village? I must think,' the dragon said, and closed his eyes.

Itty walked around him, looking for his injury, the spearhead stuck under a scale. She felt in her pocket for the fragment she'd picked up when she'd helped him last time. There was Karrin's flute, her books, the compass, something round and metallic that she couldn't recall picking up, but which seemed to push her fingers away, some sweets, but no scale. *I suppose that must be because time has wound back to before I got it*, she thought, then cleared her throat. 'Shanks—I hope you don't mind me calling you that. Shanks, I see that a spear is stuck in your, um'—she pointed at his rear end—'your down there area and causing you some distress, and I know you can't reach it. If you will permit me, sir, I can remove it for you.'

Shanks opened an eye. 'That would be a thing that is a relief. It is a nuisance with knights and their "Have at thee–"'

'And their "Die, foul creature,"' Itty continued with a smile.

The dragon raised his eyebrows and stared at her.

'You said those exact words when we met last time, too,' she said as she picked up the blacksmith's pincers. 'This might hurt a bit. Be ready to bite off the damaged scale and cauterize the wound.'

She grasped the spearhead, and placing a foot against the dragon's haunch, pulled as hard as she could. The bit of metal popped out, much more easily with the pincers than when she'd had only her hands to work with. Shanks dealt with the broken scale and quickly blasted the wound with his fire. Itty retrieved the broken-off fragment of scale, marvelling that it was identical in shape to the one she'd picked up last time, then mentally called herself an idiot, because—of course—it would be identical. She slipped it into a pocket as she said, 'I must teach you Marsh code—it'll come in handy later.'

'This all seems familiar,' Shanks mused. 'It's as if all of this is a thing that happened in a dimension that is not this one. Perhaps that is a thing that is the effect of a reversal of time, a thing that is an echo in the quantum; I will have to be a person who is thinking of it. Tell me, Itty-creature, was there a sheep, and was there a lake and a dog-creature with three heads?'

'Yes! Yes. The villagers had covered me with a fleece last time this happened, and you thought I was a sheep. And you're remembering Sir Oscar's hidden factory and Krispy—Kerr-Russ-Bey, I mean.'

The dragon's nostrils flared. 'And there was pain. Wait… sheep? You were a person-creature disguised as a sheep-creature.' He threw back his head and laughed. 'A person-sheep. What a thing! And you smelled like a sheep.'

Itty scowled. 'Never mind about that. Now, please don't take this as a criticism of your kind, but I know that dragons are long-sighted. I would like to offer you something that will help.' She dug two pits, just like before, explained about sandstone and glass, and asked Shanks to blast the pits with his flame. She got him to melt some of the iron from the village to make the frame and said, 'You can eat the rest of this metal if you like. It's a gift from the village.'

'That is a thing that is kind from you people-creatures, and that I am not accustomed to.'

'We're not too bad when you get to know us.' Then she thought about Sir Oscar. 'Well, most of us.'

By the time he'd finished eating, the spectacles were cool enough to assemble. 'Now, let me put these on your nose. They're not perfect, but they'll help a bit.' She placed the large glasses on the dragon's face, and while he was marvelling at how he could see her, and leaves, and insects, she said, 'Here are some friends I'd like you to meet.'

She waved and called to the villagers to come out from the trees.

The dragon bowed. 'Pleased to be a person who is meeting you creatures who are also people. I hope we will all be people who are friends, and I thank you for the metal.' He belched, and smoke seeped from his nostrils.

Some of the villagers screamed and ran for cover.

'No, it's all right,' shouted Itty. 'Nothing to worry about.' She patted Shanks' neck. 'See! He's safe. Come back, meet your new friend.'

Despite Nathan's suspicions about Itty's motives, as soon as he saw Shanks, he begged to ride him on the way to Yossburg. The others, somewhat more apprehensive about the dragon, made the journey on foot. When he and Itty dismounted back at the village, he shouted, 'Wow! That was awesome. Can we do it again?'

'Funny, you said the same last time,' Itty muttered.

'Pardon?' Nathan scratched his head. 'This is the first time I've ridden a dragon.'

'Never mind,' she said with a sigh. 'It's complicated.'

As before, most of the villagers were terrified at their first sight of the dragon up close, but the wide-eyed children couldn't resist approaching him. By the time the mayor and the others returned from the clearing, children were clambering all over a laughing

Shanks and scratching under his chin. Nathan regaled the youngsters waiting their turn to climb on or talk to a dragon with tales of his flight—tales which became more elaborate on each telling.

Itty asked the mayor to convene a council meeting in front of the whole village. She wanted to recount what would happen unless they did something to change the future. She told them about the other villages' difficulties and about rivers being rerouted, describing Sir Oscar's facility in as much detail as she could remember.

'We should storm the compound,' one red-faced farmer shouted from the audience. 'Tear it down. We won't stand for this!'

'I'm no expert in the arts of war, sir, but I'm not at all sure we could do that,' Itty calmly replied. 'The facility is enormous, much bigger than this village. It's also mainly underground—underwater, to be precise—and the only way in is across a narrow floating road leading to the island in the centre of the lake. What's more, the complete area is protected by the Order of the Lapsed Atheist.'

A murmur ran through the villagers, and the farmer gulped.

'Can't your dragon just get in and roast the lot of them?' a ginger-haired woman at the back called.

'No, madam, I'm afraid the facility has an invisible shield which prevents Shanks from approaching. Oh, and Shanks is not my drag–'

Questions from the worried villagers burst into a flood.

'Can we smash the walls of the lake?'

'Can the dragon get close enough t–'

'Quiet!' bellowed the mayor. 'None of these questions are helping. Let Ms Happenstance finish telling us about the compound, and then we can discuss what to do about it.'

'There's not much else to tell,' Itty said. 'The facility is deep and well-protected. I don't know how we can breach it.'

'Residents of Yossburg,' the mayor called. 'First things first. Can I have some volunteers willing to journey into the mountains to verify Ms Happenstance's claims?'

A number of hands shot up.

The mayor pointed. 'You, you, and… you.'

Itty added, 'Please take care. Don't get too close; make sure you avoid the Lapsed Atheists.'

'Next,' the mayor continued. 'Assuming all is as she says, does anyone have any suggestions about dealing with this de Montford man?' The villagers started to speak again, talking over the top of each other.

'Kidnap his children.'

'Go on strike!'

'Hypnotize him.'

'Tar and feather—'

The mayor shouted, 'Reasonable and sensible suggestions only, please.'

The villagers looked at each other and shuffled their feet.

Nathan broke the silence with a polite throat-clearing. 'I wonder if we could persuade the other villages to help. With three times as many people, perhaps we would stand a chance against de Montford. I remember our school trip to Rille's museum—they've got lots of weapons and armour there; maybe that'll help too.'

An excited buzz ran through the crowd.

'But how can we get to Rille and Tweezle?' someone asked. 'They're blocking the roads and won't let us approach.'

Itty jumped in. 'There's a Humble Monks' tunnel leading to Rille's museum. A small party could get to the village that way. We explain the story to their elders, and ask them to arrange to open the roads.'

'A brilliant idea,' the mayor said. 'And, if the village is flooded as you say, we can bring all the waterproof boots we can carry as a sign of our good intentions.'

'What about Tweezle?' someone asked.

'The tunnel goes there, too,' said Itty. 'We can send another party with fresh water.'

Chapter 23: The Three Villages

> If at first you don't succeed, for goodness'
> sake, *don't* just try again. The same damned
> thing is going to happen. Try doing it
> differently, or try something else.
>
> Or you could always just give up.
>
> Graffiti in the world-famous cave of Robby
> the Spider.

Imperceptibility led two groups of Yossburg villagers, along with Nathan, into the Humble Monks' tunnel the following morning. The six members of one group wore backpacks bulging with galoshes and wellington boots. The dozen men and women in the other group, the strongest in the village, paired up and carried bulky water skins on poles slung across their shoulders.

With memories of stumbling around the tunnels in the dark before, Itty made sure that both groups had plenty of torches and matches for the journey underground. She wondered if the passages would be exactly the same as on her last visit, but she did feel much more confident about entering the darkness this time, if only because there were many more people taking part in the expedition than just her and Nathan.

The casual chatter amongst the troupe dropped off when she opened the trapdoor at the back of the cave, revealing the dark shaft with its ladder leading down to the tunnels proper. Itty descended first, followed by the boot-carrying villagers, while the others rigged up a pulley and ropes to lower the water skins.

Sir Oscar's upper-downer would be useful right now, Itty thought.

Eventually, after a not-insignificant amount of cursing and swearing, everyone reached the bottom of the shaft with only a little water spilled, and the troupe was ready to begin their subterranean march. A few eyebrows rose at Itty's request to look out for a waist-high brass doorknob in the wall, and again, when Nathan spotted it not long after. Itty was sure it had taken longer to find the door last time. She recalled how time seemed to pass differently in the tunnels and wondered if that was another form of time travel—something else to ask the next Humble Monk she found.

She twisted the handle and, as before, it refused to turn. Two of the water carriers tried, but to no avail.

Nathan reached for it, saying, 'Maybe it's just stuck. Our back door sometimes–'

'Needs a good twist,' Itty finished with a smile and a sidelong glance at the young man.

Nathan gave her a suspicious look as he wrenched sharply, and with a crack, the hidden door swung open.

Itty peeked through the opening and was relieved to recognize the room. 'Everything's going to plan,' she said. 'We've arrived at the back of the armour room in Rille's museum.'

Nathan rushed through, excitedly zooming from the statue of King Berenice to Sir Royce's armour and the other exhibits, while the others peered around in awe. Some wanted to grab weapons right away, but Itty reminded them that they first needed to convince the Rillians that they came in peace. That would be difficult to do, she said, if they were carrying swords, pikes and maces stolen from the museum.

One of the other villagers was staring up at a window. 'It's dark.' She turned towards Itty, an expression of bewilderment on her face. 'How come it's dark?'

'The tunnels do funny things with time.' Itty shrugged apologetically. 'I think as much time passes within them as would be required when travelling normally, but I don't know how or why. The next time I meet one of the Humble Monks, I intend to ask him.'

She asked the water carriers to wait at the tunnel entrance, since they were not required in this village, while she took the others downstairs, grabbing one of the map-printed tea-towels from the museum shop. When she opened the museum door, there were gasps of disbelief at the water flooding the village, as well as murmurs of 'those poor people' and 'we didn't know anything about this' and 'no wonder they're angry.'

Itty leaned out and called, 'Officer Grigor, Officer Yonich, are you there?'

A window opposite the museum lit up in response to the noise. A nightcap-wearing head appeared in it, looked up and down the street, and muttered, 'Blasted drunkards,' before disappearing inside again.

A few moments later, the guards came splashing through the lake that was Rille's streets. 'What have we got here? Who are you lot, and what are you doing in our museum? And how do you know our names? Hey, you're robbers. Hands up!'

Itty raised her hands and calmly said, 'We mean your village no harm. And surely everyone has heard about constables as brave as you two stout men. We're here specifically to find you. We would like to ask for your help, and we can help you in return. Please come in.'

The guards entered the museum, weapons at the ready. Water seeped out of their boots onto the floor.

'Officers, judging by the puddles you're standing in, your boots must be leaking.' She pointed at their feet. 'We want to offer you replacements. What size are you?'

The guards looked at each other, then at their feet. 'Size ten,' said one. 'Size eleven and a half,' said the other. 'And no tricks.' He pointed his pike at her.

'Mr Billings, I believe you have the larger sizes. Could you bring them here, please?' Itty said over her shoulder. 'And slowly; we don't want to surprise anyone.'

''Ere, what's in the bag?' asked one of the guards.

Mr Billings emptied his backpack on the floor, boots tumbling out. 'Waterproof boots,' he said, somewhat redundantly. 'Best in Yossburg.'

Immediately, both guards pointed their weapons at Billings and Itty. 'Yossburg! You did this! You flooded our village. What are you doing now?'

'No, no!' Itty waved her arms, taking care to keep her hands raised above her head. 'Yossburg is innocent. We've come to explain what's going on and to ask for your help in dealing with the real culprit—can we talk to your mayor? We've brought as many boots as we can carry for you and the citizens of Rille, and more are on the way here via road. We need you to take news to your blockades to let them through. Please believe us; we're trying to help.'

One of the guards lifted a foot, letting water trickle out of a large hole in the sole of his boot. 'You watch them, Yonich; first sign of trouble, stick 'em. I want to check out these dry boots. Now, all of you, step back.' Officer Grigor slid off his rather worn boots.

Mr Billings pointed to a pair of boots. 'Those are the size tens.'

Grigor picked them up, tapped the soles and sniffed the uppers. 'These aren't bad. Decent leather, good waterproofing. I grant they can only have been made in Yossburg. Not saying I trust you, mind, but I'll listen to what you have to say.' He slid his feet in and marched up and down a few paces, then splashed into the water outside. His eyes glistened, and a smile pushed his jowls up, giving him the expression of a friendly bulldog. 'Oh, Yonich,' he said, 'you don't know how pleasant it is to have dry feet again. And comfortable too—it's a blessing. I don't care who these people are; they're my friends now.'

'Officer Yonich?' Itty asked, gesturing towards the pile of boots.

Yonich passed Itty his pike as he rushed to change his boots, too.

As he wiggled his toes in his new footwear and sighed happily, she asked, 'Officers, is your trainee constable not with you today? We can give him some new footwear, too.'

'Nay, lass,' replied Officer Yonich. 'He's back at the guardhouse, sorting our keys. Clumsy fool knocked the key holder off the wall and now we don't know which one fits where.'

Itty handed his weapon back to him and said, 'Now, I've got to continue to Tweezle. Perhaps one of you two gentlemen would care to accompany us, to see Tweezle's state for yourself.' She gestured towards the other Yossburgers. 'These fine people would like to meet your mayor, to discuss how we can distribute the rest of our boots and work on a plan to deal with your flooding.'

Mr Billings gathered the rest of the new boots into his backpack, and the group of six shoe-carriers followed Yonich through the water.

Itty watched them go, then ran up the stairs to the others with Officer Grigor following.

Once everyone was underground, she looked left and right. *Which way did I go last time?* Picking a direction at random, she figured that the monks' tunnels would do their magic, or perhaps Lo-La would guide their steps. The smell of roast lamb and mint reassured her, though it also made her stomach rumble. She recalled snapping at Nathan on their previous journey and saying that she was no expert on the tunnels—she wondered if, perhaps, she could call herself one this time around.

She sighed at the memory of holding hands with Nathan last time they were in this passageway. She glanced at his hand, but this version of the young man still didn't totally trust her. Maybe the darkness and anxiety when just the two of them journeyed here before, had helped to bring them together. *But*, she figured, *the needs of the three villages outweigh whatever I would like.*

'Right, everyone, this time we're looking for a black door, covered in soot or the like. A wooden door with a whatchamacallit… a latch.' As on her previous journey through the monks' tunnels to Tweezle, she gestured with her thumb.

About ten minutes later, one of the women called, 'I think I've found it.'

Itty took a few steps into the corridor behind this door, raising her torch high to see what she could make out. The tunnel veered to the left after a short distance, and she took a few more steps to peer around the corner. The tunnel switched to the right. 'Yes,' she called back, 'this is the way. Come along. This one's a long stretch with something like barn doors right at the end, painted red, green and blue. Should be easy to find.' She smiled wryly and rubbed the tip of her nose. 'I walked smack into them last time. There're chickens on the other side.'

Just as people were starting to grumble about feeling tired and to ask if she appreciated just how difficult it had been to get those water skins through the narrow part of the tunnel, they found the door and stepped through into the henhouse.

Itty tiptoed through a murmuring squabble of chickens and opened the door at the other side, just as someone else was reaching for it. 'Good day, Farmer Barnes,' she said, as the person outside jumped back in surprise. 'And hello to you too, Roscoe,' she added to the small dog who cocked his head and stared at her.

'What be ye doing in my henhouse? Come out, come out!' The man's jaw dropped as more people than could possibly fit into his henhouse stepped into the farmyard.

'We're just passing through on our way to Tweezle. That way, is it, then turn right at the end?' Itty pointed along the lane.

Mr Barnes nodded.

'Thank you, sir,' said Itty. 'Have a nice day. Come on, Nathan.'

Nathan had stopped to fuss Roscoe, and both seemed to be enjoying it.

Farmer Barnes popped his head through the henhouse door, then came back out to stare after the departing Yossburgers. His lips moved as he seemed to be silently counting them.

He scratched his head. 'Some folk be right strange, eh, Roscoe?'

Reaching down to rub between his dog's ears, he added, 'And how'd girl know tha name?'

The water carriers marvelled at the dryness of the ground and withered vegetation on the way to the village. There were grumbles about how de Montford needed to be taught a lesson. Itty warned them that things were much worse in the village itself.

As they approached, the village was eerily silent. All that could be heard above the tramp of the Yossburg feet was the squeaking of the water pump. When they turned the final corner and saw the queue, several of the water carriers gasped.

Itty called, 'We've brought fresh water, as much as we could carry. It's not enough to keep you going for long, but we hope it'll help. More Yossburg volunteers are bringing wagons full of water by road. Could you possibly send word to the blockades to let them through?'

The Tweezlins stared in weary disbelief before a woman at the end of the queue asked, 'What be this trick? This drought be Yossburg's doing, it be.'

One of the water carrier pairs hurried across and opened their water skin. 'No trick, my fine lady,' one of them said. 'We promise. Yossburg isn't doing this. It's de Montford.'

There followed a brief and somewhat confused discussion about what a 'de Montford' was and why it was doing things with their water.

Itty cut it short with, 'We want to help, and we need *your* help. We're not strong enough to defeat Mr de Montford alone, but the three villages together—you, Rille and Yossburg—

can stand up to him. But first, you all need water. Please, help yourselves.' She stood back, as the other water carriers brought their loads forward.

A day later, representatives from all three villages met in the saloon in Yossburg, to listen to the mayor explain the problem.

'Welcome, friends. Before we get down to business, as Mayor of Yossburg, I would like to invite the homeless of Tweezle and Rille into our village while we help you rebuild yours. We can make room for some of you within our own homes.' The mayor gestured at the walls of the building they were occupying. 'And in our saloon. We are erecting tents in surrounding fields for more of you.'

As a ripple of polite applause circled the room, she continued, 'We do realize that some of you do not want to leave your own villages, but we will give you all the support we can.

'Now, the reason the valley is in trouble is most certainly not natural. Sir Oscar de Montford has taken it upon himself to divert our river to serve the needs of his factory in the hills.' She looked around the gathering, meeting the eyes of everyone there. 'Your assistance is essential to attack and defeat de Montford, and drive his business out of our valley. This is not just for our village, but for all of us. Yossburg alone is not strong enough to take him on; we need your help.

'I would like to yield the floor to a brave young woman. You've met her already—it's thanks to her efforts that you're all here in the first place.' She stretched an arm towards Itty, inviting her up onto the stage.

Itty coughed to clear her throat, then started: 'As the mayor has said, Sir Oscar is a danger to the valley. Through circumstances that would take a bit too long to explain right now, I have a good idea of what he's up to and what his facility in the Karrigs looks like.'

Itty used the tea-towel map to show the location of de Montford's research facility. She described the dense wall of ensorcelled plants supporting the manufactured lake they needed to cross and the roaming squads of Lapsed Atheist soldiers they had to pass before getting there. Oh, and there was the magic invisible light that prevented Shanks from being able to help.

'We be doomed,' a thin woman from Tweezle said.

'Aye, we should drop this ridiculous idea,' added a bald man from Rille.

'Now, good people, let's not give up on the girl yet,' said Yossburg's mayor. 'She's got us all here in one place, talking to each other, hasn't she? That wouldn't have happened without her.'

All eyes turned towards Itty, who tipped her head towards the mayor in gratitude, even though she didn't have a clue what to say next.

Chapter 24: Sir Oscar de Montford

The best way to make friends is to find a common enemy, and then cast aspersions on their ability to create elegantly decorated cakes. Once you have formed a coalition of patisseries, nothing can prevent you from overwhelming your enemy with tasty baked goods. It is a far better thing to avoid war through the distribution of luscious, cream-filled honey cakes and rich almond slices topped with candied ginger than it is to swap our aprons for battle armour.

And if that doesn't work, you can hit them with your rolling pins and heavy bakeware.

Preface to *The Tart of War*, Sunny Sue.

'Uh…' Imperceptibility's eloquence deserted her as she looked around.

A sea of eyes stared back at her, people anxiously waiting for her to speak, needing her to provide them with the complete solution to the valley's problems. A lump formed in her stomach. She felt even more nervous than when she found herself in the Down-Underworld, or when she was tied up and facing a dragon.

She smiled inwardly. Back then, she didn't even believe dragons existed. An idea blossomed in her mind. *Things that don't exist…* She took a deep breath. *I can do this.*

Itty surveyed her expectant audience again. She caught Nathan's eye, and he smiled and gave her a thumbs-up. Yes, she thought, she could definitely do this. She cleared her throat.

'I won't promise that this will be easy, because it won't be. And I can't promise that I know all the answers. These are dangerous people we're up against. We need to work together to defeat them, and we'll need to use all our cunning. Here's what we'll do…'

A week later, Itty handed Nathan four sealed letters and told him to wait with Shanks. If she didn't send a message via the dragon scale before the end of the day, the pair were to fly to the capital, Khaleshka, and deliver the letters to the emperor and the city's three big newspapers: *The Times*, *The Place* and *The People*.

After that, she set off on the climb to Sir Oscar's secret facility along with the three mayors and a few other women and older children from the villages and outlying farms, as non-threatening a group of people as she could imagine. All of them carried backpacks fashioned from the cunning shoe-carrying devices they'd found in the Rille museum. These would provide sturdy protection for the packs' fragile and critically important contents.

They rode in a pair of carts to the edge of the mountaintop forest. When the horses could go no further, they were loosely tied to trees with plenty of grass within easy reach. After donning their backpacks, the villagers marched into the forest. Within a few minutes, the hikers reached the wall of dense vegetation that surrounded de Montford's lake.

Itty turned to the others and whispered, 'This is it. Watch out for the soldiers, but don't be frightened. There's no need to be quiet—we want them to find us. Don't do anything rash. Just keep calm.'

The villagers nodded and set their jaws, then the group walked around the base of the artificial lake's tall ramparts, making no effort to hide. There was much marvelling at the dense vegetation, and much less apprehension than Itty had felt when she first encountered the wall. Country dwellers must be used to such things, she thought. The farmers among them were especially impressed by the strength and solidity of the periodic buttresses.

One of them tugged at the plants and wondered, 'If we could do this to our fields' fences and hedges, we'd have less trouble with escaping sheep. Keep foxes out too.'

A resident of Tweezle replied, 'Aye, you'm right there. It would be good to have en growing by the banks of t' river, too. No more flooding.'

The villagers continued to wander through the woods, amiably chatting. Some had pulled up grass stems to chew or flowers to put in their hair.

'Halt!' a sudden voice bellowed.

One of the villagers squeaked, and another almost dropped her backpack.

Six heavily armed soldiers stepped out from behind one of the buttresses.

'What are you doing here? Don't you know this is private property?' called their leader.

Itty whispered, 'It's OK,' and stepped forward, looking up at the leader of the troop.

'Hello. Am I speaking to Reverend Major Smite And Ye Shall Receive?'

The soldier eyed her up and down for a moment before responding as if he'd expected unwanted visitors to the forest to either cower or run away, not politely greet him by name. 'Yes, miss, you are.' He didn't seem to quite know how to react. 'What can I do for you, er, ladies?'

Itty rotated both index fingers towards him. 'What can *we* do for you, Reverend Major? If I might be allowed to open my backpack…'

Smite nodded curtly, but held his sword ready.

Itty slid the clever, repurposed shoe-carrying backpack off her shoulders and gently set it on the ground, not wanting to risk damage to the contents. Making sure the soldiers could clearly see what she was doing, she opened it, revealing what was inside.

One of the soldiers let out a long 'Ahhhh' when the smell reached him.

'Kind sirs, noble guards,' said Itty, 'you work long and hard hours, bravely marching through the forest all day long, with no luxuries at all. Nothing to eat when you're out and about but dry rations, am I right? And as for the food in your mess… Well, you don't need to be reminded of that, do you? We thought we'd show some appreciation for the fine work you do by bringing some cakes and pastries. You are no doubt aware of the excellent footwear the villages of Esmiya produce, but all three have very talented bakers as well.'

She lifted a tray out of the backpack. It contained cream puffs and cinnamon whirls, iced fancies and apple muffins, coconut cookies and hazelnut tarts.

'Please do help yourselves.'

The soldier who'd reacted to the delicious aroma earlier stepped forward. Reverend Major Smite held up a hand, preventing him from passing, and bellowed, 'Not so fast, private! As you were.'

Smite reached for a sugar-coated damson surprise, sniffed it, and nibbled at the corner. He closed his mouth and pushed his tongue over his front teeth. He licked his lips, then opened wide and popped the entire cake in. He chewed briefly, eyes closing in pleasure, swallowed, and noisily sucked the remaining sugar and smears of damson juice off his fingers.

By now, all the other soldiers were licking their lips too.

'That was incredible,' Smite mumbled around his fingers. 'Might I possibly have another?'

Itty proffered the tray. 'Help yourself. And perhaps your men would like some?'

Smite nodded distractedly as he sheathed his sword and grabbed a cookie in each hand.

The mayor of Yossburg opened her backpack and displayed a flask and several cups. 'Perhaps you gentlemen would like some tea to wash down the cakes.'

While Smite continued to smack his lips in appreciation, Itty asked, 'Reverend Major, would you be so kind as to escort us to Mr de Montford's Advanced Fuel Research facility? I believe the gatehouse has a table where we can sit and enjoy our tea more comfortably and, dare I suggest it, a few more cakes. We also have some baked goods we'd like to offer him, too. Just to express our appreciation for *his* work, you know?'

Smite turned towards her and said sternly, 'I don't know what you're talking about. There're no research facilities around here.'

Itty wafted the tray under his nose and smiled.

Smite coughed, then harrumphed and said, 'That's a top-secret establishment. You shouldn't even know about it. We can't take you there.'

'Not even for some more of these?' She lifted the tray so that he could smell sugary bliss. 'Sir Oscar is expecting us. You wouldn't want to have to explain to him why he hasn't received his cakes, now, would you?'

Smite narrowed his eyes. 'How do you know Mr de Montford is here?' Then he coughed. 'If he's here. Wherever here is.'

Itty lowered the tray. 'Reverend Major, we know where the facility is,' she said, hoping that he didn't ask her to prove that—she hadn't been paying enough attention last time Smite had captured her. 'But we all felt strongly that you and your men shouldn't miss out on all this. It's only polite that we give you some cakes, and I would consider it a fair exchange for you to assist us. Now, Sir Oscar is waiting—are you going to escort us, or shall we proceed by ourselves?'

It wasn't long before the soldiers reached the entrance to the facility's gatehouse.

Itty knocked on the door. 'Mr Naimliss, coo-ee, are you in there?'

When he opened it, she repeated her story that the women wanted to donate some baked goods to the diligent, hard-working men in the mountains, and asked if he would like a cinnamon whirl.

'You're such an important man, Mr Naimliss, that we've saved the best for you,' Itty said as she passed him a plate piled high with delectable treats.

A few minutes later, Mr Naimliss, the three mayors and Itty were eating cakes and drinking tea, having displaced the other two officials who'd been playing cards at the small table in the gatehouse. The officials weren't too upset at the interruption to their game as they joined the guards and the rest of the villagers outside, working their way through more of the delicious baked goods.

Mr Naimliss emptied his teacup and leaned back, sighing contentedly. 'That was most kind, Ms…?'

'Mayor Joan Wainwright of Yossburg,' one woman replied.

'Mayor Alberta Rhinestone of Rille,' and 'Mayor Josephine Edelweiss of Tweezle,' the others added.

Mr Naimliss raised his eyebrows and looked towards Itty.

She bowed her head slightly. 'And I'm Imperceptibility Happenstance, just a visitor to the valley and no one as important as our three honoured mayors.' Then she looked up, and her expression hardened. 'But you are going to arrange for *me* to meet Sir Oscar.'

Mr Naimliss spluttered, and his face broke into a smile as if he thought she was joking. When no one laughed, he sobered and said, 'What makes you think Sir Oscar would want to meet you, regardless of the quality of your fine pastries?'

Mayor Wainwright said, with a particularly dark smile, 'What if we told you that the macaroons you ate with great relish were laced with poison? A nasty little potion distilled from a plant that grows only in this valley. Purple Tigerwort, it's called. Do you know of it?'

A rather pale Mr Naimliss shook his head.

'Then you won't know what the symptoms of tigerwort poisoning are. First, you'll feel hot, then cold, and you'll start sweating—is that a sheen of perspiration I see on your forehead? About an hour after that, you'll start to tremble, then… Well, let's just say, you might need a clean pair of trousers. Not that you could put them on, because by then, your nerves will be burning and your muscles spasming. Oh, dear boy, it'll be agony.' Mayor Wainwright's eyes shone, and her grin grew wide. 'Absolute agony. Fortunately, that phase lasts only about fifteen minutes. After that, well…' She drew a finger across her throat.

'You, you can't do this to me!' Naimliss wailed.

Itty's voice trembled with a mixture of excitement and gut-churning anxiety as she said, 'But we *have* done it. However, we do have the antidote, which you'll get when you take us to Sir Oscar.' She nodded towards the other two mayors, who retrieved identical small glass bottles from their pockets. They shook the bottles, letting the transparent liquid inside swirl around the sides. 'One of these phials contains the antidote; the other, another dose of tigerwort. That's to prevent you from attacking us and just taking the antidote, since if you drink the wrong one or both, you'll…' She tilted her head to the side and rolled her eyes up while letting her tongue loll out.

Mayor Wainwright clapped her hands and said, 'Time's a-wasting, Mr Naimliss, and you don't have much left. Take us to de Montford.' She thumped the table, rattling the crockery.

Chapter 25: The Deal

Mr Smithen-Wessen is credited with being the inventor of the portable self-igniting combusting weapon, but the explosive compound upon which it relies was devised centuries before in the savannas of Estalia. Early Estalian philosophers of nature discovered that the droppings of certain animals would give a bright, if somewhat pungent, cooking flame—and so much more. The pellets would explode, spectacularly ruining a perfectly good dinner, and were soon put to use in warfare. The most potent droppings were those of a bison-like creature known as the wildebeest, from which the modern handheld weapon takes its slang name, the gnu. Interestingly, the savannas of Estalia also gained an informal name from a corruption of the same source, the Wilde Best.

From *A History of Combusting and Non-combusting Weaponry*, Sir Ian Livingbore.

Mr Naimliss stared at the empty plates, then at the grim-faced women in front of him. He swallowed and made a whimpering sound, before lurching up from the table and bolting for the door at the back of the gatehouse.

Itty and the three mayors followed him as he ran across the floating road towards the island in the middle of the lake, stumbling in his haste. The three older women grasped each other's arms as the pontoon bridge bobbed underneath their feet.

'Hangar two, isn't that right, Mr Naimliss?' Itty called when they'd reached solid ground again, on the island.

Naimliss nodded, unable to speak.

The mirrored room was a tight squeeze with all five occupants. The mayors stared around them wide-eyed, and all three emitted surprised squeaks when the room started to move.

The donkey harnessed to the upper-downer mechanism brayed, complaining about the weight, as Mr Naimliss muttered, 'Faster, faster.'

He raced along the corridor to Sir Oscar's office and burst in without knocking.

Mr de Montford's personal assistant's eyes bulged when she saw the crowd in her doorway, but before she could say anything, Mr Naimliss panted, 'It's urgent! Please, Ms Stone, these women must see Sir Oscar right away.'

Ever the professional P.A., Clara Stone replied coolly, 'I'm afraid that's not possible. Mr de Montford is a very busy man.'

'It's a matter of life or–'

Just then, a door at the other end of the room banged open. A fat, bald man in a suit stomped in. 'Clara, where are the notes from my—Who are you? Clara, what are these people doing down here?'

Itty spoke. 'Mr de Montford—Sir Oscar— may I say what a privilege it is to meet you.'

Mr Naimliss made hurry-up gestures with his hands while she continued, 'I think what you're doing in the aeronautical industry is amazing.'

She stuck out a hand.

'Erm, harrumph.' Oscar de Montford switched his expression to a smile and shook her hand. 'Thank you, young lady. It's nice to have one's achievements recognized. I like to think—'

'However, you are also a despicable individual whose fuel factory is destroying the valley and the lives of all who live in it, through your single-minded pursuit of profit.'

Sir Oscar's mouth gaped. He snapped it shut, as his face went red, and he looked as if he would explode.

Mr Naimliss squeaked, 'The antidote. You promised me the antidote!'

Sir Oscar turned towards him, a frown of confusion crossing his face. 'What are you blathering about, whatsyername?'

Mayor Wainwright ignored him and waved a hand towards Mr Naimliss. 'There never was any poison. You're perfectly fine. Those phials contain nothing more than water. Pull yourself together, man.'

Mr Naimliss stood up straight. He pulled out his gun and pointed it at Itty. 'Sir Oscar, I'll call the guards and have these people taken away. They're here under false pretences. I'm sorry for disturbing y–'

'No,' Itty said quietly. 'It's not as simple as that. We know what's going on here. We know all about your secret fuel formulation. See.' She brandished a piece of paper. 'Here's the recipe for the orange mash you feed the pigs.' She'd remembered the recipe she'd found when she was being chased by Sir Oscar's soldiers last time she was here—at least, enough of it, she hoped, to convince him her threat was real.

Sir Oscar snatched the sheet of paper from Itty's hand and glanced at it. Then his eyes widened as he read it properly. Then he smiled, showing his array of blackened teeth. 'But you're all here. Who will you be able to tell? What can you do?'

'More than you think.' She pulled Shanks' scale from her jacket. 'You know what this is, don't you? I've got a dragon waiting to take the recipe and word about the illegal goings-on here to Khaleshka's newspapers, unless he hears from me before the end of the day. Just think of the effect of competition and litigation on your bottom line.'

'What? How? No!' Sir Oscar blustered, then he paused and glared at her. 'Wait a minute. How do I know you've really got a dragon and haven't just picked up that scale in some flea market?'

'Are you willing to take the risk?' She held up the scale. 'Shall I tell Shanks—that's his name—to deliver his message right away?'

Sir Oscar paled. 'You wouldn't.'

'We would.' Itty leaned towards him. 'But we don't want to.' She put the scale back into her pocket and gestured towards the three village leaders. 'Madame Wainwright, Madame Rhinestone and Madame Edelweiss are the mayors of Yossburg, Tweezle and Rille, respectively, and they would prefer to come to a mutually beneficial agreement than to ruin you. You're not a very nice person, but you could help the valley without affecting your profits. And the villages could help you.'

The three mayors nodded.

Itty continued. 'The last time I was here–'

Sir Oscar's eyebrows rose again, and his mouth opened.

'Don't ask,' muttered Mayor Wainwright.

Itty frowned at her and turned back to Sir Oscar. 'Last time I was here, I saw the conditions of your pigs. I'm sure they'd thrive much better outdoors. There's no reason to keep them confined inside all the time. The villages could help look after them and would be willing to keep visitors away. Who's going to think twice about perfectly ordinary pig farms in the perfectly ordinary countryside, regardless of what the animals are being fed and what happens to their waste? With the space available in the valley, you could generate much more fuel than you could ever produce in this facility alone.'

Sir Oscar rubbed his chin and seemed to consider this.

Mayor Wainwright said, 'By my estimate, and from what this young lady has told us, we should be able to support ten times as many pigs as you have here currently, and they'll be more comfortable.' She smiled. 'And happy pigs will produce more… raw material for your fuel manufacturing process.'

Itty added, 'I'm sure your workers will be happier, too. It's not very pleasant down on the animal floor, is it?'

Sir Oscar shrugged, and Itty guessed he probably didn't know what it was like to work on the floor with the pigs, nor would he care very much. Perhaps they should have thought of 'poisoning' him and making him spend some time there before giving him the imaginary antidote, but, she realized, that wouldn't help matters with the villages.

'What we ask for in return,' Yossburg's mayor said, 'is rerouting of the river back to normal, and a small share of your profits. We're not greedy. Let's say, a mere ten per cent.'

Sir Oscar's eyebrows shot up yet again. '*Ten per cent!*'

'Stop your blustering, man,' Mayor Wainwright countered, hands on hips. 'What difference does ten per cent make if we can increase your profits tenfold?'

Sir Oscar bristled some more, a tic developing below his left eye as he spluttered wordlessly, but it was obvious he was doing the calculations.

'Deal.' He stuck out his hand.

The three mayors shook his hand, but Itty refused, crossing her arms tightly.

'I don't like you, Sir Oscar,' she said, 'but this outcome is what's best for the villages. I will let these three ladies work through their contracts with you, but I'll be keeping an eye on you, as will Shanks.'

A sly smile crept across Sir Oscar's face.

'And don't think I'm not aware of your anti-dragon force field things. I expect you to disable them—dragons are no danger to you or your business, as long as you behave. If you threaten the villages or dragons again, those letters will be delivered.'

Sir Oscar's smile vanished.

Itty leaned towards him. 'Do I make myself clear? Oh, by the way, I suggest you *don't* light up a celebratory cigar on your facility's main floor—I don't want to go through that again.'

Sir Oscar nodded, only half paying attention. He let his gaze drift off into the distance, clearly thinking about the extra money that would be making its way towards his coffers.

'Let's get down to business,' said Mayor Wainwright as she passed Sir Oscar a folder containing details of plans, estimates and financial predictions. 'By the way, Sir Oscar, as you undoubtedly know, our villages produce some of the most exquisite footwear in existence, and I'm sure we can find it mutually profitable to include your engagement as our worldwide distributor in these negotiations.'

She pulled out a complicated-looking graph. 'Here are sales to date.' She tapped on the chart. 'The downward spike here is attributable to your activities in the valley, but if we ignore that, our projections for the next calendar year are healthy.' Turning to another brightly coloured page, she continued, 'If we assume efficient worldwide distribution, then those projections are much more than merely healthy…'

Itty tuned them out and turned towards Mr Naimliss. 'Now, Mr Naimliss, you can take me back to the surface while the others work out the details. It'll be quite pleasant to breathe fresh air again. Perhaps you would like another of those macaroons you seemed to enjoy so much earlier.'

The official turned pale again.

The other villagers looked at Itty anxiously when she returned to the gatehouse.

'Yes, we've done it,' she confirmed.

The villagers cheered.

'Our trick with the fake poison worked, and your mayors guessed correctly that Sir Oscar's desire for profit would outweigh any disagreements he could possibly have with anyone else.' Itty knew full well that the mayors wouldn't have reached their conclusion without her nudging, but she thought it diplomatic to let them have the glory.

She smiled grimly. 'Let's hope he doesn't think about getting into politics—he'd do very well.'

She pulled out Shanks' scale and tapped a quick message to call off the delivery of the reports that would have financially ruined Sir

Oscar. Finally, with her village rescue mission complete, she realized how tense she'd been and how exhausted she was now. Slumping into one of the chairs in the gatehouse and deflating, Itty poured herself a cup of tea. She took a sip, grimacing when she discovered it was totally cold. She folded her arms on the table, and resting her head on top, nodded off to sleep.

Sometime later, she was awakened by the three mayors' return to the gatehouse accompanied by a beaming Sir Oscar.

'It's been my pleasure to meet you three remarkable women, and I hope we can do wonderful business together over the coming years.' He stabbed his cigar in Itty's direction and scowled, the tic at his left eye starting up again. 'And you, young lady… I hope to never see you again.'

The tired villagers and Itty trudged downhill again, escorted to the edge of the forested area by Reverend Major Smite And Ye Shall Receive and his soldiers.

Mayor Edelweiss pointed at the backpacks containing the remainder of the cakes and pastries. 'We don't really want to carry these all the way back, and you nice men look like you need to keep your strength up.'

The soldiers practically tore the backpacks off the villagers' shoulders in their eagerness to get hold of their contents. Reverend Major Smite struck a salute while the other soldiers waved to Itty and the others as they continued their walk downhill.

Chapter 26: The End, Almost

Dealing with the Supernatural
1. Never trust a supernatural being.
2. Demons, djinn and their varied kindred never lie; why should they when the truth can be even more damning?
3. There ain't no such thing as a free wish.
4. Never, ever trust a supernatural being, especially an apparently honest one offering free wishes.

From *Making Money Through Miracles, Metaphysics and Magic*, Leonora Soothsayer.

'We'll miss you, young Ms Happenstance,' the mayor of Yossburg said as they stood at the edge of the village three weeks later.

Imperceptibility's purse now contained enough money for passage on a ship or dirigible to Hyrhia as well as payment for a stagecoach to take her to her departure point, and Mr Johansenn, his wagon wheels now fixed, had offered to take her to the coach stop.

The water was once again flowing where it should be, and Rille had a river wall of ensorcelled plants protecting its green. Sir Oscar's botanomancers had even managed to transform some tree roots into a sprinkler system for watering the grass without human intervention.

Many of the sheep farms in the valley had switched to pig farming with little fuss, though Mr Barnes' chickens weren't so sure about the newcomers; the pigs were a lot noisier and more inquisitive than the docile balls of wool they'd shared fields with before. Daily wagons from the facility in the hills brought food supplements and left full of pig manure, using wonderfully smooth roads Sir Oscar had financed. The original plan had been for weekly visits, but the number of pigs that the farms could support, and thus the amount of 'raw product' they could produce, was higher even than their best estimates. Shanks helped with some of these deliveries too, but he was preparing to leave soon.

Shoemaking was back on track as well, though one of Yossburg's shops had been converted to stock pig-related products—ceramic pigs in amusing poses, tea-towels featuring pigs, and tiny toy pigs which grunted when you squeezed them. A few of these could also be found in the Rille museum shop, and tourism was booming across the valley.

'It's certainly been exciting,' the mayor said. 'Yossburg, Twęezle and Rille are all back to normal, and we see a profitable future ahead of us, all thanks to you, young lady.'

Nathan rushed up to give her a tentative hug. 'Come back anytime. You're a friend to the whole village.'

Itty sighed at the thought that, to Nathan, she was merely a friend of the village and not anything more. She'd tried talking to him, but she couldn't work out the right words to explain—everything she could think of would have him staring at her as if she were deranged. Besides, he was too excited about the return to normality of life in the valley to pay much attention to her. Although her chest ached when she thought about what might have been, it was undoubtedly better to be friends and alive rather than romantically involved and trapped in the afterlife with a dying dragon.

She put on her best smile and thanked Nathan and the mayor, then she turned to the waiting ranks of villagers. 'I've enjoyed meeting you all, even though it's been a very strange visit. Two visits! I'll be sure to come back soon, but I really do want to go home now.'

Despite her words, she'd been away from Hyrhia for so long she wasn't sure if she belonged there anymore. The *Invigilator* with Captain Smart and the Down-Underworld with Karrin felt more like home. Even the villages felt more real than Hyrhia, which seemed like a dream from a distant childhood.

She decided that, regardless of the full purse, she wouldn't sail or fly to Hyrhia, but instead, step into the Humble Monks' tunnels to see where they might take her. Perhaps she'd meet Brother Nobody 231 again, Lo-La permitting.

She was trudging across the field at the edge of the village, blinking her eyes so that she wouldn't cry, when the flap of enormous wings dragged her from her reverie.

'Itty person-sheep, it has been a time that was interesting that I have spent in company that is yours—and if I think upon it, perhaps more than one time. I will be a dragon-person that misses your shee– person-person.' Shanks smiled at her.

Itty flung her arms around the dragon's neck and wailed, 'I don't want to lose all my friends again. We may have fixed the villages, but I've got no one left. We didn't get to meet Captain Smart again, and the only way I'll see Karrin is when I die.' She gulped, tears in full flow now. 'This Nathan doesn't know me at all; I miss him, and he doesn't remember anything about us. And now… And now, you're leaving too.'

Shanks pulled himself free. 'There, there, Itty-person. I will be a dragon leaving here, that is a statement that is a true fact, but I do not have to be a dragon leaving *you*. Why don't you become a person who is not by herself, but accompanying a dragon-person while that dragon-creature finds out more about this world?'

She sniffed and wiped her eyes with her sleeve. 'Really? I can come with you?'

The dragon nodded.

Itty hugged Shanks' neck again and cried, 'Yes! Yes!'

He knelt low, as if formally bowing to her. 'Be a person climbing on my back.'

As Itty scrambled up, the dragon asked, 'Where shall be the place we visit first? The place can be anywhere.' He squinted at the sky and scratched his head with a long talon, then looked back to the young woman on his back. 'Anywhere that is a place I can find.'

She was about to say Hyrhia, the obvious choice, when she remembered that he didn't know the city, so couldn't find it in his windows. Besides, she thought, that wasn't her home anymore. Nowhere was home. After all her travels, she felt untethered. She had a vision of herself floating free, high above the world, disconnected from it and belonging nowhere. *Somewhere new. I want to go somewhere new, where I'll be too busy to think.*

She recalled The Adventurers' Guild; there ought to be enough there to keep her mind occupied. 'I know. What about Khaleshka? I want to meet some real adventurers. And I reckon there ought to be someone there who can make you a better pair of glasses, too.'

Shanks said, 'Khaleshka is a place I know. We'll be persons getting there quickly.'

The dragon started to run, and flapping his enormous wings, launched himself into the air. The familiar ruby tendrils extended from his long, feathery wing scales, crackling and pinging as they met above Itty's head and thickened. Soon she and the dragon were once again enclosed in his crystal-windowed shell, and the sound of rushing air vanished.

Itty could see snowscapes, turbulent seas, busy cities, peaceful countryside, and a thousand other sights through the many panes. She was certain she caught a glimpse of Krispy through one window—that was surely his deep rowlf she heard as the scene raced past the pane. Some of the images were so still that they seemed to be detailed paintings and not real landscapes; some hurtled by so quickly that she felt dizzy and had to cling tightly to Shanks' neck.

The dragon oriented towards one particular ruby pane, which grew and became a view over a massive, densely packed, multi-spired city. As they approached, faint animal noises could be heard, along with the buzz of industry and the hum of hundreds of conversations.

Buildings flashed by.

Itty recognized the central clock tower of the Grand Library from pictures she'd seen an age ago, back in what felt like a previous life. A life before the Esmiyan villages; before her rescue; before the Down-Underworld; before the ship. Only a few months had passed since she was snatched from Hyrhia, but it seemed like years.

Seven storeys high and with numerous slim towers soaring higher still, Khaleshka's Grand Library was the largest in the world. Who knew what treasures she might find within it? Shanks hovered above the emperor's palace, a building even more magnificent than the library, with its dazzling golden turrets and massive colourful tapestries hanging on its outer walls. The brightly coloured tapestries depicted the emperor and his children, smiling beatifically with arms spread in welcome.

Shanks looked around and asked, 'Where shall we be persons making a landing?'

Itty spotted the place she'd always dreamed of visiting, The Adventurers' Guild. The building was very plain compared to the others. The squat, boxy affair had austere stone walls decked with rather dreary flags and pennants. It sat in the centre of expansive grounds, which showed off the best of the fauna and flora retrieved by enthusiastic explorers. There were several gardens cultivated with curious plants from many countries, along with some fenced-off areas dedicated to zoological exhibits of animals brought back from far-flung parts of the world. She pointed to an open field. 'There.'

Shanks landed, scattering a herd of long-necked, stripy horses, who ran off in a slow but graceful gallop. 'I think I should be a person who stays here, away from the building, while you are a person who goes in.'

Itty slid off and patted his shoulder. 'Are you sure?'

'These people who are adventurers in this place are often persons who are knights, and I am still not a creature who trusts them.' He yawned. 'And I am a person who is tired. I will wait in this place for you to be a returning person.' With that, the dragon curled up for a snooze, tail wrapped under his chin, and one eye still open in case a knight dared to appear.

Itty set off across the field to the building itself. As she approached it, she noticed that some of the pennants had writing on them:

ANNUAL ENTRANCE CONTEST FOR NEW ADVENTURERS

TODAY!

FROM THE TENTH HOUR OF THE MORNING UNTIL THE SEVENTH OF THE EVENING

She stopped, mouth dropping open, palms prickling in excitement. Itty knew all about the contest. Once a year, The Adventurers' Guild opened its doors to all-comers. Anyone could present the Guild with something precious, and if the item was deemed acceptable, he would be recruited as a bona fide adventurer. Anyone who was a man, that is, because as everybody knew, only men could be adventurers.

Even with nothing to offer, she could at least see what it would be like to walk through the doors, and perhaps catch sight of this year's contestants and their treasures.

She set off again, but stepped in a hole made by an animal hoof and tumbled. As she fell, something dropped from her pocket.

What's that? I don't remember having a lamp.

Itty picked up the lamp, wondering how that had got into her pocket. As she stared at it, a faint noise came from inside, along with the scent of cardamom, vanilla and sulphur. She brought it close to her ear. The noise seemed to be an indistinct voice, but it sounded familiar, and she was certain she'd encountered that smell before. A vague recollection came to mind of a smile with large white teeth.

She shook her head to clear it.

Perhaps the new version of Nathan had hidden it in her pocket as a surprise going-away present. A rather eccentric present, but still. As she examined the lamp, the clouds stifling her memory melted away, revealing a clear image. The djinn! Her wishes! Itty remembered his tricks as well, but she had one wish left.

She could ask for something to offer the Guild and enter the contest. *No, wait*, she thought. *That would be cheating.* She looked hungrily at the building and read the pennants' message again, then looked at the lamp in her hand. She licked her lips. She wanted to be an adventurer so very much. Would it really matter how she got her object, whatever it was? Surely there were no rules *against* using a djinn.

Before she could change her mind, Itty rubbed the lamp and was only slightly surprised by the flash and cloud of smoke.

'What is your third wish, O mistress?' intoned the djinn.

'You know, I've always wanted to join The Adventurers' Guild and, now that we're in Khaleshka, I think it's time.' She thought carefully, making sure she used the correct phrasing to avoid any tricks from the djinn. 'What I wish for is the gift I need to get into the Guild's halls.'

The djinn held up a finger. 'Might I briefly pause the proceedings before we make a mistake? You need not waste a wish on that, O mistress, when there are so many things here which will suffice.'

'But you're a djinn. You grant wishes.'

'Of course, my mistress, but surely you can see the advantage of using wishes only when you absolutely need to. After all, once I grant your final wish, I will vanish, and you will have no more wishes.' The djinn leaned closer, whispering conspiratorially, 'Wouldn't it be much better if I furnished what you need without wasting a wish?' He spread his arms wide. 'We could be together for so much longer, you and I.'

Itty felt uneasy but had to admit that the djinn's words did make sense.

A pair of geese landed nearby and waddled past the two, obviously very used to people in their fields. The djinn stretched out a sinuous, elongating arm and plucked a soft feather from the belly of one. It honked and stared back indignantly, before turning and continuing on its way, grumbling as it went in the low-key manner of all mildly put-upon fowl.

'There you go. A graceful and delicate feather from a common Arcanian goose, and no need to waste a precious wish. How could anyone say that's not a unique gift to the Guild, something they've never seen before? That'll get you in and will most certainly grant you'—he smiled, showing a very wide mouthful of shining teeth—'everything you deserve.'

With that, the djinn vanished into the lamp.

'Wait! Come back.'

The djinn's head reappeared, floating in the air above the lamp. 'What?' he snapped.

'Listen. I know that The Adventurers' Guild has very strict rules for what people bring them. They execute timewasters! And this feather sure looks to me like a waste of time.'

'Ah, dead—sorry, slip of the tongue—dear Imperceptibility, if I may call you that, let me explain my clever plan.' The djinn's body flowed from the lamp until he was whole again, and he hooked a conspiratorial arm over her shoulder. 'You're right, most perceptive of mistresses, there is indeed a trick involved. However, O mistress, it's not on you at all, cross my heart and hope to— well, I'm not really alive, but you know what I mean. Those bigheads at the Guild are bored of seeing the same exotic objects. What does an ice crystal from the cold fires of Eridon mean to them, or a gregarious spacklebeast from the Itranian jungles? They've seen all that before—one unique object is the same as the next. On the other hand, most blessed of mistresses, they'll jump at the chance to have a feather, something from their very own doorstep. Why, I imagine that almost none of them have actually seen a goose feather. Not a single one of them would ever think to look at a goose, even if it was standing right in front of them.'

He smiled broadly. 'Think of the wonders that will be bestowed upon you as the bringer of such a wondrous item.'

The djinn vanished again, rattling the lamp in her hand.

Itty studied the feather for several seconds as she absently slid the lamp back into her pocket, instantly forgetting about the djinn.

A feather? Will a feather work?

She felt something cold and round in her pocket as she withdrew her hand. *What's that?*

No matter. The feather. That's something they've never seen before.

Who told me that?

She thought for a bit longer, twizzling her prize, then shrugged and started walking to the Guild's headquarters.

As she paused to look at what appeared to be a horse's head and part of a chariot wheel made from paper, somewhat damp and squashed, the Grand Library clock sounded seven chimes. She looked up and started to run towards the entrance.

Chapter 27: Back at The Adventurers' Guild

Dragon Gate-crashes Annual Contest

Entrants for this year's Rare and Unique Objects contest were not put off by yesterday's inclement weather. In fact, Gatekeeper to The Adventurers' Guild, Dame Octavia Bluminsheim (67), had a record-breaking fifty-two applicants to assess, though one fled before presenting his treasure.

Everyone's favourite bad boy, handsome Prince Ollipher of Plenipont (21), demonstrated his adventuring prowess with a magnificent fragment of the fabled god-king Amoncolata's funeral shroud. Lady Sebastienetta Holtenstoque (18) disclosed, 'Lawks, I practically swooned, so I did, at the brave prince's tale of derring-do. He's only gone and invited me back to his tent after the contest, don't you know!'

Our sympathies lie with the two unfortunates who were taken away to await execution. We can only hope that the senior Adventurers show leniency and reduce their punishments, as has been the case in recent years.

More on the winners and losers later, but first, the surprise of the evening was a late entry by a Ms Imperceptibility Happenstance (17, or possibly 19 or 16, depending on how time passes in the afterlife and the effects of time travel), who entered the hall with a feather. She… *[contd pages 4–8]*

Front page, *The Khaleshkan Times*, 17th day of Nontemps, 39th year of the 8th Emperor.

'And that's the story of how I got here, Madame Gatekeeper,' Imperceptibility said. 'With this.' She brandished her feather.

There was a hush in the hall.

After what seemed like several minutes, the silence was broken by a cough, and the gatekeeper said, 'Let me see if I've understood what you've told us… You were press-ganged into the Estalian navy, but were cast adrift because of a mutiny. You then arrived in the underworld where you seem to expect us to believe you spent some time with the great Kharon, who then simply let you wander out through the tunnels of the Humble Monks. But, alas, this was not the end of your misfortunes. Instead, you were sacrificed to a dragon, then blown up by the well-respected Sir Oscar de Montford, which was followed by another visit to the world of the dead. As if that wasn't enough, you wound back time to before this alleged explosion, then persuaded Sir Oscar to take up pig farming. I must say, young woman, even if we ignore the several gaps in your memory, this is a remarkable story. Especially the ending—do tell me if I've got this wrong… Just a few minutes before your arrival, someone—you don't recall who—handed you this…' She gesticulated. 'This *feather*. A feather from the sort of common goose that gets served as dinner here twice a month! When the kitchen skivvies pluck those geese, they save the feathers for stuffing pillows. Everyone in the Guild…' She waved her arms around more violently, and her voice became shriller. 'No, everyone in the *entire city* rests their head on feathers such as that you hold in your hand.'

Laughter erupted in the chamber. Prince Ollipher was barely recognizable, curled up and gasping, clutching his sides. The guards' armour rattled as they tried to contain their mirth. Even the sullen crows nesting at the tops of the hall's columns were cawing and thrashing their wings as if joining in the commotion below.

Itty's face dropped. How could she have been so stupid? And what was wrong with her memory? She stared at the feather.

Where exactly did that come from?

Who had given it to her, persuading her that it would be a good prize? Someone who didn't have her best interests at heart, obviously. Underneath the cacophony in the chamber, she heard a faint cackle, and a hint of cardamom and vanilla wafted in the air.

Only one other person wasn't laughing: the stern-faced gatekeeper. Itty shrank under her glower as she spoke quietly through gritted teeth. 'You are an unbelievably stupid girl and undoubtedly the most utterly feeble-minded time-waster I've ever encountered. Possibly in the entire history of the Guild. Your execution will serve to increase the average level of intelligence within the city.'

The gatekeeper raised her eyes and bellowed, 'Guard! Take this embarrassing excuse for a human being to the dungeon.'

A shiny-armoured guard grasped Itty's upper arms and started to direct her out of the hall. He was still somewhat wobbly, having barely got his laughter under control. As he unsteadily twisted her around, Itty stumbled. Several objects fell from her waistcoat and pantaloon pockets, clattering across the floor.

'Stop!' the gatekeeper barked.

She was leaning so far across her tall desk that she was in danger of toppling over it and peered intently at the objects spread out on the floor.

'Bring that here,' the gatekeeper said to a guard, pointing at a small circular box. She inspected it closely, then held it up to Itty. 'Is this the compass of Captain Estobilius Smarrette?'

'Yes, ma'am, Captain Smart is—was—his great-great…' She started to count on her fingers but gave up. 'Great-something-grandson, and he gave it to me just before he…' Tears threatened her eyes, more for the captain than for her own fate. 'Before he died. I told you about that.'

But the woman had stopped listening. She pointed at another of the objects scattered at Itty's feet. 'Is that a scale from a dragon? A Great Red, if I'm not mistaken.'

'Yes, ma'am, I told you Shanks had a spear stu–'

'That thing. That stick. There, by your left foot.'

Itty picked it up. 'This? The flute that Karrin gave me that I told–'

After a deep inhalation, the gatekeeper choked out, 'The great Kharon actually gave you that? A fragment of the fabled plants of the River Sticks.'

'Her name's Karrin, actually, but yes, ma'am. She carved it into a flute for me. If you blow on it, Krispy will come. I can do that if you want to see.'

Once again, the gatekeeper wasn't listening.

'No, no, no. These must be fake. You're lying. What tricks are you up to, girl?'

'Ma'am, I'm not trying to trick you. Really, I'm not. They're real. My story is true!'

'You must have stolen them.'

'No, I didn't.' Itty stood up straight. She picked up Shanks' scale. 'I'll ask Shanks to come in here and tell you. He's just outside, in one of your fields.'

The woman paled and asked in a dazed tone of voice, 'You brought a dragon here?'

The laughter in the hall stopped, and a few people started to casually shuffle towards the door.

Itty nodded, then licked her lips as she considered that she might have done something bad.

'Are you really telling us there's a dragon waiting *outside?*' the gatekeeper said more loudly.

Those retreating towards the exit slowed upon hearing that a dragon might be beyond the doors and nonchalantly changed direction to huddle in the corners of the room. The crows glanced around uneasily and tried to shrink themselves into the columns' carvings.

'Yes, he's quite friendly.'

The gatekeeper beckoned a guard and whispered something to him. The guard scurried out of the hall, leaving everyone staring at each other. The hall was silent apart from nervous shuffling of feet and the occasional scared whisper.

The guard ran back in a minute later, looking somewhat shaken.

'Yes, ma'am,' he said, saluting the gatekeeper. 'Ruddy great thing, just lying there in the ziraffe pen, snoring. Took a while to find 'im in the dark. Tripped over 'is tail, I did—luckily 'e didn't wake up and eat me.'

Several people gasped before glancing in the direction of the ziraffe pen as if they thought they might be able to see through the walls.

Eyes widening, the gatekeeper stared at Itty. She took a deep breath and said tonelessly, 'You confronted a fire-breathing dragon, something few people return from, and then you met Kharon, Master of the Underworld. And you're still here. Are you a witch, or some supernatural spirit with mystical dark powers?'

Some members of the audience whimpered and pressed themselves deeper into their corners. Even Itty's guard took a half step away from her. He still held on to her arms, though not as securely as before.

'No, ma'am, not at all. I'm a normal living and breathing human being, nothing special.' She shrugged. 'It all just sort of happened.'

The gatekeeper moaned. Her hands were trembling, and she seemed to be about to fall off her stool. 'Kharon gave you a flute. And you're alive.' Her face was pale. 'And you have your own dragon.'

'I don't *have* Shanks. He's my friend. And she prefers to be called Karrin.' Itty snapped. She pulled one arm free of the guard's limp grasp.

The other occupants of the hall all stared at Itty in total silence. Not even a breath could be heard.

After an awkward moment, just as Itty started to wonder if she should do something—perhaps run away, while she still could—the gatekeeper blinked. She took off her glasses with trembling hands and slowly and carefully cleaned the lenses with a cloth she fetched from somewhere within her desk. A simple, familiar, soothing task. She sighed and put her glasses back on. She coughed twice and stared at Itty for a long time.

Itty tried to swallow, but her mouth was too dry.

'Free the girl,' the gatekeeper called to the guard, before turning her attention to Itty. 'Imperceptibility Happenstance, if you would consent to the display of those treasures in our museum—not permanently, just now and then, when you can spare them—we will gladly grant you membership of The Adventurers' Guild.'

Itty looked around at her wide-eyed audience, then back to the gatekeeper's waiting expression, and after a second's thought, she nodded.

'I bid you welcome to the Adventurers' Guild, Mistress Imperceptibility Happenstance, Adventurer!'

After a few seconds of stunned silence, the crowd of onlookers cheered wildly and burst into applause.

Prince Ollipher strode across the floor with a look of fury on his face. 'Madame Gatekeeper,' he shouted, 'you cannot, just cannot, do this. She's a commoner and she's a… a… a woman. She arrived late and she offered nothing more than a ridiculous feather. How can she be offered membership for all the other things she happened to have? Why, my hirelings—I mean, *I*—have collected many extraordinary items, but I was required to choose one to present to you. Just one. This mere *girl* doesn't deserve to be an Adventurer!'

'Sit down and shut up, Master Ollipher,' the gatekeeper roared, 'or I will change my mind about your membership of our venerable society. No one in this chamber truly believes that you fetched your fragment of shroud unaided, but we are forced to accept an objectionable weasel like you into the Guild because we cannot actually prove beyond any doubt that you didn't. This young woman— and there is no rule whatsoever that prevents women from becoming members, just archaic tradition—has done braver and more worthy deeds than you ever have in your entire over-indulged life.' She cast a glance around the chamber. 'Than many in this hall, for that matter. It is a privilege to have such a person join our esteemed number, and I feel honoured to be the one to greet her.'

The rest of the chamber started to applaud and cheer again, and Itty's heart felt like it would explode. She was going to be an Adventurer! Her smile almost reached her ears.

As she tingled with delight, Itty caught a sudden waft of sulphur and spice, and could distinctly hear muttered cursing coming from within her waistcoat. She wasn't the only person to hear the voice, because the gatekeeper and guard suddenly looked at her. But what on Earth was it?

The gatekeeper squinted at her and asked, 'Is that an Estalian Djinn Lamp in your pocket? I thought all of the djinn had escaped, destroying every last lamp in the world. But that voice… And that smell… It can't be anything else.'

'Lamp, what lamp?' Itty put her hand in her pocket and touched something metallic. The lamp! How could she have forgotten? Again. Itty extracted the lamp and held it up for all to see.

For the first time, the gatekeeper genuinely smiled. Her fingers twitched as if she wanted to rub it, then she pulled her hands back to her lap. She peered at the lamp and pursed her lips, tilting her head. She murmured, almost to herself, 'That explains the memory lapses,' then cautiously asked, 'You must have some wishes left—is that correct?'

Itty frowned. 'Yes. One, I think.'

The gatekeeper crooked a finger in her direction, so Itty strode to the desk and reached up high to hand the lamp over.

As the lamp passed from Itty's hand to the gatekeeper's, a faint wail came from within it: 'So close. Escape so close.'

The gatekeeper turned the lamp this way and that, scrutinizing it as if it was the most precious thing in the world while taking care not to accidentally touch it in any way that could be construed as rubbing. She set it down on the desk in front of her and her smile widened still further.

She licked her lips. 'I wonder, Mistress Happenstance, if we might prevail upon you to let us show this djinn lamp, most certainly the last in existence, and a veritable treasure. It would make the Guild's museum the envy of the world. Please don't cast your final wish, otherwise the lamp will vanish to the next owner. Now, as I'm sure you're aware, the more ancient djinn are capable of injuring their owners in a bid to escape their servitude.'

Itty's eyes widened, and she gulped.

The gatekeeper continued. 'In return for your donation, we will place a djinn ward on the lamp which will prevent him from escaping and harming you or anyone else. Is this agreeable?'

Itty nodded, then asked, 'Will this ward thing hurt the djinn?'

It was the gatekeeper's turn to widen her eyes. 'You care about the well-being of a lamp demon? A creature who would not think twice before destroying you.'

Itty nodded again.

'Professor Albright and Dr Plately, our experts in djinn and other demons, will take the utmost care when placing the ward.' The gatekeeper spread her hands. 'If anything, I'm certain your djinn will feel a load taken off his shoulders. No more need to grant wishes, no worries about what sort of owner he might have next, no pressure to escape.'

Itty wasn't sure if she believed the gatekeeper's concern for the djinn's well-being, but she had to admit that her own well-being would undoubtedly be better served without the djinn's presence. 'Well, OK, if you're sure.'

The gatekeeper held up the lamp and admired it. 'This is an artefact we'll look after ever so carefully, Mistress Happenstance. We'll make sure to put it somewhere safe, suitably guarded and protected, so that no one can rub it ever again.'

She looked at Itty. 'Now, what are we going to do with your dragon?'

'He's not my… Oh, never mind.'

End

For more of Imperceptibility Happenstance…

This is my first novel, but Imperceptibility's adventures will continue in *The Djinn and the Moonflower*, and you can find pointers to some of my writing via

https://www.amazon.com/~/e/B0BC99FYGK

and

https://www.facebook.com/L.N.Hunter.writer.

Author Bio

L.N. Hunter is a tangly web of off-kilter ideas and eccentric thoughts, masquerading as a human being—and sometimes as a writer, which is much more fun. And harder work. Some of those weird notions have appeared in Short Édition's *Short Circuit*, as well as anthologies *Obscura* and *Trickster's Treats 3*, among other places. There have also been papers in the IEEE *Transactions on Neural Networks*, which are somewhat less entertaining. When not writing, L.N. unwinds in a disorganised home in rural Cambridgeshire, UK, along with two cats and a soulmate.